AMICUS 101

A Story
About the
**PURSUIT OF
PURPOSE**
and Overcoming
Life's Chaos

SHAWN ANDERSON

Also by Shawn Anderson:

Countdown to College: Preparing Your Student for Success in the Collegiate Universe

SOAR to the TOP: Rise Above the Crowd and Fly Away to Your Dream

Amicus 101: A Story About the Pursuit of Purpose and Overcoming Life's Chaos

by Shawn Anderson

copyright © 2009 by Shawn Anderson

ISBN: 978-0-9820974-0-3

Printed in the United States of America
Limited First Printing

cover artist George Foster
design Dawn King
set in Adobe Garamond Pro

Published by

Goldmind Press®™

Goldmind Press
Marina del Rey, CA 90292
USA

Order this book online at www.GoldmindPress.com
To e-mail Goldmind Press: info@GoldmindPress.com

Library of Congress Control Number: 2009923133

To those who are inspired to overcome the chaos in life and create their own destiny... this book is for you.

10/16/17

To Kristen...
Never stop believing in YOUR dreams. That is where great lives begin.
I am rooting for you.
With gratitude...

Shawn

Acknowledgements

*O*ver the course of my life, there have been tens of people who have encouraged in me a mind-set that has led to writing Amicus 101: A Story About the Pursuit of Purpose and Overcoming Life's Chaos. *In writing this book, however, there are four people who played a significant role.*

To George...thank you. In addition to designing a fantastic cover, you gave freely of your knowledge and contacts. You are a rare professional...and gentleman.

To Dawn...thank you. The countless hours you spent working with the manuscript truly did make it a better product. You are an extraordinary, extra-mile person.

To Jinx...thank you. I have never met any person in life who claps as loudly. This world needs more cheerleaders like you.

And most of all...

To Christine...thank you. From beginning to end, you generously gave me the benefit of your feedback, your time, and your energy. You are a true model of what it means to give unconditionally.

Why not chase rainbows?

Why not build castles and paint mountains?

—Amicus

Amicus 101:

A Story About the Pursuit of Purpose
and Overcoming Life's Chaos

Wednesday
May 7th...6:30 A.M.

The day started out very much the same as any other Wednesday. The 6:30 A.M. alarm went off far too early and thoughts of calling in sick and sleeping until noon seemed to be rather popular in Jay's head. Staying up late to watch *The Tonight Show* had proven once again to have been a flawed decision. A grumbling of unrecognizable sounds escaped Jay's mouth as he threw his favorite pillow over his head and desperately hoped that it was still only 3:00 A.M.

"Oh, man! I need more sleep!"

Jay desperately wanted to close his eyes and again slip back into the world of dreams and make-believe. If he fell asleep right away, Jay thought he could probably get back to his dream...and the golf course... and finish the head-to-head U.S. Open battle he was having with Tiger. Birdies over the last three holes were eminent for Jay, and he alone would bring golf's greatest player to his merciful knees. The problem for Jay was, however, it wasn't going to happen this morning. Jay knew he had to get his tired butt out of bed and into the office.

Vicki, Jay's wife of six years, could be heard noisily shuffling through her dresser as she looked to put her wardrobe together for the day. Vicki's ever-dependable morning noisiness was a source of strong contention for her and Jay. Their morning sparring sessions never helped either of the two get off to the best of morning starts. Jay would argue from the bed that Vicki couldn't be quiet if she were standing still holding her breath, while Vicki fired back that Jay could hear a snail crawl across the sidewalk a block away. Whatever the truth, mornings in the Garfield house were never to be replayed on a *Focus on the Family* broadcast.

Fifteen minutes after the dream-crashing alarm clock's wake-up call, Jay slowly dragged himself out of bed and allowed his legs to hit the floor. Slumped over with his head hanging into his lap, Jay was oblivious to the fresh optimism that a new day brought with it.

The hopeful promise of the morning sun penetrated the bedroom window blinds, but Jay was trapped in his limiting, self-created morning ritual.

First thing every morning, his mind focused on three survival objectives and nothing was going to distract him from achieving any one of them: #1 take a wake-up shower, #2 get dressed, and #3 get coffee. Passionlessly, he rose to take on the first.

With shower completed and now dressed in his best suit...a handsome, dark blue, Calvin Klein pinstripe he found on the sales rack at a clothing discount store...Jay stepped into his new car. With a tie dangling from his neck as it usually did at this point in the morning, Jay looked to fasten one of his quick no-look knots at the first available traffic light. Jay could still smell the newness of the Japanese-made automobile. At one time, he found the smell invigorating, but now it reminded him of the fact that he had another thirty-four months to go in car payments.

Jay Garfield had watched one too many car dealer commercials and was hooked on buying *something* on that fateful Saturday two months ago. He wished now that he had taken to heart Vicki's words of warning and bought a less expensive car or even a car a couple of years old, but no, no, no, he had to have top-of-the-line, and he had to have new. Now, he was snared in the obligation net of having to work to pay for his car, his wife's car, his house mortgage...and cat food. The cat food was obviously important as Vicki had taped a note to his steering wheel: *Punkin needs food. She likes the tuna.* Yes, today was going to be a day where Jay worked to fulfill all ninety-nine of his life's never-ending financial responsibilities.

For a Wednesday morning, Jay found the traffic congestion on the highway to be incredibly tame by normal work day standards. Jay thought that there must have been a lot of other commuters who had stayed up late watching Leno or Letterman's "Stupid Pet Tricks" also. Unlike Jay, however, they had conveniently called in to work with early morning doctor appointments signaling their tardiness. Fewer cars meant less traffic stress, and for the first time that morning, Jay took a moment to smile.

Eleven minutes and two point eight miles from work (he had the time and distance down to a science), Jay pulled into his regular coffee stop, Java Now! As he had hoped, his favorite server Julie was tending to the customers in the drive-thru. Jay loved to harmlessly tease Julie with his morning order.

"Good morning, beautiful! Whatcha' doin' here so early?"

As if on cue, Julie giggled. "Why waiting for you, of course! Let's see…one blueberry muffin and one large Swiss Vanilla Macadamia with two packs of sugar. Oh, and less muffin and more blueberries, right?" Julie knew Jay's whole routine and delivered her supporting lines like a veteran actor.

"You got it, Julie! Just load that blueberry dude up with more berries and fewer calories! I am watching my boyish figure, you know!"

Jay got a kick out of this little morning ritual. He pretended to be cute and funny, and Julie pretended to think he was the same. The fact that Jay had been going there for ten months and she had served him on most of these trips was a fact that Jay seemed to easily ignore. Wishful thinking had Jay assuming that his sense of humor must have made him Julie's favorite customer in the whole world. For the second time that morning, Jay smiled.

Quite pleased with his conversational performance, Jay happily bit into his enormously oversized muffin. Balancing the coffee expertly in his lap and holding his morning breakfast securely with one hand, Jay turned right out of the parking lot and headed the final miles to work. As he neared his Lincoln Boulevard office, Jay for some strange reason remembered the movie that he and Vicki had rented a couple of weeks prior…*Dead Man Walking*. The phrase "dead man walking," he had learned, was in reference to a death row inmate's final walk to the execution chamber. Jay thought that it was peculiar that thoughts of this movie would strike his conscious mind now; there was no real explanation why they would. His skin broke out in goose bumps as a cold shiver ran through his body. Jay took a quick gulp of coffee, hoping that the hot caffeine hit would relax his momentarily tweaked nerves. Little did Jay know, but this eerie feeling was simply a forecast of what was soon to come.

Uncharacteristically, Jay took extra time getting out of the car before walking into the office. He sat in the front seat and cranked on the stereo in an attempt to shake the foreboding feeling that had hit him just moments ago. Two songs later, Jay turned off the stereo and got out of the car. Steadying his coffee cup in his left hand, Jay reached into the back seat and grabbed his briefcase. He still hadn't had time to finish the muffin, so it was a rather impressive feat to grab the briefcase with the same hand that was holding his half-eaten pastry. With a little hand manipulation, he accomplished the feat successfully for the umpteenth time in his life. A bit more at ease after listening to a couple of Christina Aguilera songs, Jay shut the car's back door and demonstrated his speed-walking skill as he sped towards his office building.

Narrowly pushing the 8:00 o'clock hour, Jay slipped like a shadow through the entrance doors and past the empty receptionist desk. "Boy, I am good!" he thought, "I made it past ole Shirls, again!"

This was actually quite an important accomplishment. Everyone who worked at Jay's company knew that the grandmotherly, gray-haired lady posted at the front had been there since the business's inception twenty-four years ago. Nobody or nothing ever got past her watchdog glance without a judging eyebrow or a quick word. Today, however, Jay's timing was perfect and he was saved from being videotaped by Shirley's overseeing eye.

Shirley Davis had been offered numerous promotion opportunities to move out from behind the circus atmosphere of the reception desk, but she never wanted to. Shirley was like family to James L. Jefferson, the owner and President of JLJ Advertising, and she stood like a loyal overseer reporting who came in late and who went home early.

"Once again," Jay competitively thought, "I have escaped the jaws of danger! Indiana Jones has nothing on me!" Jay's small but meaningful victory brought a third smile to his face that morning. Unfortunately, this would be his final smile for many, many days.

7:59 A.M.

Jay slipped into his office down the hall without being noticed and closed his door. Immediately, his brief case flew open and out cascaded a wave of papers. Jay systematically scattered them over the top of his desk in order to create the impression that he had been hard at work all morning. He then sat back in his big, comfy office chair and wolfed down what was left of his morning muffin. The remainder of his coffee, however, he treated more gingerly. Drinking it as if it were a fine glass of wine, Jay imagined that he was a writer testing the delicacies of a twenty year-old bottle of Merlot. He slowly breathed in the aroma of the coffee and then let its gentle taste run in and around his pallet. Although the temperature of the coffee was now cold, Jay was having too much fun in his imaginary world to notice. This little escape ritual was a part of Jay's morning pattern and a way of entertaining himself before he dug in and finished an unappealing report that was to be on his boss's desk by ten o'clock.

Some days, Jay liked his job or at least moderately tolerated it. Other days, he couldn't push the minute hand around the clock fast enough. With his head seemingly on a swivel, Jay would longingly turn to the wall clock every ten minutes hoping thirty minutes had somehow escaped. Although Jay had been working for JLJ Advertising for eleven years and it had become an integral part of his identity, he wouldn't have been there unless necessity required it. Jay would have preferred spending Monday-Friday absorbed in his favorite pastime, but real life was simply too big from which to run.

Jay's business card officially read "Senior Account Executive" which was actually his third job title since he had been at JLJ. Initially, he had been hired in an administrative capacity handling payables and receivables, but when he showed a knack for spinning a phrase during brainstorming water cooler conversations, the company VP gave him a shot as a copywriter. The copy writing position had been a creative outlet and a new experience for a time, but what the position failed to provide Jay was something his outgoing personality and depressing checkbook required...more people contact and larger paychecks. So after four years in the Accounting office hounding past due accounts and three years bringing dull brochures to life, Jay changed career directions and entered the world of sales. Instead of polishing a client's image with his creative pen, he now hit the pavement as a foot soldier selling his own company's image and capability.

This last job change, now going on four years, had been good for Jay. He liked the autonomy of his outside sales position and enjoyed wining and dining potential clients on the company tab. Most of all, however, Jay was fond of the significant pay increase that came with a JLJ sales position. At JLJ Advertising, account executives had a very attractive base salary. James Jefferson had a special and somewhat unique philosophy about paying his sales team: straight salary, no commission. Mr. Jefferson didn't want a member of his sales team walking into a potential client's office with an attitude or look of financial desperation. Instead, he thought that by giving his sales team the knowledge that their own financial world was secure, they in turn would exude a more relaxed and polished confidence regarding JLJ.

Despite Jefferson's best intentions, however, a secure paycheck wasn't without its stress for his sales people. The pressure to bring new clients into the JLJ world was intense. Like a tape recording stuck on permanent rewind, Mr. Jefferson concluded all Monday morning sales meetings with the same unbending diatribe: "Listen people…we know advertising! Yes, we do! But all that knowing doesn't make a pig's ear worth of difference if we don't have clients to make things happen for! C'mon folks! New clients or more dollars from old clients…that's what we need here, damn it! Smile and dial! Hit those phones! Feet on the floor…butt out the door! Make something happen!"

Sometimes at night while sleeping, Jay was haunted by visions of Jefferson dressed as General Patton authoritatively barking out this same call-to-action speech. Restless nights with darker dreams were often met by tired mornings, but as he often rationalized to Vicki, "It comes with the check, Vic…it comes with the check."

Having now finished his coffee/wine taste test, Jay came back to the morning's reality after noticing the clock on the wall ticked its way to 8:16. Jay knew that the sooner he got the April report done, the sooner he could get out of the office and out on the road. Actually, Jay was looking forward to today. He was scheduled to have lunch with the CEO of a sporting goods company at noon in a new restaurant he had been dying to try, and later tonight he was taking another client to see the Dodgers play the Mets. As he thought about what the day still held for him, Jay heard a less than convincing voice inside his head whisper, "Yeah, the job perks are worth it, buddy!"

Jay turned on his computer and started reading through his

e-mail. As he scanned through each new message, Jay noticed an e-mail from Jefferson. This was indeed rare. Although technology was what pushed JLJ Advertising to be a top-notch agency, Jim Jefferson was not known to use modern technology personally. In fact, Jay couldn't ever recall the president of the company sending him a personal e-mail message. Jay clicked on Jefferson's mail and opened it. The message read simply, "Jay, please come to my office first thing this morning. Important." That was it. Nothing else.

"Hmmm…important, huh?" Jay's mind raced in a quick nano-second wondering what in the world Jefferson could want with him that was so important. Not having the time to ponder what the possible intent of the message might be, Jay leaped up, straightened his tie and tugged on the back of his suit coat thus tightening the lines on his shoulders. He headed to Jefferson's office with adrenalin racing.

Jay had already been at work for nearly twenty minutes and the note did read "…first thing this morning." He was angry with himself for goofing off with his stupid wine tasting game earlier and not reading his mail sooner. He made a mental note to not let that happen again: "Note to self…stop being a goof and check your e-mail immediately!" Jay took an extra deep breath as he turned right out of his office and headed for the stairwell leading to the second floor. His legs were feeling weak and wobbly as he ascended the steps.

With his customary lack of warmth, Jim Jefferson greeted Jay as he entered the impressive executive office. The non-personal greeting was nothing unusual as Jefferson was not an individual known for exuding warm fuzzies. Except for Shirley out front, Mr. Jefferson rarely showed a personal side to any of his employees. Everybody knew Jefferson was always about business…nothing more, nothing less. Using a simple hand signal to point out his wishes, Jefferson directed Jay to sit in one of the two chairs in front of the president's huge, antique mahogany desk.

Like a good soldier, Jay followed the unspoken command and took a seat. Feeling as if he had an imaginary steel rod inserted into the back of his suit coat, Jay sat up as straight and tall in his chair as humanly possible. He was barely breathing, and hoped he wouldn't have to talk much. Jay thought that a sentence coming out of his own mouth now wouldn't last for more than ten words before he would run out of enough air to push more words out. He desperately hoped Jefferson couldn't tell how nervous he really was.

"How stupid!" Jay thought. "Why did I have to run up here so darn fast without first getting a grip on myself!" After silently swearing to himself, Jay fired off a second mental reminder, "Note to self #2… It's okay to walk before running!"

Although Jay was used to controlling his nerves in pressured situations, this situation was proving to be remarkably unique. As he sat there waiting, he pinched himself and took long, slow, quiet breaths, but nothing seemed to bring his emotional state to a place of effective calm. With hands folded in his lap, Jay said nothing as he waited for Jefferson to give the conversation direction.

In quietly observing Jefferson while in his current numbed state, Jay noted for the umpteenth time that Jefferson was ten years older than all the press release and marketing material photos that JLJ used to showcase their president. Additionally, his marketing pictures seemed to cast Jefferson as a man with considerably more hair than he had now.

Jay had joked with Vicki about this many times before. Now Jay was desperately biting his lower lip in order to avoid breaking out in a nervous, uncontrolled laugh as the thought struck him in that moment as completely hysterical. "My boss has ten strands of hair arranged to try and cover his bald head! C'mon, Jay…that's not funny. Hold it together…don't laugh now! C'mon…look away! Think of something else!" Jay pinched himself harder in order not to lose it.

"Oh, crap! I forgot my notepad!" Suddenly he realized that in his panic to run up the stairs and get to this meeting, he had forgotten to bring the mandatory meeting tools of pen and paper. He panicked. His mind turned to a new concern, "Man! I hope I don't have to write anything down." Too late. Jefferson was speaking.

"Jay, let me begin by saying that I have appreciated your work for JLJ. Sincerely. I know you have worked hard for this company, son, and have done your best. I know that you have been with us for a long time and have been open to the changes we have required of you. Tough changes, no doubt, but you have gone with them…you've gone with the flow. You have proven you bleed JLJ blue."

"Well, Jay, I am sorry to say, however, there comes a time when the survival changes that are often necessary for an executive to make are not always consistent with what an employee would like. Today, I am forced to make one of those tough changes that you won't like. Son, as the President of this company, I am required to make the biggies… the tough ones…the decisions that involve people…my people…my employees."

Jay began feeling nauseous as his mind began to race at Jefferson's words. It didn't take extraordinary brain power to figure out that the "tough ones" comment was targeted at him. Like a heat-seeking missile, Jefferson's words were moving in on their target, and it didn't take a rocket scientist to know what was coming. Jay glanced at the clock on the wall above Jefferson's shoulder and noticed that it read "8:23." Right then, the answer to the mystery of *Dead Man Walking,* which had crossed Jay's mind earlier, began to reveal itself.

Having had trouble deciphering it earlier, Jay heard the answer in his head now as clearly as if a sixty person firing squad had come into the room and shouted it out simultaneously. The ominous thought of that unsettling movie forty-five minutes earlier was undoubtedly a warning signal for what he was now experiencing. He was about to be executed. The universe in all its infinite wisdom must have been throwing a huge hint Jay's direction preparing him for what was to happen later that morning.

"Hilarious!" he thought. "Great sense of humor, God!" Truly, though, it could not have been a more fitting match for the moment Jay was now experiencing. Sitting there in the chair, Jay knew then that he was about to get fired and would be making his own fatal walk out of the building shortly.

"Jay, I'm sorry, but I don't know any easy way to say this. Starting today, JLJ is going to have to let you go."

The rest of Jefferson's termination speech was nothing more than a hodgepodge of sounds that went in one ear and out the other. All Jay kept hearing now were the words, "Starting today, JLJ is going to have to let you go… Starting today, JLJ is going to have to let you go…" The words "starting today" seem to be repeated and emphasized in his brain with a particular cruelty.

"What was happening? Is this real? Wake up, Jay…wake up!" Unfortunately, there would be no waking up from this unsettling moment. What was happening was very, very real. The situation Jay was living was neither a dream nor a movie.

"I am being fired! Dismissed! Terminated! Axed! Jefferson's right! There's no easy way to say it! I've just lost my damn job!"

Three minutes later, Jay Garfield stood and took an envelope from the extended hand of the man whose "tough decision" had just thrown Jay's life directly into the path of an emotional hurricane. Jay's thoughts and feelings were spiraling wildly out of control. "This can't be happening! Are you kidding me? C'mon, Jay, think! Say something to him to make him change his mind!"

Jay's thoughts, however, were not to be translated into words. As much as his inner world was racing to come up with job-saving answers, Jay's outer expression was as composed as a fisherman sitting calmly in his boat with pole cast. Sixty more seconds passed as Jefferson wound down his great speech, and still Jay was stuck on quiet. Nothing. No defense…no response. Finally, the moment had come and gone. It was too late to respond. The bloodshed had ended.

Jay walked out of the office and away from the face of a man whom he would never see again. With slow, deliberate steps, Jay walked like a "dead man walking" back to his office. The sounds were dead quiet all around him. He felt as if he was in the eye of a hurricane, floating peacefully in the air, but waiting to get violently hurled at any moment by a very angry supernatural wind force.

Staring at the envelope that he now carried in both hands, Jay stepped into the office with the nameplate "Jay Garfield" across the door. As he collapsed into his once comfortable chair, Jay felt his entire muscle system tighten like a Nerf ball being squeezed. In that single instant, Jay felt the crushing pain of leaving the emotional hurricane's eye as his gut was now tossed violently to the earth with the realization that he was now unemployed.

"I've been fired!" The repercussions of Jay's brutal crash back to reality were about to hit him hard.

8:39 A.M.

After staring blankly for ten minutes at the envelope in his hand, Jay pulled up the scotch-taped seal and removed the contents. The first of the two items enclosed was a paycheck. Jay noticed that the check was typed and dated May 7th. "Today…May 7th…today," he whispered to himself dispassionately.

The check was typed and not handwritten which Jay interpreted to mean that his JLJ fate had been sealed not this morning, but yesterday, or maybe even weeks ago. "They knew this was coming! They knew I was getting canned!" Who *they* were right now didn't seem to even matter. "They" were everyone as far as Jay was concerned.

"Did I miss something? Were the signs there and I just didn't see them?" If there had been any indication that Jay was going to be fired, he had missed it completely. Unlike footprints after a first snow, there had been no visible indicators. All the people who might possibly have been in the information loop had covered their tracks completely and had been very discrete about not letting any information out regarding Jay's demise.

"They knew it and didn't even give me a heads-up! Pffffff…I can't believe it!" At that moment, Jay's anger was directed at every one of the twenty-five people employed by JLJ. In his raging mind, Jay thought every single one of them to be a plotting enemy.

"I don't have a single person here who cares enough to look out for me! No one! They knew what was happening and no one told me a thing! I could have been warned ahead of time so that I could do something to have stopped this!"

Overwhelmed with bitter anger, Jay lashed out with desperate thoughts looking to blame someone. His ability to think rationally had disappeared fifteen minutes ago and was not to return any time close to today.

On first glance, the amount on the check was an unusual amount to Jay. He read the number out loud, "$4,135.17." Studying the figure further, however, he realized that it was twice his two-week salary. His check represented what he would make in a month which meant the additional two weeks extra obviously represented a two-week severance pay. "Amazing! Eleven years gets you two lousy weeks!" Jay shook his head in absolute disgust.

He took the second and final item out of the envelope. On company letterhead were typed three sentences: *Enclosed you will find your final check with two weeks' severance. Your work for JLJ has been appreciated. If there is anything that I can do in regards to providing you with a reference, please let me know. Regretfully, James L. Jefferson.* That was it. No personal signature. To Jay, it was a note of stunning impersonal finality.

Jay reread the letter. "That's great!" he thought sarcastically. "If I need a reference, the company that just fired me will be happy to provide me with one! I'm sure that'll go over great with someone looking to hire me!"

His thoughts raced forward in an imaginary interview with a prospective employer. "Yeah, I wasn't good enough for JLJ Advertising, but here's a great letter from them telling you why I'm so fantastic!" Jay closed his eyes. His anger briefly subsided as desperate hopelessness slipped into its place. "What am I going to do?"

At 9:10, Jay was carrying a box out of the building with his personal possessions. He had cleaned out his office as quickly as possible throwing everything that belonged to him in an Office Depot box once reserved for copy paper. He crept out of the office as quietly as possible without drawing attention to himself, but when he saw no one loitering around the front desk as usual, he knew that everybody had probably barricaded themselves into their own offices in order to avoid an uncomfortable run-in on his way out. Even Shirley managed to duck away when she saw that Jay was coming down the hall.

"I'll miss that old gal," he thought. A quick pang of regret seeped its way into Jay's conscious. He was starting to miss a place that he never really appreciated. Ironic.

Jay was actually glad that no one had come up to him to say anything. "What would I say anyway? Hey, Sara…I'm fired and you're not! I guess the fact that I was ahead of you last month on the sale's charts really didn't matter. Hey…John, better go easy on that expense report or Big Brother will be gunning for you next! Okay, Shirley… take care. You won't have my sorry rear-end to kick around anymore!"

The truth is Jay wouldn't have known what to say, others wouldn't have known what to say, and both parties would have stood there feeling absolutely silly. Good-byes are never easy, especially when they surround awkward circumstances like a firing.

Jay quickly stuffed his briefcase and box of possessions into the back seat. As he shifted his car into reverse and began backing out of his designated parking spot, he had no idea where he was heading. All that seemed to matter right now was to escape from where he was. Jay frantically wished that he could be a long, long way from where he was now. It wasn't a physical location he wished to escape from; it wasn't the building or parking lot. No, he wanted to escape from how he was feeling and what he was going through emotionally. He wanted to escape from his reality.

Jay pulled out of the parking lot up to the street. He had no idea whether he should turn right or left. Going home had zero appeal; for that reason, he turned right, toward the freeway and opposite from the way home. Driving through busy city streets and stopping for endless minutes at one stoplight after another had less appeal than ever. Thoughts of waiting for a light to turn green so he could hurry up and wait at the next "stupid" stoplight made Jay's blood boil. He felt like racing—going fast. He felt that if he went fast enough he could outrun his problems. Irritated with the world, he pounded on the steering wheel with his fist. He cranked his stereo as loud as his ears could handle.

Finally, Jay made it through the last stoplight and accelerated up the freeway on-ramp. As he hit a smoother flow of freeway traffic, Jay took out his CD case and removed the latest arrival from his CD-of-the-month club. He didn't even notice who the artist was, and right now he didn't care. He just wanted loud. Who the artist was, what the words were, what the song was…none of it mattered. Jay's mind was one hundred percent focused on having been fired.

"Why? Why? Why?" Thoughts of Jefferson, JLJ and losing his job dominated Jay's thinking as an imaginary thought librarian raced through the aisles of his mind looking for answers. The car stereo blasted out the latest in pop music, but the noise in Jay's brain was so loud that he was immune to the stereo's sound.

Jay replayed the events of the morning…rewinding over and over again his meeting with Jefferson…hoping to hear something on second play, third play, fourth play that he hadn't heard before. "Why was it me? Why was I the one and not Mark or Sara or Nicole? Why me? Why!"

Jay came up with a hundred reasons why he should have been the one to stay, but identifying each one individually only compounded his irritation. Everything that entered Jay's mind fired up his irritation to another level: slow traffic, coworkers, lousy employers. It didn't matter what it was. Jay was emotionally out of control. And he was flying.

For the rest of the day, Jay just drove. Shouting unheard expletives to other drivers to speed up every few minutes served to release a bit of the pressure geyser building up in Jay, but it really did little to speed up the slower pace of the traffic. At one particular slow point, Jay decided that he had had enough of the slow pace and headed for the off-ramp and the nearest fast food drive-thru. "Heck with this! I'm getting a burger!"

As could be expected, a burger and fries wasn't going to change how Jay was feeling or thinking. The negative thoughts kept drumming through his head with the same beat over and over. And like the thoughts, the yelling didn't stop either. Instead of slow drivers, Jay vented his anger at the unfortunate high school girl behind the fast food order window who forgot to add the three extra catsups for which Jay had asked.

"Look…customer service matters! If you don't listen to what customers want they may never come back! If they don't come back, the business won't make money, and you'll be out of a job! Do you get it? Do you understand? Sheesh!"

Now having another lightening rod spark the intensity of his anger…the customer service skills of young people…Jay forgot all about the hamburger and three catsups and the fact that he was even hungry to begin with. The unopened lunch bag sat next to him growing cold in the front seat.

A few hours later with his car's gas gauge steadily winding its way down, Jay Garfield headed home. Nothing, of course, had been fixed. He hadn't succeeded in getting his job back or in finding a new job. He hadn't found a renewed sense of peace or cast his mind towards a new life goal. No, Jay Garfield really didn't accomplish anything other than letting the natural healing process begin to run its course. It was 5:39 P.M. and 298 miles since Jay had started his mad driving venture before he finally pulled into his home garage…worn-out, defeated, and a tank of gas poorer.

Jay dragged himself through the garage door entrance into the house and immediately smelled spaghetti on the stove. The delicious homemade pasta smell which normally served to click-on Jay's hunger switch did nothing of the sort today. Ordinarily, Jay would have made a beeline for the pot simmering on the stove. He was fond of teasing Vicki that one great advantage of marrying an Italian was that she knew how to cook amazing pasta dishes…his favorite.

He loved Vicki's spaghetti more than any other meal in the world, and although his stomach was certainly calling out for him to sit down and have a plate, his mind wasn't. Jay skipped the kitchen visit altogether and slipped upstairs before Vicki could even notice him. He hastily disrobed, throwing his suit coat and slacks over the back of a corner chair. He quickly disappeared beneath the covers, and with head barely peeking out from under the top blanket, Jay would sleep undisturbed until morning.

Thursday, May 8th…The Day After

Vicki had let Jay sleep without waking him up to ask why he hadn't gone to the Dodgers game the night before. She was still miffed that Jay had snuck upstairs without saying anything, but she made a conscious decision to let it go and not create a morning world war Garfield style. She thought that there must have been a good reason in Jay's mind to have avoided her (although at that moment she had no clue what it could have been). The answer to that riddle would have to wait until later. She had learned a long time ago that the saying "let sleeping dogs lie" actually meant, "don't wake Jay while he's sleeping." She even tried extra hard to tip-toe around the room that morning as she got ready for work so she wouldn't wake the pit bull that occupied the left side of the bed.

Of course when the time was right for discussion, Vicki had a few sure fire question grenades to lob in Jay's direction. "Why didn't you go to the game? Why did you go straight to bed without saying anything? Why didn't you hang up your good suit? Why did you forget to buy cat food?"

Sure it was easy to forgive him for slipping upstairs without saying anything to her; most likely Jay hadn't felt well. What was temporarily less forgivable, however, was that Jay had forgotten to buy Punkin's food as she had written on her morning steering wheel note. She had been forced to make a late night market run in order to quell the constant kitty crying that had been following her in and out of every room. Additionally, the truth was that if Jay really was sick he needed the rest, and if he wasn't sick, well then, she wasn't ready to talk to him quite yet. She thought they could catch up on what was going on later tonight and that in turn would give her all day to calm down in regard to Jay's failed obligation to his cat.

Jay and Vicki had a rather average relationship as measured by the silly magazine quizzes Vicki was known to put them through. "Hey, Jay, answer this for me: Do you consider our communication: A) Fantastic! We could teach a couples' class; B) Okay, but we could benefit from a joint trip to Dr. Phil or, C) Sorely lacking and headed towards TV's *Divorce Court?*"

Of course, Jay was trained to always throw out the answer Vicki expected to hear, but it was true that the two had grown "comfortable" with each other and that their marriage had turned routine with little excitement. Neither one of them went out of the way to brighten the day of their spouse with an extra-mile surprise, but yet each considered the other to be the most important person in his and her life.

This had been the second marriage for both, and deep down neither one of them wanted #2 to end like #1. Jay had a thirteen year old son, Josh, with his first wife, but they lived on the other side of the country and Josh visited for only two weeks during the summer. On the other hand, Vicki, thirty-four, had no biological children. She often tested the water with Jay and hinted about having a child of their own, but she wasn't a hundred percent sold on the idea herself.

"Am I ready to take care of a baby? Can we afford for me not to work?"

She lingered over questions like this, but couldn't help but believe that maybe a child was exactly what the two of them needed in order to grow closer. For his part, Jay, 39, had absolutely no interest in having another child, let alone a newborn. To him, his life seemed chaotic enough already without making it any crazier. Thrown into the mix, too, was the stinging notion that Jay felt he had been a considerably less than stellar father to Josh and that weighed heavily in his thinking. He didn't want to make the same mistakes again in raising a child, and furthermore, he wasn't confident that he really was cut out to be a father to begin with.

Both Jay and Vicki were cat-like in their personal need for independence and allowed each other a lot of room in their day-to-day lives. Deep down both knew that their communication practices with each other could be sharpened, but neither felt a desire to make the effort and push to strengthen that area. Overall, they were both content with how things were, even though they recognized that they were not soon to be nominated for the "Couples Communication of the Year Award."

Vicki assumed Jay obviously had his reasons for going to bed early and getting up late, and by giving Jay a "conversational pass" for the moment, she was just giving Jay space…good or bad. Obviously, it came as a complete shock later that morning when Vicki received a phone call at work. It was Jay.

"Jefferson canned me."

Vicki knew immediately that Jay hadn't been kidding. The pieces had fit together too well. Jay home early…sleeping in late…not talking to her…forgetting the cat food…she knew it was no joke. She knew it was real. Immediately, Vicki's first thought was to support her husband.

"I'll be right there and we can talk about it."

Jay however, had other ideas. "No, no…I've rented a few movies and I'd rather just hang out and veg by myself for awhile. I think what I need to do is just let my brain find something else to dwell on for a bit. I need to take a mental breather. I can tell you about the details of things later if that's okay." Vicki knew Jay well enough to imagine that he was probably beating himself up pretty good over being fired, and agreed that a few *Rambo* movies was a good escape.

That night at dinner they talked. Vicki could see the agonizing pain in Jay's eyes. She just wanted to reach out and hug him with her arms and her words, but she knew Jay wasn't the mothering type. With elbows on the table and her chin resting in the palms of her hands, Vicki just sat and listened to Jay vent. Within moments, his conversational mood would quickly change from anger to sadness to hopelessness. Being a problem solver, Vicki wanted to talk about what Jay was going to do next, but she knew the question at this point would have been futile. She knew Jay really had no idea.

"Let it go," she thought to herself. "Let Jay just deal with his pain right now. Just let him talk."

There would be a time for moving forward she knew, but now was not it. So Jay talked and Vicki listened. She watched his movements, his face, and listened intently to every single word that came out of Jay's mouth. Vicki loved her husband very much and she wanted to ease his pain, but she knew there was little that she could really do right now to glue his world back together except offer her listening support.

Before the phone call earlier that day, Jay had dreaded sharing the news of his firing with Vicki. "She's going to think I'm such a loser! Who gets fired? How totally embarrassing!" he thought distressingly.

Fortunately for Jay, a humongous wave of relief surged through his core when her first response back to him wasn't something along the lines of "What in the world are you going to do now? What are we going to do?" Instead, Vicki had been terrific about what had happened and had not pushed him. She reminded him that everything would be fine and that they had saved for times like this.

"Jay, don't worry. We'll just take things a day at a time and I know everything will work out!"

Vicki's overwhelming support felt good. It was exactly what he had needed to hear. She didn't exacerbate his downward spiral with her own panic, but instead gave him an extended arm to brace his fall. Vicki's reaction had been perfect in stopping Jay's ever-building negative momentum.

Friday, May 9th – Thursday, May 15th

Jay did nothing on the Friday after "Doomsday Wednesday," nor did he do anything the whole following week. He would usually sleep until after 10:00 A.M. and then get up, turn on the TV, and watch soap operas and talk shows for the rest of the day. He knew it was a gigantic waste of time, but in a cynical sort-of-way, the talk shows made Jay feel better. By realizing that the world was full of thousands…even millions of people whose situations were far more screwed up and desperate than his own, Jay felt relief. In a "Thank God, I'm not him!" sort of way, Jay found immense personal consolation in comparing Jerry Springer's guests with himself.

As a matter of obligation, Jay had begun to flip through the job ads in the newspaper, but was not having luck finding anything that appealed to him. Sure, there were hundreds of sales positions, but the thought of going back into a new sales position made his gut turn.

"I'm about to turn forty and starting over for crying out loud! Nice, Jay…really, really nice! Your boss will probably end up being ten years younger than you! Idiot!"

Jay knew enough about the pay structure of most sales positions to realize that the compensation packages would be strongly related to performance. Today's "Help Wanted" ads supported his thinking: "Commission based"…"Top achievers make a hundred thousand dollars a year!"…"Three months paid training!" Jay believed that if he went back to knocking on unwelcoming doors, making cold calls that were rarely returned, and working off commission, he would have a nervous breakdown.

"I can't do it! I can't do it again…especially working for commission!" Developing a client base from ground zero like he had done at JLJ was motivating once, but not twice. "Should I go back into payables and receivables? Copy writing? Heck…should I go back to school?" None of the ideas being thrown around in his head had appeal. Jay was completely and totally lost and had no clue as to what to do next.

The days soon began to melt into each other; ten days had gone by since that infamous meeting with Jefferson. Jay had picked up the phone a few times and answered job ads, but he had yet to motivate himself to the point of writing a resume.

"Oh geez…it's been so long! Where do I even begin?" he mused.

The thought of summarizing his life's work in a single page seemed daunting at best, but he knew procrastination was not the answer. "C'mon, Jay…just do it! Just start!" Finally on the eleventh day after getting fired, Jay found the discipline to get past his raining doubts and found himself turning on his computer for the first time in what seemed like ages. Even the keyboard seemed foreign to Jay.

Before getting busy with the priority at hand, Jay signed online and checked his e-mail. Besides the ordinary barrage of junk mail, Brent and John from the office had sent "I'm sorry" notes. Of course, both let him know how terrible they felt regarding what had happened, and both expressed a desire to do whatever they could to help him. It felt good to know they cared…embarrassing…but good.

Jay wrote back, and in a good humor, "everything is great" sort of way told them that he was fine and that there were a "number of great opportunities" that were presenting themselves. Of course this wasn't true, but it made Jay feel better to let them think that. Jay wrote that he would stay in touch and keep them filled in on his "next great adventure," but deep down he knew that it probably wouldn't happen, and they would both slip away from his life without the common bond of JLJ Advertising. Additionally, the truth was that if Jay really did share a lunch date with either of his former coworkers, they would be able to see through his "I am fine" charade, and that was a bit too much for Jay to bear. With mask firmly in place, Jay sent the two e-mails painting a far rosier outlook for his life than actually existed.

With this first task painfully completed…the easy task…Jay blew out a deep breath. As each extra second of air passed through his mouth, Jay slumped even lower into his seat. Sitting dejectedly like a puppet whose master had failed to pull up his shoulder strings, Jay closed his eyes and prayed. "Please, God…whoever you are…give me the strength to write this resume and get through this time in my life. Help me…please. Won't you?"

To an unbiased observer, Jay looked as if every ounce of life had been drained from his defeated body. With eyes fixated blankly at the monitor, Jay looked as if every trace of possible hope had long exited his downcast spirit. Like Frasier's famous *End of the Trail* bronze, Jay's body position one hundred percent resembled the once great American Indian warrior slumped on top of his horse, broken down at the end of a long and hard-fought battle. Like the proud Indian, Jay's world appeared to have no hope…it was over. His career battle had been fought, and he had lost.

After what seemed like a lifetime of non-movement, Jay took one extra deep breath as if the additional oxygen in his system would ignite a new life fire within him. Perhaps it was the extra deep breath, or the prayer, or just the knowledge that he needed to do it, but Jay finally found the will to take the most forward-looking step he had taken in days; he brought up Windows on his computer and opened up a new document. On the top of the page, Jay quickly typed his name…*Jason "Jay" Garfield*. But then he stopped. Instead of continuing to hit the key strokes that would list his education background and work history, Jay decided it would be much less painful to beat himself up again with the same questions that he had already asked a hundred times:

"Where did I go wrong? What am I going to do now? Who is going to hire a thirty-nine-year-old laid-off has-been account executive?"

The negative momentum again began to build, and all Jay could do to stop this depressing and destructive mental roller coaster was to simply stop altogether. Without hesitation, Jay closed the file. He had come close to starting, but his new resume would not take life today.

"Tomorrow. Yeah…tomorrow I'll do it. Perhaps I'll be in the mood."

Friday, May 16th…9:22 A.M.

Twenty-four hours later, Jay honored his own wishes and found himself back in the same chair staring at the same *Jason "Jay" Garfield* heading. The mental block that seemed to impede his fingers' movement on the keyboard yesterday, however, had not gone away. Jay was still locked in his dark prison of doubt and uncertainty and he had no idea where to even to begin. He was stuck…flat-out stuck. Thirty minutes painstakingly slipped by for Jay without even a cursory attempt at typing something that was helpful or made sense. Typing and then cutting and pasting "Jay is a very stupid boy" over and over was not something that could really be called a good start. But this is what he did.

Clearly, this writing effort was not going well. At the rate he was progressing, Jay may have sat there staring indefinitely, but a life changing occurrence broke his do-nothing trance. Of course, Jay had no clue what affect this single moment would eventually have on his life. Then again, who would recognize the sound of a simple computer beep as having such pivotal power?

"Beep!" The computer spoke on its own.

Jay's eyes grew large. He was shocked to see that words had mysteriously appeared on his computer screen.

Hey, Jay!

"Hey, Jay?" he said to himself. "What the…? Where in the world did that come from? I didn't even know I'd signed onto Instant Messenger?" Then Jay smiled, "I must have typed the words to myself."

The computer beeped again and three more sentences were added to the first:

No, Jay. You didn't type the words. I typed the words.

"Huh?" To say Jay sat flabbergasted would be an understatement. "What the heck is this? Am I going crazy or what?" Jay stared straight ahead. With mouth slightly ajar, he began to open and close his eyes over and over again as if to clear-up a slight focus problem he must be having. "Am I seeing things?" He blinked one more time hoping that the four sentences would disappear. Instead he was greeted by three more.

Think you are seeing things, huh? Don't worry, my friend, you aren't hallucinating. This is real.

"Real? Real? What do you mean real! There's nothing real about what's going on here!" Jay spoke out loud as if he could be heard. "I don't believe anything I'm seeing!" His fingers, not convinced by the tone of his voice, set themselves on the keyboard, preparing to type back to the mysterious stranger. "Oh, how freaking silly!" Before he could fire a sentence off in response, Jay removed his hands and started to laugh.

"Fantastic, Jay! Now you have no job *and* need to be checked into the loony bin!" Reassuring himself that his imagination had taken an extra giant step, Jay laughed harder. It felt good to laugh again. "But wait…I swear I can see those words!" Doubt sprinted back.

As if following a perfectly orchestrated script, the computer beeped a third time and, magically, new words popped onto the screen.

Great to hear you laugh again, Jay! Feels good, huh? But I have a secret for you: I'm not your imagination, and yes, you can talk with me. Just type away.

With great caution, Jay slowly let his hands find their way back to the keyboard. This time, however, he didn't pull them back. He typed: "Who are you? How do you know my name? How did you know I was laughing?"

Hit by a sudden epiphany, Jay jerked his chair around, searching for a camera. In a loud voice he said: "Vicki, you must be playing a prank!"

No response. Jay drew in a breath, "What am I thinking? There's no way she'd do that! Is someone watching me through the window?"

Looking out and seeing nothing, Jay was greeted by disappointment as he realized his first instinct was wrong. It's not that he wished to have been on an episode of *Candid Camera*, but at least that was a reasonable answer to what he was experiencing. Jay's attention returned to the monitor. Five minutes ago, Jay's face was carved in absolute despair as he sat down to work on his resume. Now his face shined with sheer bewilderment as he contemplated the fact that he was not alone.

Just call me for now: A. Friend. You seem like you could use one, Jay, and that's what I'm good at being. So, adding one

plus one, since you need what I'm good at, I thought that we'd probably make a pretty good match. What do you think?

As far as me knowing you, let's just say, yes, I am quite familiar with a lot about you, Jay. I believe practicing humility is so much more appealing, but if the truth was to be revealed, I know a lot about a lot of things. And what I do know about you is that you're going through some tough times, my friend.

"Wow! This is mind-blowingly crazy!" Jay thought. "This is absolutely insane! This can't be happening!" Jay found it additionally bizarre that as soon as he finished typing his response, the stranger's reply came back at him immediately with seemingly no time taken for thought or keying in words. There was zero time delay!

All of this was more than Jay could take. "Impossible! It's all impossible!" Without even closing down his file, Jay reached down and turned off the computer tower. "I may be out of work, unemployable, and maybe even a bit desperate, but I'm not crazy!"

Temporarily comforted by the resoluteness with which he had handled the *stranger of the computer* mystery, Jay bolted from the computer and headed back downstairs to disappear into the world of television escapism. Finding an old re-run of a favorite *I Love Lucy* episode, Jay lost himself in Lucy pretending a huge wedge of cheese that she had brought onto the plane was as an infant wrapped in a blanket. Laughing at Lucy's attempt to pull one over on a fellow passenger and a flight attendant, Jay pushed the idiotic computer incident as far out of his mind as possible. Lucy's escapades were much more believable than a faceless computer that knew his name.

Sunday, May 18th…11:43 P.M.

Vicki had gone to bed long ago. It was only Jay who was up, and he was antsy. His energy circuits were firing on all cylinders and he knew why. Two-and-a-half days had slipped by since the strange experience on the computer and he wasn't completely sold on the idea of going upstairs to re-visit the situation again. Part of Jay didn't want to believe that what had happened was real; the unexplainable incident had been a crazy lapse in his nighttime imagination. Another part of Jay was nervous that the encounter actually had been real. That thought was far more difficult to comprehend.

"If it really did happen, then I'm going bonkers!" So whether real or not real, Jay's mental spin on the incident was terribly unappealing to accept.

At last, human nature's need to know what's hidden in a wrapped package won out, and the temptation to solve this disturbing mystery was too much for Jay to avoid. "I need to figure this out! Besides, I can't put off doing my resume any longer! Go, Jay, dang it! Get up there! Now!"

With self-permission, Jay popped open a second bottle of evening courage. Beer in hand, he headed upstairs to the unknown. Gingerly he eased himself into the same seat in front of his computer that he had a hundred times prior, although this time the chair…the monitor… the keyboard… each seemed as unfamiliar as the moment he had unwrapped them from their individual shipping boxes. Jay chuckled to himself as his mind played out a macabre visit to his home office from Rod Serling introducing a new episode of *The Twilight Zone.*

The computer quickly buzzed to life, and Jay watched the machine wind through its start-up machinations. A hundred imaginary butterflies fluttered inside Jay. This jumpy feeling reminded Jay of how he had felt five years earlier when the arena announcer called out his name to take a halftime, half-court shot at the UCLA-USC basketball game. Standing there at the mid-court line, Jay dribbled the ball in front of a full house of cheering fans with the distant chance of winning a seventy-thousand dollar new car. Nervous tension made Jay feel as if his legs were going to give out as he tried to muster the strength to accurately catapult the basketball forty-seven feet into the very small basket at the other end of the floor. The end result of that moment in Jay's history was legendary in his mind.

"I thought the hoop was only forty feet away!" Jay would say in recounting the event to friends throughout the years. "And if it had been forty feet, my shot would have hit nothing but net! I was dead-on pure, baby!"

Without the supportive assistance of thirteen thousand screaming fans, Jay now felt the same awkward tension of that moment kick in. After finally finishing its own pre-game gyrations, the computer was ready to take on all incoming keystrokes. With leery fingers, Jay again pulled up the shortest resume in resume history. The words *Jason "Jay" Garfield* were humbly positioned at the top of the page with nothing but empty type space underneath it.

"Just as I left it," he whispered reassuringly to himself.

What he had been expecting or afraid of he couldn't be sure. He was certain, however, that he was just flat-out ecstatic to have entered into a world of normalcy as he delightedly stared at the simple, uncompleted document. Jay sat staring and hoping that nothing would happen as three minutes crawled by. Still nothing. No computer beeps. The coast seemed clear.

"Perfect!" Jay was beginning to feel as if the world, his world, once again made sense. "All is as it should be. What a lark!" Five more minutes passed and still, gratefully, nothing. Jay smiled at his temporary ridiculousness, very much pleased that he had returned to the here-and-now.

With all computer surprises an occurrence of the imaginary past, Jay took a huge swig of beer and focused his mind on filling in the rest of the required resume steps. "Write, Jay...write! You can do this! Think...think! Hmmm...do I start with my most current job? Yeah... that's right! No wait...let me start with my education first!" Jay was now picturing a resume template in his mind and everything was beginning to flow.

A cut-and-paste here, a few typing deletions and additions there, and Jay's resume was taking first draft shape. "Oh yeah! That sounds good.... Let's go with that!" Jay had just had a fresh spin-of-phrase idea pop into his mind when it finally happened again.

"Beep!"

Well, hello, Jay!

Feeling as if he had suddenly been hit by a tsunami of adrenaline, Jay froze. Actually, he stopped breathing, too. On the top of the resume he was writing there appeared a dialogue box. There was no doubt it was "him." For a moment, Jay's eyes didn't budge as he stared blankly at the block of writing. He was too afraid. Finally, he read:

Well, hello, Jay!
I'm absolutely pleased to see you again! I detect, however, that you have a few reservations about seeing my words. LOL. And just so you know, I actually am laughing out loud right now! I think it would do wonders for your spirit and how you're feeling if you followed suit and laughed, too! Laugh more in life, Jay! You would feel so much better if you let out a few more belly busters and didn't take everything so darn seriously! Laugh! And laugh hard!

"You've got to be freakin' kidding me! Not again!" Jay exclaimed in an irritated volume loud enough to be heard by Punkin who had just wandered into the room on an investigative mission to see what the big person was doing. Obviously the tone of Jay's voice was startling enough to the little cat that she stopped in her tracks scared, with tail raised, before darting out of the room assuming the angry tone must have been intended for her.

Oblivious to Punkin's quick entrance and departure, Jay continued out loud, "I have no clue who this is…but I'm not running scared this time!"

"So, hot shot, know-it-all," Jay began typing, "You think you know me, huh? Who are you and what do you *think* you know about me?"

Without being too braggadocios…fun word, huh, Jay… where do you want me to begin? I can pretty much start anywhere. School? Work? Family? Friends? I could share almost

any part of your life with you! Would you like me to tell you about the first time that you met Vicki at your friend Tricia's party? Do you remember your first date with her? Of course, how could you forget! You spilled a whole bucket of popcorn on her! Great movie that night though, huh? Audrey was so perfect in *Sabrina*, wasn't she?

Or how about when you coughed yourself blue in the face after your first cigar puff when Josh was born? Now that was funny! Or I could even go back to a time when another man named Garfield pulled out a cigar at the birth of his own son...a young boy named Jason William Garfield. I don't suppose that you'd remember that one though...would you, Jason William? LOL.

With jaw dropped and brain stuck on numb, Jay just stared with eyes wide. If his face had been captured on camera, one could interpret the picture to say that he had just realized that his lottery numbers had gone six-for-six and he was about to unbelievably cash in on "the big one." Of course, this wasn't true. Instead, Jay was getting a personal life history lesson of unfathomable proportion.

The blocks of words on the screen continued:

Let's see...your first grade teacher was Cahill...your second grade teacher was Taylor...boy, did you have a crush on her! Thought you were quite clever standing in front of the mistletoe near her desk at Christmas, didn't you, Jay? No pretending on your behalf there! The first time might have been an innocent mistake, but the third time! LOL. Your favorite teacher of all-time was your third grade teacher, Mrs. Waters. Fourth grade was Roush, fifth grade Metcalf, sixth grade Woofter...should I go on? Nah...new topic.

Remember your first baseball glove? Boy, you were proud, weren't you? You must have spent hours on that Rawlings mitt breaking it in. How about the end of the game winning shot you made to help your team go undefeated in middle school? You name it and we can talk about it! You see, Jay, there is really nothing I don't know about you. Your all-time best golf score is

a 76…darn those two 3 putts and that one out-of-bounds ball on 17 or you could have been looking at an even par round! Oh, and you love Indiana Jones, but who doesn't?

Jay quickly tried to process the information overload, but it was overwhelming. If someone had asked him to name his teachers in grades first through sixth, he probably would have had a difficult time coming up with the answers right away. But of course, the computer was right. "Cahill, Taylor, Waters…yep…and yeah…76 is right, but wait! How in the world?" Like a losing debater, Jay lashed back in frustration and aggressive anger. "How could the computer know this? Where in the world was this computer character coming from anyway?" Jay hit the keyboard with an indignant flurry.

"Look! I have no idea who you are! I have no idea how you know this information about me, but I demand that you tell me immediately! Tell me who in the world you are!"

The computer voice didn't answer right away. Sixty seconds passed before the typed conversation continued. It was as if the computer voice was either thinking, or giving his conversational partner a chance to quiet his pressed nerves.

Perhaps that's where your trouble lays, Jay. You're looking in this world…in everything around you…for answers when you should be looking inside yourself. As for who I am? It doesn't really matter. Knowing your current skepticism, you wouldn't believe it anyway. What I do encourage you to believe in, however, are my words. They are more than real. They are universally powerful.

You also need to believe that I truly do know the struggles that you now face, Jay. I know what you are feeling. I know the pain that you are experiencing and the doubts that are dominating your thinking. I know, too, that you have lost your confidence. And you know what else I know, Jay? I know I can help you find it again.

"Ouch!" The painfully true words on the screen struck a nerve. "Find my confidence, huh? Hmmm…."

The thought struck Jay somewhere in the middle of wanting to be defensive and wanting to acknowledge that it was true. That level of self-awareness wasn't an area that Jay liked to wade into and think about, but Jay knew that the mysterious stranger had been right on target. Jay would never admit it verbally. Never. But it was true. He had lost his confidence. Getting fired at this point in his life was almost more than his ego could handle. No amount of mirror self-talks could convince him that his best career days with a new company were still on the horizon. While looking in the mirror brushing his teeth, Jay would internally attempt to motivate himself to believe that his best days were ahead, but it was a tough sell to make.

"Jay…focus…c'mon focus! You can still do it! You still have it in you. Don't you?" Pleading eyes staring back at him in the mirror seemed to reinforce the idea that maybe he really didn't have it in him. He considered the notion that maybe he really had achieved all that he was destined to achieve. It was not a good thought. Yes, *confidence* was not an attitude Jay Garfield currently subscribed to in life.

"But how does this guy know that?"

What was also true was that Jay had lost his life passion. He had lost that little extra *edge*…that second wind that allowed him to achieve earlier in life. It was the *edge* that enabled him to work a twenty-hour-a-week job and still take a full college workload. It was that added desire that pushed him to work a professor's extra credit questions until he had the answer. It was that *edge* that sparked his passion to want to excel and make a difference. It was that *edge* that fed an internal craving to make his life count. When he was younger, he had it, although right now Jay even doubted that.

"Was I ever passionate about my life?" The person Jay now saw in the mirror was old and tired. His eyes looked dead. The smile was weak and so was his courage. What Jay saw in the mirror now was a man who barely existed. No dreams…no life…no energy. He was not a risk-taker, but a condition-acceptor. He was a settler.

"Why even try? I'll just end up being disappointed," were words that zapped his conscious mind. Of course, Jay didn't like the man in the mirror. He despised him.

"I've always been like this, haven't I? I've always been a mediocre loser destined to finish somewhere in the middle of the race." Brutal words polished a brutal self-affirming attitude.

Now, when the words on the computer appeared on the screen and pointed out that he'd lost his confidence, Jay felt the truth hit him like a sledgehammer making contact with a half-inch nail. It was shear devastation. Hit to the core, Jay was defenseless. Any strength that he had in trying to fend off the harsh truth to the mysterious messenger's words was long gone.

"It's true. I'm the man in the mirror." The life in Jay's body began to leave him like air escaping a rapidly leaking balloon. He sagged further in his chair.

C'mon, Jay! Lighten up! You need to begin by stopping this ugly mental game of convincing yourself that you're meant for a life of mediocre living! Nothing could be further from the truth, and that's why I am here, my friend!

My job is to build your esteem and belief in yourself again! My role here is to help you reach a new and more profound level of brilliance by showing you how to have confidence in yourself! My job is to add helium into your life balloon so that you can float even higher than previously imaginable in a world that is full of intrigue, adventure…and reward!

"I don't even type, and he still knows what I am thinking. He seems to see into me. How?" Too mystified with how much truth was being exposed, Jay no longer wanted to argue with the "how's" and "why's" of what was happening. Emotionally he was too tired to fight the "voice" any longer. Apparently, the voice was not going away and Jay didn't have the physical energy to leave anyway, so he decided to just go with the moment.

"What do I have to lose? My sanity, I suppose…but apparently I've already lost that." Jay pondered quietly.

Committed now to taking off his verbal boxing gloves against a force he didn't understand, Jay placed his fingers shakily back on the keyboard. For the first time since their conversation had begun,

Jay typed not from an attitude of angry frustration, but from a place of child-like hopefulness.

Jay typed. "Well, if you are here to help me as you say that you are, can I at least ask your name?"

Of course! My name is Amicus.

"Amicus…Amicus." Jay repeated the name out loud a couple of times. "Amicus…where do I know that name from? Amicus… Amicus…."

Suddenly, Jay remembered. "It's Latin! *Amicus* means *friend*!"

Many years ago, Jay had greatly struggled to pass a Latin course. The small victory of remembering a single Latin word from years ago now seemed to be so much more meaningful than the hard-earned "C+" he had been able to coax out of his instructor back then.

"Friend," he said the translation again out loud. With signs of resurgence, the former student of Latin sat up a bit straighter and typed back. Hitting the keys with determined fingers, Jay continued typing: Nice to meet you, Amicus. Cool name. I like it. It's promisingly friendly.

"Promisingly friendly," huh? How interesting that you'd use those two words. I'm quite certain those are the same two words that Abraham used when he first heard my name, too. But thank you, Jay. Thank you, also, for thinking my name is "cool." I'm not sure if I've ever heard that description before, however! LOL.

"Abraham…who's Abraham? Another computer friend of yours? Am I going to meet him, too?" Jay caught himself smiling as he typed. And although it was a rather small smile, it was a large miracle considering where Jay's state of mind had been just minutes prior.

Ahhh…Abraham! Well, actually I have befriended a number of Abraham's over the years, but the one whose words you duplicated unknowingly had a rather famous last name… Lincoln.

"Lincoln? Abraham Lincoln?! Any relation? No, no, no…wait! Not THAT Abraham Lincoln!!!" Jay's fingers never moved across the keyboard so quickly and without error. He was typing his thoughts into sentences almost as fast as they entered his mind. Being a two-fingered typist, Jay was not known to be a very fast "pecker," but suddenly his fingers were on a world-record setting pace.

"You can't mean Abraham Lincoln…#16?" Jay gulped down the last of his beer.

Yes, that Abraham, Jay…#16. There was a stretch of time where Abraham's world became pretty dark, and he was anguishing over a few decisions that he had to make. I remember him sitting at his writing desk feeling the weight of the world. When I first met him, he'd reached a desperate point and he was losing hope that things would ever get better.

"Hold on! You're telling me that you TALKED to Abraham Lincoln? That's impossible! How old are you pretending to be?"

As to your belief that "it's impossible,"…nothing is truly impossible, Jay. Some things in life may be more improbable, but nothing is impossible. In fact, when things seem impossible, I'm known for doing some of my most creative work. And to answer your first question, yes, I did spend time with Abraham. As to your second question, the answer is irrelevant.

You may know Mr. Lincoln for what he did as far as uniting your country, Jay, but I know him as a man of immense personal commitment who desired to find a way to be of service to his fellow man. Abe was truly dedicated to making a difference and he never gave up on that mission. At times, he may have considered throwing in the towel, but he persevered through the toughest of trials. It's true that Abraham was a sensitive man who took the lows of life exceptionally hard. In fact, I know that he appreciated my presence a great deal when things were the most painful for him. It was during those tough times when we became friends.

"You were friends with Lincoln? You met him? You've shaken Lincoln's hand?"

LOL. Shaken his hand? No, Jay. I didn't meet Abraham in an "I can see you!" physical sort of way. There are other ways to meet people that you might not yet be able to consider…like the way we are meeting. The first time I greeted him was right after the death of his dear Ann. He was so heart-broken by Ms. Rutledge's passing that I even wondered if his broken spirit would ever mend. During that very hard time, I came to him simply as "opportunity." His life was once again given hope, and he was able to move forward and away from his personal anguish by setting his sights on a renewed life purpose. For him that purpose became business and politics.

"You came to him as 'opportunity'? I'm not quite sure I understand. What I think you're telling me, though, is that you really never talked to him…right?"

That's not what I'm saying, Jay. Remember, there are different ways I can communicate. Sometimes it might be through a new opportunity created. Other times it may be through the pages of a book or through the words of a friend. It could be in an epiphany of inspirational thought motivated by a powerful, crashing ocean wave or in the beautiful simplicity of watching a dutiful ant go about his work. It all depends.

As Abraham grew in age and wisdom, he realized that my presence in his life had been wordlessly apparent for years in many forms. It was, however, when he called the White House home that Abraham had need for me in a far more direct fashion. It was there that I came to him most directly, and it was also there that much of our writing became indistinguishable.

"What is he saying?" Jay thought. "I have no idea what to think. I don't understand at all. Who in the world is Amicus? I can see the words in front of me. They are real. Is Amicus a prophet, an angel…or even more…is Amicus God?" The question struck Jay like a hot ember striking his skin from a bellowing fire.

"Was it even possible? Am I talking to God?" Jay shook his head as if trying to release the temporary blindfold of what could have been the fantasy of a simple daydream. "Do I ask him if he is? Do I even want to know?" Jay chose the safe route. "Avoid the question and ask about something else."

"Okay…what did you like most about Lincoln?" Jay typed.

Abraham was a man of great conviction. Of course, history will always remember him for his passionate fight for the equality of all men. I'll remember him as a man that didn't let others' fervent feelings sway his belief system. Despite being bombarded regularly by the harsh criticism of the press, Congress, an entire region of the country, and the not-so-silent voices of his friends, Abraham never looked to others for affirmation; he looked to himself.

I remember one particular letter where Abraham wrote:

> *I desire to so conduct the affairs of this adminis-tration that if at the end, when I come to lay down the reigns of power, I have lost every friend on earth, I shall at least have one friend left, and that friend shall be down inside of me.*

Powerful conviction, don't you think, Jay?

Jay read Lincoln's words through a second time. "…If at the end, when I come to lay down the reigns of power, I have lost every friend on earth, I shall at least have one friend left, and that friend shall be down inside of me." Without Jay realizing it consciously, the first seed of personal empowerment had just been planted.

It was 3:18 in the morning when Jay and Amicus parted ways. Jay had asked dozens of questions about other footprint-leaving people with whom Amicus had met. Jay listened to the inspiring stories of historical giants and learned about the seemingly insurmountable obstacles that they had each overcome throughout life. Later before falling off into a hard sleep, Jay again felt connected to the world. As obvious as the thought would seem, Jay recognized that he wasn't the first person to ever face a dramatic life-altering moment. He felt great comfort in outwardly acknowledging that he was a part of mankind… a universal group that had felt defeat and pain and struggle since the beginning of time. Jay went to bed more hopeful and peaceful than he had in months.

"I'm going to be okay. I'm going to survive this and even be better for having gone through it."

Monday, May 19th…9:30 A.M.

After barely six hours of sleep for a guy who liked to push the sleep limits considerably past eight hours, Jay woke up feeling energized. "Wow! I feel great! This is going to be a great day!"

Inadvertently programming his brain to expect good things today, Jay quickly slipped on his green army camouflage shorts, and a favorite, old, holey T-shirt. He ran his hand twice over his scalp with the purpose of livening up still sleeping hair, brushed his teeth with a cursory sixty second once-over, and then proceeded down the stairs doing a quick-step drill similar to a football player high-stepping in a tire exercise. Jay was whistling his own rendition of an old Bob Seger song, *Like a Rock*, which probably would have even stumped the best of *Name That Tune* players. His new friend Amicus was on his mind and the source of his morning revitalization.

Jay grabbed a gallon jug of two-percent milk out of the refrigerator, took his favorite brand of cereal from the cupboard, grabbed a bowl and spoon, and sat down at the kitchen table to enjoy his favorite breakfast…a big bowl of cold cereal.

"I have so much to ask him! So much I want to know!" Thoughts of Amicus' true identity currently seemed irrelevant. It didn't matter. What did matter was how spending time with Amicus last night made him feel now.

"Alive! I feel alive again! It feels so fantastic to feel good again!" Jay enthusiastically pumped his fist to reinforce the feeling.

Jay felt healthier emotionally than he had in a long time; the feeling was so freeing. With energy at a maximum level ten, he wolfed down his first bowl of cereal. This was definitely a two-bowl morning, but before Jay could pour bowl #2, he noticed a note on the corner of the table that he hadn't noticed initially. His ravenous craving to devour the entire box of Life cereal sitting in front of him caused such single-mindedness of focus that he probably wouldn't have noticed even if Punkin had been laying on the table as she sometimes was mischievously known for doing. The note was from Vicki.

Jay! I am so proud of you! Your resume looks fantastic! This morning when I got up, I noticed that the computer was still on, but before I shut it down, I noticed that your resume file was open. You did it! You finished it…and it looks great! I'll stop by the Office Store on the way home and pick up some letterhead and envelopes so that you can start sending it out! Wait till the world sees you now! I'm so proud of you, Jay! Love, V.

With forehead lines scrunching together in a sign of definite uncertainty, Jay thought to himself. "I finished my resume? Did I? I don't think so!" Thoughts of a second bowl of morning cereal were now relegated to a possible lunchtime option as Jay bounded back up the stairs taking two at a time.

"C'mon…c'mon! Hurry…hurry…hurry!" Jay's fingers tapped anxiously on the keyboard as he waited impatiently for the computer to start. Finally receiving the green light to move forward, Jay brought up the file marked "resume." He began to read.

"Hmmm…I did all of this? Geez…I don't remember polishing this up like this! Wow!"

Jay was surprisingly impressed. Articulately worded, the resume highlighted his professional achievements with colorful accuracy. "Man…this does looks good! I look great on paper! This should impress someone!" Giving himself a small ovation with a flurry of small hand claps, Jay barely heard the computer.

"Beep!"

What do you think, Jay? Impressive, huh? There's no doubt

that you sure dress-up well on paper, my friend! You have developed terrific experience that a number of employers will surely welcome!

Amicus was back.

"AMICUS!!!!" Jay typed back with on-fire energy. "Good morning …good morning! Hey, Amicus…I don't remember finishing my resume at all…but I love it! I remember talking to you about Lincoln and Obama…Oprah and Gates…but I don't remember finishing my resume!" Amicus' response was short.

Even the greatest of ocean going ships could benefit with a little help from the wind, Jay.

"What? I don't get it. What does he mean?" Jay pondered. "Wait! No way! He didn't…did he? How?" Jay was talking to himself. "Did Amicus help me finish this?" The thought was stunning, but what other explanation was there? "It wasn't Vicki…and I'm darn sure I didn't finish it…so…could it really be?"

Ideas in Jay's world that once seemed ridiculously impossible were now modestly more acceptable. "Hmmm…maybe he means that I am the ship and Amicus…I think…is the wind. Is that what he means? Oh, man…Wow!" A wave of gratefulness washed over Jay as he came to grips with this undoubtedly true realization. The resume that had once hung over his head like undone taxes on April 10th was now finished. Not only was it finished, but it was perfect! Absolutely perfect!

Jay started typing. "Amicus…thank you! I don't know what else to really say. I'm very grateful!"

You're welcome, Jay, but don't give me too much credit. I, perhaps, provided a little inspiration, but you're the one who did it, Jay. You're the one who has lived the life to which the resume points.

Jay thought about that for a minute. He reviewed each of the jobs and experiences listed on the completed resume. Again he read each sentence mulling it over like a red-penned editor would mull over an article waiting to go to print.

After five minutes spent thoroughly reading it, Jay typed back. "Yes, I suppose it's true…I really did do all of these things!" Beaming with pride, Jay felt great at seeing his past accomplishments and experiences on paper. "Well," Jay continued typing, "no matter how it got done …it is! And that makes me ecstatic! Thank you, Amicus! Thank you for your support!"

Although my contribution to the effort is not worthy of note, you're welcome, Jay. I'm pleased that you are pleased!

"Vicki loved it! Her feedback this morning made me feel great! It feels so good to think that she is proud of me again." Jay continued typing. "In fact, she's going to be picking up letterhead today so that I can start mailing them out." He paused then continued, "But I guess that means I need to find somewhere that I really want to send them… right? Geez, Amicus, I have no idea what I want to do! Do you need an assistant?" Jay was only half joking.

Amicus' words quickly hit the screen…full of energy and passion.

Jay! Stop for a second and look to your right. See the window? Well, look outside! Today is a great day! A new day! A great, new day for YOU! New days mean new starts! The future is completely yours to do with as you wish! You have no limits except the limits you give yourself…so don't hold yourself back! Yesterday and the mistakes you think you made? Forget about them! They've come and gone! Look at the potential of today… and tomorrow! That's what exists! That's where your focus should be! So when you start thinking about what you want to do…be bold! Be a possibility thinker! Be an opportunity seeker! Get a job doing something that you know you'd love to do!

The words landed like a ton of bricks and hit Jay brutally hard. He had felt completely optimistic just minutes ago, but then the emotional roller coaster that seemed to keep Jay trapped as a perennial rider swept him away again. His smile…outer and inner…disappeared. Optimistic truth can be so unsettling for someone not ready for its lessons.

"Yeah right, Amicus. Nice thoughts…but my reality is not your reality. You might be able to do what you want in life…but I can't. Did you forget I just got fired?" Jay's writing took on a sarcastic tone. "In case you didn't know, getting fired means the company doesn't need you. It means you're dead wood. It means you suck!" Jay was on a negative roll and happy to stay on it. "Look…the time that I have spent with you has been dandy, but MY truth is I don't have a job! Even worse, if I don't find one soon, I could be in serious financial trouble! That's what's real in my world, Amicus! Your stories about Lincoln and all the other people overcoming stuff? Blah, blah, blah. They're great stories…but they aren't real to me. They don't help me get what I need. A JOB!!!" Jay had definitely gone overboard on his self-thrown pity party.

Amicus was not holding up his end of the conversation. All was silent. There was no "beep." Nothing. A minute went by. Three minutes went by and Jay was getting nervous. "Uh oh!" he said to himself. "I think I chased him away! Oh, crap!"

"Amicus, are you there?" Jay typed. "Amicus??? Amicus…where are you?????? Jay to Amicus…hellooooooo?" Four painfully slow minutes passed before the sound came again.

"Beep!"

A block of words appeared on the screen.

I'm here, Jay…and it appears that I'll be here for quite some time. It's now one hundred percent clear that you needed more than a nudge getting your resume done. Even the small jumpstart I gave your personal battery last night seems to have run out of juice already! No, I think what you need, Jay, is a total mental attitude overhaul!

Now it was Jay's turn to grow silent. Jay didn't type back, and Amicus continued.

Just remember, Jay, I'm a friend. I care about your life…. I care about what you think…. I care about what you feel. You can trust me, Jay.

I know you. I know the sort of passion that hides within you. I know your fears, and I know your dreams…even the ones that you currently don't know exist. And most importantly, I know this: today is the first day of the rest of your life! And you know what else, Jay?

Jay was embarrassingly forced to type back. "What?"

I know that this is supposed to be a secret to you, but I will tell you anyway. The rest of your life? It's going to be incredible!

Jay! Look inside yourself! See what I see! You have a tenacious spirit that has been dying to escape and chase adventure for a long time! You were born to do great things! You have incredible talent and there are thousands of people who need to be touched by the gift that only you can give them. So now is your chance, Jay! Now is your time! It's time for those hidden dreams inside you to see the light of day! It's time for you to give yourself to the world and really live!

This was all too much for Jay to handle. A defensive spirit grew angrily and sarcastically inside him as he shot back to Amicus, "Really live? What in the world are you talking about? What do you think I'm doing now? Hear me breathing, Amicus? See me moving in this chair? I can assure you that I'm very alive and not ready to be picked up by the coroner anytime soon!"

Ignoring Jay's feeble attempt to defend himself, Amicus continued.

Jay, there's opportunity and adventure all around you! Open your eyes! Open your mind's eye! With the rising of a new sun comes new intrigue, new purpose, and new celebration! You've been given a brand new chance to be great again! You've been given the chance to take on motivating new challenges and to feel the exhilaration of incredible new victories!

41

What would I like to see you do? I'd love to see you go out and jump onto the playground of life again! You've been living a dull routine for far too long! You were built for exploring! You were created to build! Now is your time to explore and build! Capture your new moment, Jay! Have confidence in yourself and watch your destiny unfold in a brilliant way! It's time that you learn to SOAR in life, my friend! Really SOAR!

The words tackled Jay's heart and mind like a three-hundred-pound defensive lineman going after a frightened skinny quarterback. Jay felt their brutal smack. He knew once again that Amicus was right. He wasn't really living. But he desperately wanted to.

10:45 A.M.

Still feeling deflated by his morning conversation with Amicus, Jay went downstairs and, out of guilty obligation, spread out the employment section of the paper on the kitchen table. He retrieved his notebook, a pair of scissors, and a dispenser of scotch tape.

Jay's job hunting approach was basically lacking any real strategy. Choosing to ignore internet resources at this time was a strong indicator that Jay had not yet fully embraced the job finding challenge in front of him. Instead he studied the *Help Wanted* section of the paper, starting with "Accounting." When a job had even the slightest appeal, Jay would cut it out of the paper and tape it in the notebook.

Thus he moved page after page, letter after letter, to the "Z's" and "Zoo Guide:" *Outgoing person needed to give public tours and community presentations for Los Angeles Zoo. B.A. and strong public relations background preferred. Must be good with all age groups. Strong telephone and presentation skills necessary. Competitive salary commensurate with experience.*

"Hmmm...maybe working for the zoo would be fun. Is this what Amicus meant by *Go out and experience the playground of life?*" Jay pictured himself wearing an oversized safari hat and throwing peanuts to the elephants in order to encourage them to pay attention to his group.

"Daisy over there is an Asian elephant. You can tell the difference between Daisy and her female African counterpart by the much smaller size of her ears." A glimpse of a smile parted Jay's lips.

"Funny if that happened...showcasing Daisy! Maybe it isn't that far out of the question. It would be fun!" Jay let his mind delve a bit longer into the zoo possibility and his imaginary tour before he refolded the dissected LA Times. He finished by diligently reviewing the three notebook pages of job ads that he had cut out.

"Not bad...twenty-three possibilities." Jay mumbled audibly as he counted the result of his nearly two hour effort. Jay was pleased with what he'd accomplished, not in the sense that he'd found "I want it!" positions that excited him, but rather because he was finally getting his act together and seriously looking. Jay's spirits began to rise once again. Just putting in a solid effort in the morning's job hunt was reason to be more hopeful.

"I wonder what Amicus meant when he said that my future was going to be incredible? What does he know that I don't know? I hope he's right...."

Jay dared not allow the hope of Amicus' premonition to linger. Achieving the opposite result of "incredible" currently seemed far more realistic in his life and he didn't need any more meteor-like disappointments bashing into his world.

Jay grabbed the phone and brought it to the table. "Well, I might as well begin tackling these dudes." He sighed unenthusiastically. He really wasn't looking forward to this next part of job hunting...the calling. Most of the ads had phone numbers listed and although the thought of picking up the phone and making contact turned Jay's stomach, he knew it was what he needed to do. With fleeting courage, he dialed the eighteen business ads that had listed numbers.

The majority of Jay's calls were met by either a receptionist taking names (*Ms. Kennedy is only taking names and numbers of interested candidates at this time.*) or a voice mail informing him to fax or e-mail his resume. For those few businesses that did volunteer more information about their job, Jay wrote applicable notes under the ad in his notebook: *Lousy pay!"...100% cold calling...Group interview on the 26th...Sounds good! Send resume!*

Out of the twenty-three original ads and eighteen calls, Jay decided to pursue eleven of the opportunities.

Feeling victorious with his day's job seeking effort, Jay decided that hopping on his bike for some afternoon exercise sounded like a great idea. After giving both tires a quick boost of air with the hand pump, Jay hastily pushed his bike out of the garage before the electric door came down completely. With weary legs that felt great to be challenged again, Jay pedaled the four miles to the post office to buy stamps for the resumes he planned on sending out.

As he pedaled, Jay enjoyed the sun on his back; warm rays penetrated his shirt. His exhilarating efforts caused his body to sweat. It felt invigorating to exercise and to celebrate his efforts toward exploring a new career opportunity. Jay's thoughts soon turned to his new friend …Amicus.

"Who is this guy? What's going on? Whatever…whoever… he's just what I needed! I feel like I'm starting to make things happen again!"

Jay pondered Amicus' morning words, "You have a very tenacious spirit…dying to escape…you were born to do great things…allow your dreams to spill out…learn to SOAR!"

Jay played the words over and over in his head, like he would have played Session One of a *Learn Spanish in 30 Days* CD series. Jay carefully listened to the Amicus tape until the end and then he rewound it and played it again. The words permeated his tired body. Like a mantra sparking his final half-mile bike sprint home, a few key words attached themselves to each of Jay's pedal strokes. *Believe…dream… SOAR! Believe…dream…SOAR!* Like a gold medal winning cyclist, Jay crossed the imaginary finish line of his driveway feeling fantastic. Unknowingly, Jay was slowly re-wiring his body and brain to create great things.

3:31 *P.M.*

Feeling exhilarated from his day's effort, Jay decided to keep the positive momentum going and write a simple cover letter that could be sent along with his resume. In his letter folder, Jay tweaked eleven different versions of the same letter adding destination addresses and recipient names so that they would all be ready to be printed and mailed once Vicki brought home the paper and matching envelopes.

"There it is…number eleven! Done! Great day, Jay! Way to go!" he proudly reflected. "Vicki's going to be totally jazzed when she sees this!"

Rising up out of the chair to stretch, Jay took Amicus' earlier lead and glanced out the window at the beautiful sunny day that still remained. The picture was stunning as the late afternoon sun brightly highlighted nature's dazzling colors on a myriad of amazing flower and leaf forms.

"Wow! Everything looks so beautiful!" Jay thought. "The trees… the leaves…the floating clouds…why don't I take the time to notice this more? Amicus is right. I've been blind to so much! I don't want to be…I want to change!"

For the first time not only in weeks, but in years, Jay began to see things differently. For a brief instant, he was looking at the world through fresh eyes. With a new-found spirit of awareness awakening within him, Jay was feeling the life-affirming power of hope. Maybe it was the emotional hell that he had gone through or maybe it was the jolt of Amicus' empowering words this morning. Maybe it was the afternoon bike ride, Vicki's confidence, or possibly the eleven finished job letters that were ready to hit the mail. Actually, it didn't even matter what the root cause of Jay's momentary revitalization was. What did matter was that Jay felt like climbing his way back up the mountain. Turning his back on the intense disappointment that he'd felt just hours earlier, Jay was setting his sights on the exciting possibilities of the future. At that moment, Jay felt encouraged. Life again felt hopeful.

"Beep!"

Breaking his trance, the interrupting sound sent Jay's focus back to the computer screen. Of course it was Amicus, but this time the words on the screen appeared differently. The words were not written in a manner seeking to create conversation, but they came in the form of a letter:

Dear Jay,
I want to applaud you for taking action on the *Help Wanted* ads! Good work!

For a brief second, Jay stopped and wondered how Amicus could have known that. He shook his head in puzzlement and continued reading:

But, being productive for a single day isn't the same as being productive for a lifetime, Jay. And frankly, after our morning conversation, I'm concerned about how long the positive energy you're now feeling will last. You're too valuable for me to let you slip again, and I feel there is the potential for you to do that. Because of this, I have decided to enroll you in a unique class called *Bamboo Farming 101*. You might wonder at the title, but as the course continues, you will come to know what is meant by its name.

I will be your instructor in this course, and it will be a mix of written lesson and self-directed lab application. Again, all of the pieces will begin to fit together nicely as we progress. Each day I want you to check the computer for your lesson. It will always be there.

During the course, you will not have the chance to directly interact with me as you have become accustomed to during our last conversations. If I allow you to ask direct questions, you may seek to chase tangents that are less important. I want you to focus and reflect on the message of the lessons.

I will set expectations high from the beginning when I tell you that this course has the potential to change everything about your life. Of course, your personal change will be in direct relation to your own

dedication and effort. Remember when I told you that there are big things in store for you, my friend? This is the beginning of it. This is where you take ownership of your life, and your eyes are opened to all the amazing possibilities that are out there waiting for you.

You will have twenty-one lessons to complete in this course. After the last lesson, I will return and you will take a Final. However, this Final will be different from all others that you have ever taken. In this Final, you will not be quizzed by the professor's questions, but rather you will ask me three questions. Do not worry about what you shall ask; it will be evident to you when the day comes.

So my very special student, be prepared tomorrow for *Lesson #1*.

In service to you,
Amicus

It had been only three short days ago when Jay Garfield first sat at the computer with the simple goal of writing a resume. To say his life had been rocked emotionally by the termination events on that infamous May 7th day would be accurate, but potentially more life changing was what he was experiencing now. Of course like most people, Jay thought he would have been crazy to consider the truth of what was happening. Not only was he writing to a stranger whose words magically appeared on the computer screen, a stranger who knew everything about his life and was quite proficient in polishing resumes, but evidently this character named Amicus was also a teacher who thought it necessary to enroll him in a class called *Bamboo Farming 101*.

This crazy comedy of events might have seemed unbelievable unless you had been Jay Garfield and were experiencing it firsthand. So how did Jay respond? Surprisingly for Jay, he didn't respond with defiance or with irritation. Instead, he internally responded with expectant hope. He was sincerely looking forward to reading what Amicus had to teach. Externally? Jay laughed. He laughed the sort of hearty laugh that his teacher Amicus had earlier prescribed. "Boy, would Professor

Amicus be proud of me for learning so quickly!" In the forefront of Jay's mind was the exploding thought of going back to school. Taking classes had never been this invigorating to Jay in his whole life.

Tuesday, May 20th

There would be no early morning wake-up conflict in the Garfield house this morning. Jay energetically popped out of bed, at the same time as Vicki, ready to experience a new day. The previous night had been one of great optimism in the Garfield home. There was a shared excitement and hope as Jay had proudly showed off his day's job development work. Vicki insisted on reading through each of the eleven cover letters separately and talking about the merits of each potential opportunity. Although she didn't share what she was doing, Jay knew that with each resume and cover letter that made it to the final sealed envelope stage, Vicki was saying a quick, silent prayer for the person who would be opening it. Jay didn't mind though. Although he'd never been a religious man, Jay had recently come to the conclusion that it didn't hurt to have "someone" looking out for you.

As Vicki hurried to get ready for work, Jay followed her around the house. From the bedroom, to the bathroom, to the kitchen, and then back to the bedroom…Jay was sharing with Vicki his plans for the day. He was going to extensively search on internet job sites; then he planned on calling and registering with a few employment agencies.

"Who knows? Maybe the agencies have something great. It doesn't hurt to cast every possible line out there." Jay enthusiastically spoke.

Vicki was happy to listen and share in Jay's eagerness about the upcoming day. There wasn't any talk about what Vicki's day would entail, but that didn't matter to her right now. Jay had never been one to share much about what he was thinking and feeling so Vicki found this new connection to be revitalizing. Jay's positive energy was contagious.

Jay stood at the door that led from the garage into the house and waved to Vicki as she pulled her car out and headed to work. There was no doubt that Jay was feeling animated this morning. The reason was obvious, of course. Sure the job hunting adventure was motivating, but the real intrigue was about starting the first day of class and *Bamboo Farming 101*. As soon as the garage door shut, Jay sprinted upstairs.

Little surprised Jay about Amicus anymore. Therefore, as soon as Jay entered the home office, it wasn't startling to see that the computer was somehow turned on and Amicus' message was glowing from the monitor. Jay hurriedly slipped into his class seat like an eager, but tardy student. With attention fully captured, Jay began to read his first lesson.

LESSON 1: AWAKEN YOUR GIANT!
(Dream Again)

In order for you to live big, my friend, we need to turn you back into a person who dreams big. We need you to see life once again as something that is exciting, fresh, and new. We need you to look at life again through the eyes of a child.

Remember when you believed you could do anything? Remember when you dreamed you could be a professional golfer or a U.S. Senator? Remember a time when you had no idea how tough life was and believed everything was truly possible? Well, let's go there again. Let's start your very first lesson by shedding the restraints of adulthood by playing a child's game. Let's take a moment and pretend.

By accident, you've rediscovered a key which unlocks an old treasure chest that has been kept locked and in the attic for years. Over time, you'd forgotten all about the old chest, but with exciting memories from the past now racing through your mind, you bound up the stairs thinking about all the great stuff that might be stored in it.

You hustle up the ladder, hoist yourself into the attic, and quickly survey the contents of the dimly lit room. Years of accumulated cobwebs and dark shadows attempt to hide the object of your search, but very quickly your eyes find the old trunk. Excited and out of breath, you uncharacteristically

slide across the dusty floor and fall to your knees in front of this glorious, magical, treasure chest. Mere seconds seem like minutes as you clumsily attempt to use the key. Wildly flinging the chest open, you discover to your disappointment that nothing is in it except a dusty document rolled up and laying next to a very old and tarnished lamp.

Somewhat perplexed, you unroll the document, blowing dust off of it so you can begin to read. Ah, but wait! You quickly learn that this is no ordinary lamp! The document reveals that by simply rubbing the ancient lamp, you'll set free a powerful genie who lives inside and is prepared to fulfill the deepest desires of your heart! All of the amazing dreams stored in the back of your mind now have a chance of becoming reality! The magical genie has the power to change your life from the ordinary into the extraordinary! Great news, huh?

As you continue reading the document, you learn that in order to release the genie…your genie…all you need do is polish the lamp and restore its original shine. Sounds easy, doesn't it? So what do you do next? Do you start scrubbing and polishing as fast as you can, or out of uncertainty and fear, do you set the magical lamp back in the treasure chest and lock it forever?

Well, Jay, certainly very few would turn their back on such an amazing, life-changing opportunity. I know you wouldn't. If you really did find the proverbial genie in the lamp, I know you wouldn't pass up this unique opportunity to reshape your own destiny and create the life you want. Or would you? Would anybody?

Sadly, the answer is "yes" they would. You would. Every single day you and millions of others close the lid and walk away from the hope of turning deeply seeded dreams into reality. Every day millions turn their backs on chasing a passionate purpose and settle for an ordinary existence.

Somewhere deep inside you, Jay, a magical genie truly does exist. It has a name; it is called "Potential." Unfortunately, most people are too lazy, too afraid, or too preoccupied to spend the time and effort required to release their genie on the world. The result is that all of these people never even realize a fraction of their true potential. With a very heavy heart, I can say that there's little in the world that I find more upsetting than unrealized potential.

Life is too precious and too short to live without giving your best effort, Jay. With so many amazing things to do, with so many interesting people to meet, with so much opportunity all around, there should be no excuse that should ever hold you back from going for it! Why not live up to your potential? Why not chase rainbows? Why not build castles and paint mountains? Dream again! Then take action; make those dreams materialize!

Sure, it's easy to become a victim of life and fall prey to the negative circumstances and events that derail your dreams. But is that really any way to live? Is that what you truly want? Rise above setbacks, overcome obstacles, and live the life that you desire! Shape your own destiny! Make your journey through life your journey and not one that is pushed and pulled by other people. Lock the door forever on excuses and rationalizations and open the door wide for your dreams to enter the world!

Jay, it's time. It's time that you make the decision to start scrubbing and shining your "lamp of potential." It's time to release your genie! You have a unique destiny to fulfill, my friend, and it's time for you to start dreaming to make it happen! Dream powerfully! Dream purposefully! Dream passionately! Dream, Jay, dream!

At the bottom of the page, there was a single question:

What would you like to do in your life?

It was followed by a short notation:

PS: You will find each lesson immeasurably more valuable if you answer the question that follows. Keep your answers in a notebook and you'll start the process of making the invisible… visible. You will soon understand.

Jay read the lesson a second time. He then opened a drawer in his desk and pulled out a note pad. At the top of the page, he wrote:

DAY 1: AWAKEN YOUR GENIE! (Dream Again).
Skipping a line, he then wrote down the first question:
What would I like to do in my life?

Uncertain what to write or where to begin, Jay sat quietly and thought. Soon, however, the pen was flying across the paper as he took on an exercise whose answers came from deep within him. For the first time in a long time, Jay was actually wiping the corrosion off of his inner lamp. The sleeping genie inside Jay began to wake from slumber.

Wednesday, May 21st…9:30 A.M.

Twenty-four hours later, Jay was in front of the computer once again. In his notebook, which lay opened on the desk in front of him, he copied down the title of today's lesson in his neatest penmanship. Then he began to read:

LESSON 2: JUST IMAGINE!
(Dream without Limits)

As the writer picked up his pen in preparation to write, he closed his eyes. To him, the vision of what tomorrow might be seemed clearer when the realities of today were blocked out. He imagined the future. He imagined a new world. In this world, the people traveled by incredible moving machines that were controlled by a steering mechanism and foot pedals. In this world, he visualized a device that allowed people to transport the written word over long distances so that others could read it. In this world, he imagined machines that could think and solve complex problems involving numbers. In this world, he pictured a society run by technology.

A profile of the future? I think not. Cars, fax machines and computers are commonplace. They're a part of everyday life. But at one time they weren't. At one time, they were the fantasies of a science fiction writer. The year was 1863 and the person was Jules Verne.

In his novel, *Paris in the Twentieth Century*, Jules Verne opened up his imagination and pictured a world completely foreign to anything that even closely resembled the reality of his time. He looked beyond the walls that society had built around him, and flooded his brain with vivid pictures of what might exist outside those walls. This great visionary was not afraid to close his eyes and imagine.

Now it's your turn. Imagine the future. Imagine YOUR future. Imagine what would happen in your career if you performed your job with excellence every single day. Imagine what would happen in the relationships in your life if you greeted every person you met as if they were the most important person in the world. Imagine what would happen in your life if you dedicated thirty minutes every day to pursuing your ultimate dreams.

Although our imagining exercises might be a bit different from the questions Mr. Verne asked himself, the answers are no less thrilling or life changing. Jules saw the future as it might be. You can see your own future as it can be. Different from our teacher, Mr. Verne, you don't have to wait a hundred years for the images of your future to come true. They can start coming true now!

Let's go back to the three preceding "imagine" situations above:

1. Imagine what would happen in your career if you performed your job with passion and purpose every single day. What do you picture? A raise or promotion perhaps? Those

are the quick and easy answers. Add more detail! Imagine a personnel search firm contacting you because you'd been referred to them as a dynamite prospect. And the job that they eventually offer you? It's more incredible than any you've ever had! It could happen. If you can imagine it.

2. Imagine what would happen in the relationships in your life if you greeted every person that you met as if he or she was the most important person in the world. At the very least, others would recognize you as a person who is warm and friendly. But imagine harder. Suppose that a stranger who is the recipient of your friendliness, encouragement, and positive attitude is the owner of a multi-million dollar business that caters to celebrities and dignitaries. Just suppose, too, that she happens to be in the market for someone with remarkable people skills to communicate with her clientele. Of course the job is crucial to the long term success of her company and it pays very, very well. Preposterous? Not if you can imagine it.

3. Imagine what would happen in your life if you dedicated thirty minutes every day to pursuing a dream. With daily focus there's no doubt that your passion and commitment to achieving your dream would increase. Want to write a book? Write for thirty minutes every day and watch the great novel that the world has never read come to fruition. When you strive consistently towards achieving your goal, you reinforce your motivation and confidence. You also ignite that amazing success pilot light inside you, and when that pilot light is lit one hundred percent of the time, watch out! Before you know it, page one materializes into "The End!" It could happen. If you can imagine it.

Imagine, my friend. Imagine all the great things that you can do with your life. Imagine the amazing places, the interesting people, the fantastic life opportunities, and the valuable social contributions that are simply out there waiting for your imagination and effort to kick in. Follow the example cast by Mr. Verne and dare to step outside of your comfort zone and s-t-r-e-t-c-h your vision for what your life could be. Your future is limitless, my friend. If you can imagine it.

Question:
With absolutely no limits to your thinking, what crazy things can you imagine accomplishing in life?

"What crazy things can I imagine accomplishing? You mean, besides peace on earth and goodwill to all men?" Jay laughed. "Okay… fun question…why not? I'll go with it!"

With imagination shifting into full gear, Jay Garfield started to have some fun as he wrote his answers. A half-dozen half-hearted and playful dreams like *Win an Oscar!* were soon followed by the same number of entries saving the world such as *End hunger on earth.*

"What can I really and truly imagine myself accomplishing?" The inspired genie within him seemed to breathe its divine breath into Jay's conscious mind as answers to the question began filling the notebook page.

Thursday, May 22nd…9:09 A.M.

Jay continued to call on employers and send his resume to the new ads that he found in the Help Wanted section of the newspapers and on the internet. Jay hadn't received any calls back from his resume yet, but he was still hopeful. Having been in sales, Jay understood the "numbers game" of making as many contacts as possible in order to generate that one golden opportunity. *"Keep on dialing. Keep on inquiring!"* was a note he had taped to his office computer at JLJ Advertising. He had read it so many times before that it was now a mantra repeated at the first sign of failure fatigue. Understanding and accepting the ups-and-downs of job hunting, Jay felt anxious for sure…but he wasn't ready to hit the panic button quite yet.

There was no doubt that Jay's confidence was slowly growing. Perhaps his self-assurance wasn't Trump-like in magnitude and his mind was still frequently attacked by the uncertainty monster, but Jay was feeling much better overall about himself and the potential of finding something new. One week earlier, Jay would have begged for a job. Now, not weighed down by the desperate fear that he and Vicki would be out on the street within the month, Jay had cautious optimism that maybe he could even find something that he liked.

"Heck, maybe I can find a job that I look forward to spending eight hours a day and five days a week doing! Is that too much to ask? And if I really want to push my luck, why not take this chance to find a job I love? Why shouldn't I find a job that makes me feel great and motivates me?" Vicki overwhelmingly endorsed Jay's thinking. "I couldn't have a more supportive and encouraging fan!" Jay thought. Her unwavering belief in him boosted his confidence in himself.

Jay had yet to share with Vicki the major source of what was behind Jay's revitalized spirit. Maybe some people would have come clean and shared with a friend or spouse the truth about Amicus if the same thing would have happened to them. However, like Jay, a greater percentage of us might have decided to keep the super-natural Amicus phenomenon under wraps. Jay was not one for taking a chance and spilling the beans. Too much risk.

"Yeah, right! Where do I even begin explaining the story of Amicus? Vicki will think I'm a loon when I say: 'You see, Hon, I met this really cool guy named Amicus on the computer...and, well, he knows everything about my life. But don't be nervous or weirded out. He knows everything about Lincoln's life, too. No...no...no! Not Carl Lincoln down the street...but Abe Lincoln. You see, he hung out with him a bit, and....'" Jay mocked himself. There was no choice. Everything had been going so great at home that Jay honestly felt this would turn the home apple cart upside down...back up...and upside down again.

Of course, Jay was dying to tell somebody...anybody...about his unusual friend. Jay honestly felt like one of the luckiest people in the world to be experiencing what was happening, but it was the sort of luck that was perhaps best not bragged about. Sure Jay knew that his mysterious friend was one hundred percent responsible for having thrown him a life preserver and keeping him from going under, but he also knew that sharing the story of his real life lifeguard was bound to send Vicki to www.HelpMyMixedUpHusband.com looking for world-wide-web answers.

"No…everything is fine just as it is," Jay concluded. "I'm not ready to begin answering questions about something I don't even know about. And maybe I never will be. Let's just see how this whole thing plays out."

9:30 A.M.

Something felt different in his makeshift home office, but Jay couldn't quite place it. Curious, he walked to his new classroom seat, sat down, turned on the computer and waited for his professor's lesson. Nothing happened. No Amicus. No lesson. He waited longer. Still nothing. Not knowing what to do, Jay typed on the screen in bold capital letters: "AMICUS!! YOUR STUDENT IS HERE! WHERE ARE YOU?" Still, there was no response.

Feeling more dejected than he had in days, Jay reached under the desk and turned off the computer tower. "Hmmm…I guess that's that," he thought. "Another disappointment. Now what?" Amicus' disheartening absence sent Jay's emotions yo-yoing once more.

Disappointed, and rising to head downstairs, Jay noticed out of the corner of his eye some goldenrod colored paper laying in the printer tray. He hadn't noticed it before. There were six pieces. He picked them up and read them. The first and second sheets were a reprint of *Lesson 1*, the third and forth sheets were a printed copy of *Lesson 2*, and the bottom two sheets were titled *Lesson 3*. With a wave of relief flooding his spirit, Jay smiled big at his discovery. The teacher had shown up for lecture after all!

"Thank goodness!" Jay exclaimed aloud in relief. "For a moment there, I thought I'd lost my inspiration coach!" He dove into reading the hardcopy of the day's lesson.

LESSON 3: BLOCK OUT NAYSAYERS!
(Believe in Your Dreams)

Believe for a moment that you have the ability to travel back in time. Setting your time dial back to the 1940s, you set your sights on visiting three different places on three different dates: the White House in 1945, Hollywood in 1946, and an everyday New York City news stand in 1948.

On your time travel vacation, you have two objectives: listen and learn. On your brief excursion into the past, you'll hear the profound words of three cutting-edge influencers of yesteryear. This real life trio had the ears of national business and industry leaders, scientists, educators, and even the President of the United States. Each was at the pinnacle of his profession.

Your first stop is 1945. Stepping out of your time capsule unseen, you quietly slip into a high level meeting in the Oval Office of United States President Harry S. Truman. He is easy to recognize and obviously the center of attention. He's seeking input from a group of high level officials regarding the atomic bomb.

Fascinated to be watching history unfold, you listen as an agitated man wearing an impressively decorated military uniform addresses the President. With total conviction, Admiral William Leahy of the U.S. Navy boldly tells Mr. Truman: "That is the biggest fool thing we have ever done...the bomb will never go off, and I speak as an expert in explosives." History, however, recorded a different story, didn't it? The events in Hiroshima and Nagasaki that shortly followed the Admiral's critique proved him to be explosively wrong. The bomb did work.

After hearing the not-so-expert advice of the Admiral, you head to a lighter meeting. Your second destination is a 1946 gathering in the world of Hollywood. Fun, huh? Eavesdropping on the conversation of 20th Century-Fox's head honcho, you prepare to hear a visionary remark about the movie industry or one of Hollywood's big stars. Instead you hear this: "Television won't be able to hold onto any market it captures after the first six months. People will soon get tired of staring at a plywood box every night." What? Did he just say the television would be a flop? Obviously, this major prediction didn't pan out as decades later the facts tell us that the average American watches in excess of four hours of television each day! This statement looks even sillier when we know that some companies will pay millions of dollars just to catch the viewing public's attention for a mere thirty seconds!

Wow! So here we have a top military leader telling the President of the United States that the atomic bomb won't work and the head of a major motion picture studio completely missing the boat on one of the hottest waves of American entertainment. And these people were the experts! It makes you stop and think about some of the "expert" advice that you've personally been given and accepted to be true over time, doesn't it?

But wait. Your time travel includes one more stop... New York City, 1948. Reading your itinerary, you discover that you're to locate a newsstand, find the August issue of *Science Digest*, then read an article concerning moon travel. Starting to feel a bit skeptical about prognosticators of the future, you locate the magazine and begin to read: "Landing and moving around the moon offers so many serious problems for human beings that it may take science two hundred years to lick them." Two hundred years? Well, the history of 1969, a mere twenty-one years after this prediction, proved *Science Digest* to be emphatically wrong...like the Admiral and the Hollywood big shot.

So what can we learn from this? What is the lesson? Look at your life, my friend. Do you have people telling you that something that you want to do "can't be done"? And more importantly, are you believing them?

Thank goodness the people working at NASA defied the experts, or the world would never have known the thrill of seeing a man walk on the moon. If knowledgeable and passionate experts such as these three naysayers could make such glaring miscalculations, doesn't it make you wonder about some of the people in your personal history whose words have dimmed your own "moon walking" dreams?

Believe in your dreams! Believe in what you can accomplish when you set your determination in motion! Limited thinking influencers who say "you can't" or "that won't work" are everywhere. Don't listen to them! Block out reasons why you can't do something and focus on why you can do it! Remember, greatness is measured by what you try to accomplish...not by what you don't try to accomplish. If you want to climb the mountain, close your ears and listen to your heart! In the end, you'll find the journal of your life...and your own personal legend...to be far more exciting.

Question:
Think of a time that you held back on pursuing something you wanted because of someone's *expert* advice. What did that expert's advice stop you from getting?

PS: No doubt you were surprised to find today's lesson somewhere other than where you have grown accustomed to expect it. Well, I printed it out for a reason. First, I want you to make sure that you have a copy of each lesson to put inside the notebook that you are keeping. (This may be useful in referencing lessons in the future.) Second, I want to reinforce today's lesson. Sometimes the answers to your questions are not where you have grown accustomed to looking. When you open your eyes to possibility, you need to close your ears to probability. Sometimes that even means closing your ears to your own voice.

"Hmmm..." Jay considered Amicus' words. His thoughts zoomed back to earlier days when those close to him had discouraged him from traveling abroad after finishing college. "You need to pay those loans off! Act responsible and find a job!" He thought about how he was discouraged from joining the fraternity...of how he was discouraged from going to grad school...of how moving to that new development was a terrible decision. Jay now regretted listening to that "wisdom." Time had proven it all to be misdirected...and even selfish...advice.

Over the next forty minutes, Jay listed other times where he'd let conventional wisdom sway his decision. In looking back at the times when others had discouraged him…and he had discouraged himself…he now realized that if life were ever meant to be an amazing adventure, he would have to learn that it was smart to listen to the opinions of others, but not necessarily wise to accept them. Deep down inside of Jay, his genie…his potential…was stretching his muscles. And smiling.

Friday, May 23rd

Jay woke up excited…and nervous. Today was a big day. Two interested employers had called late Thursday afternoon and had requested Friday interviews. The two interviews brought with them a combination of good news and less-than-good news. The good news was that Jay's effort in sending out resumes had garnered interest and was starting to produce results. The less-than-good news was that neither position triggered Jay's adrenalin switch. More good news was that Jay was going to be able to dust off his rusty interviewing skills and get some practice. More less-than-good news was that Jay really was going to have to confront one of his least favorite activities in the world…the dreaded job interview.

Like most, Jay found the idea of sitting in front of a stuffy interviewer answering questions to be about as appealing as sitting in a dentist's chair having his teeth drilled. "So, tell me, where do you see yourself in five years?" "What do you think our company could expect you to bring to the table if you were to join us?" "What do you think your greatest strengths…and weaknesses…are?" Jay knew all the questions. He just hated answering them.

The bottom line was that Jay had absolutely no clear direction in mind for his career to go. Although he was no longer drowning in "stinking thinking" like he'd been just a week prior, Jay still felt he didn't know how to answer the ultimate stress producing question that he was asking himself multiple times daily: "What do I want to do with my life?"

As long as the unemployment checks kept rolling in, the monthly bills were still a few months away from gaining a strangle-hold on the Garfield house. Jay knew, however, that if he didn't get his act together, there would come a day in the near future when they would begin to feel the financial heat. Of course the answer to turning down the temperature and relieving that ever-present gut knot would be to get a job. It was nice to talk about the luxury of taking time to find that "Perfect, I love it!" job, but today Jay felt the sand of the hour glass falling ever faster. If he happened to find something that he liked... great! If it was something less than great, Jay felt that he might just have to suck it up and learn to live with it.

"C'mon...keep an open mind today! You need a job!" Jay said to himself.

Was Jay backtracking on finding his dream job? Possibly. Hadn't only twenty-four hours lapsed since he had given himself the okay to find a job that really motivated him? Yes, again. The problem was that without a written plan to keep him emotionally steady and focused, Jay had given permission for doubt to creep in regularly. With no real strategy or time deadlines outlining levels of urgency in his job hunt, Jay was emotionally unanchored and subject to drift from feeling to feeling.

Some moments Jay felt like the little engine that could. At other moments the dark realization that a financial grim reaper was right around the corner melted his self-assurance. Sure Jay's personal confidence was three sizes larger than when his world initially collapsed, but even the new XL confidence he now wore didn't allow him to one hundred percent commit to the idea of being patient in his job search. At this point in his quest for new employment, Jay was caught between two opposing mentalities. Part of him wanted to look skyward at the future with hopeful eyes, while the other part of him looked at the future with both feet firmly planted in freshly poured concrete. Jay's career spirit wanted to fly, but his mind wasn't quite convinced that was possible.

Jay's day-to-day self-doubt was absolutely normal. Anybody who's ever been in the position of looking for a job can surely relate. "Rent money...or happiness?" What compounded Jay's internal chaos even more was that he enthusiastically embraced the messages of Amicus' first three lessons on an emotional level, but his brain hadn't fully claimed them to be a part of its full-time mental makeup. As Amicus had pointed out in his *Dear Jay* letter, it's easy to get fired up for a moment or even a day, but it's consistently keeping charged-up that's the most challenging. Jay wanted more…sure. But settling for the next best seemed to be the most realistic to Jay. Unfortunately, "settling" is just something that seems to get added into the DNA as people age. Jay was no exception.

With the first of his two interviews scheduled in two-and-a-half hours, Jay eased into his chair in front of the terminal and opened his notebook. "Well, let's see if Dr. Amicus can offer a remedy to calm these interview jitters, huh?" Pushing interview anxiety out temporarily, Jay focused on what he was reading on the computer.

LESSON 4: 5,110 DAYS!
(Visualize Long Term)

Good morning, friend! What a great day today…yes? Who knows what new adventures and experiences lay ahead! Let's see what we can spark with today's lesson….

I know that you've never had the privilege of gazing up at the awesome creation called Mt. Rushmore, but one day I hope that you'll be able to stand before the incredible magnificence of this monument. I remember when that determined fellow, Gutzon Borglum, began carving into the side of that massive mountain of granite in 1927. Of course, most everybody thought that sculpting the gigantic faces of four presidents into a stone wall seemed ridiculously impossible. To my friend the sculptor, however, it was a burning desire. It was a mission.

Decades after the first pieces of granite were chipped off, Gutzon's mission…and his achievement…stands not only as a tribute to greatness, but also as an incredible testimony to what can happen when an individual dares to dream…and to create…and to master.

I remember the day quite clearly when Gutzon, proudly looking up at his historic masterpiece, proclaimed, "…until the

wind and rain alone shall wear them away." Now that was an impressive vision, don't you think?

Mt. Rushmore is a brilliant example of the power of the human spirit. And although the finished product is incredibly inspiring, it's Gutzon's vision that I want you to grow to appreciate...and even model. It's his self-confidence and overwhelming purpose that you, my friend, have the opportunity to duplicate in your own life. Self-confidence and purpose...these are the powerful life-changing qualities that can enable you to "sculpt" your own amazing Mt. JAYmore.

You can, you know. You have the power to make a profound mark. Like Gutzon, you have the ability to do something extraordinarily dramatic.

So tell me, what are you *sculpting*? Tell me, what are you doing that drives you...that thrills you...that gives you a deep sense of knowing that you're making a great contribution to your world? Tell me, Jay, what great masterpiece are you chiseling out of your life?

My friend Gutzon's remarkable feat took fourteen focused years. Let's suppose that I give you the same amount of time right now. Let's suppose that right now I hand you a *life chisel*. What do you think that you could accomplish over the next fourteen years? What inspiring life undertaking could you begin?

The older you get, the more you realize the inevitable fact that life is not long enough. Eventually time runs out. When you understand this inevitable Law of Life, there should never be a reason for you to get off the scaffold. There should never be a reason for you to stop chipping, carving, sculpting, designing, building, and sharing. There is simply no reason that should ever stop you from making this life as incredible, exciting, and lasting as possible for yourself...and for others.

What your Mt. Rushmore is, friend, I cannot tell you. What I can tell you, though, is that I have absolutely no doubt that you have one in you. Did you hear me? I say again with bold and complete confidence...you have a Mt. Rushmore in you! Your goal is to dream it...and then *sculpt* it.

I want you to realize that each day of the next fourteen years is a precious gift. Each of the next 5,110 days (and I will even throw in a few leap year days as a bonus) is a chance to continue to chip away at something that is meaningful and lasting. As Gutzon discovered, the trick is to dream big and then take it one day at a time…one face at a time…one eye at a time…one pupil at a time. You do the same!

Starting today, don't let a single day pass by without making your contribution known and felt. Pick up that chisel and hammer! Share your Mt. JAYmore with the world! Don't wait another moment! Fourteen years from today, your project will be unveiled, my friend…and I will be there to see it! Until then, make every day count!

Question:
What will you accomplish 5,110 days from now?

"Wow!" The number popped out. "5,110! That's a lot of days! Do I really even live that long?" Doubting Jay pulled out a desk calculator and did the math. "365 days times 14 years…and…yep…5,110. He's right. Hmmm…"

For some strange reason, the job interviewer asking Jay, "Where do you see yourself in five years?" seemed so much less emotionally powerful than Amicus' fourteen year version of the same question. Why? Who knows exactly. Maybe because the answer to Amicus' version pointed to the notion of making one's life matter. The *five-year* version was shaded with giving the *politically correct* answer so that the person being interviewed would impress the interviewer enough to get hired. Amicus' version was bigger…eye opening…mind awakening.

"What can I accomplish in 5,110 days? Possibilities…possibilities …but what?" Jay pondered the size of the question. Leaning back in his chair, he closed his eyes and let mental doors open. And they did. Twenty minutes later, Jay's pen raced across his notebook pages as his thoughts were translated into words.

Saturday, May 24th

A7:45 A.M. call to Vicki's cell phone broke the Saturday sleep of both Garfield residents. One of Vicki's store employees called in sick at the last hour and Vicki was racing to get in and cover her shift. Jay got up and chatted with her while she stood before the bathroom mirror applying the last touches of her morning make-up. They had extensively gone over the details of Jay's Friday interviews the night before, but some of the previously discussed particulars seemed to need an extra dose of analysis.

"You know, I really am pretty good at that outside stuff. Maybe selling phone systems wouldn't be that bad. I mean the commissions are great and I really don't need to make that many sales to make my quota. I could probably nail it."

Yes, both positions were in outside sales. Of course, Jay knew this going into the interviews. Sure it wasn't what he preferred, but then again there weren't a whole lot of jobs available for playing eighteen holes daily at the area's best country clubs. Jay had hoped initially that the percentage of time that he'd have to spend outside pounding the streets would be minimal, but it was what it was.

Jay loved the autonomy of outside sales, but in the summer heat…in the winter rain…yuck. The brutal asphalt days of summer appealed only to people selling air conditioners and swimming pools. Getting out of an air-conditioned car, which hopefully hadn't over-heated, and heading into shirt-sticking heat was not a thing from which dreams were made in Jay's estimation. As far as the rainy season? Too many times Jay had soaked his shoes trying to avoid stepping in rainy day water puddles. Add to both of these bad weather scenarios the unenviable position of always trying to find street parking in order to call on a prospect and you had the make-up for a frustrating day on the job. Even so, Jay spent this morning writing two thank-you letters. Just in case.

Jay's Saturday was short of big events. Yard work, exercise… and Amicus. There was no doubt that Amicus had thumb-tacked a Rushmore-size question in Jay's mind and he wanted to give it considerable more thought.

"What great masterpiece is waiting for me to sculpt?"

Although Jay didn't know, he was determined to find a Rushmore sized answer. With yesterday's 5,110 day question still rattling around in his head like a toy top with an extended life, Jay sat down for his next lesson. He turned on the computer.

LESSON 5: THE POWER OF ONE!
(Focus Short Term)

Thinking big today, Jay? Great!! As we learned yesterday, big visions lead to big results. But in today's lesson, I would like to shrink what might seem overwhelmingly large into something attainably small. You'll understand what I mean soon enough. Ready?

Let me start by telling you about one of the more determined people that I've ever known. I'm sure you've heard of Hubert Humphrey. He was a famous Minnesotan who rose to the office of United States Senator and then Vice President. I remember one particular day when I was sitting with Hubert during his first visit to Washington, D.C. He was a young man then, and as one would expect from a first time visitor to his nation's capitol, very excited about his trip. In a letter to his wife, he wrote: "I can see how someday, if you and I just apply ourselves and make up our minds for bigger things, we can someday live here in Washington and probably be in government, politics, or service. Oh, I hope my dreams come true…I'm going to try anyhow."

Wishful thinking on Hubert's part? Most people might have said so at the time of his correspondence, but history teaches us otherwise. After writing his letter, Hubert soon returned home and focused one hundred percent on making his dream happen simply by working towards his dream one day at a time.

History has given you so many great examples to illustrate this point of *one-day-at-a-time*. You see, the road less traveled is definitely not a road that has never been traveled. What's more,

you don't need to look back years and years to find examples of individuals who have chosen the road of self-determination. They exist all around you.

One contemporary that is in the process of leaving her own set of distinguishable footprints is Caroline Kennedy...yes... that's correct...President Kennedy's daughter. Caroline spent three years writing *In Our Defense*, a book examining the U.S. Bill of Rights in action. And although you might not think that writing a book is a big deal, what is amazing is that during the time that she wrote it, she also managed to graduate from law school, pass the bar exam, and give birth to two children! I remember someone asking her how in the world she had been able to write a book and juggle all of the other major events in her life. Caroline just shrugged and said, "Just work at it...a little bit every day."

"Just work at it...a little bit every day." And that, Jay, is the answer. That's the secret to making great dreams come true. It's one of life's most powerful secrets. Just work at it...a little bit every day...one day at a time.

Successful lives, you see, are built one moment at a time... one step at a time...one day at a time. If you commit to doing the best that you can each day of the week, each day of the month, each day of the year, you have an excellent chance of making all of those successful days add up to equal one thrilling and exhilarating life. And isn't that what you desire, my friend? Isn't that what you long for?

To my great disappointment, too many people forget *The Power of One*. They forget that successful careers are built one step at a time and that great lives are built one day at a time. They forget how much can be done in a single day. And when they begin to lose sight of this golden secret, they have difficulty maintaining focus and purpose. One day slips into the next, and the great opportunity that each new rising of the sun brings is lost.

Making your dreams a reality, like Hubert and Caroline, requires understanding a principle I call *The Power of One*. Happiness and fulfillment aren't things that happen automatically; you have to want and work for them daily! Just giving lip service and telling others that you're going to the top doesn't cut it. What does bring success is telling yourself that you will go the distance, then utilizing the power of every single day to get there. Be passionate about bringing your best to the every-day table of life. Be committed. If you want to write a book, write a page a day. If you want to go back to school, take it one class at a time. Whatever you want, just work at it a little every day. That's the secret.

Pledge to yourself to make each day count! Do something every single day that pushes you a little bit closer to achieving your goal. Baby step…baby step…baby step. That's all it is, Jay. Big life dreams…small daily steps. Use this tool…*The Power of One*…and watch a whole series of successful baby steps lead you all the way to the success and life you crave. And deserve.

Question:
How would your life change if you started practicing *The Power of One* today?

"*The Power of One…The Power of One…The Power of One.*" Jay silently repeated the words over and over again. "One day after another…baby steps…a little bit every day…hmmm…that doesn't seem hard at all."

A thought flashed into Jay's mind. He remembered, as a boy, watching his father building a brick wall around a home rose garden. Brick by brick his father carefully worked to build the wall. With a deliberate and steady hand, his dad slowly added one brick next to or on top of another until soon there was one row after another, and eventually, a really great wall.

The vision of his mason-working dad building a brick wall cemented itself into Jay's mind. "Hmmm…just like the wall, I'm building brick by brick, too…except instead of bricks being laid one after another, I'm building a life one day after another. Interesting."

Jay liked this new concept. Thinking in this brick-by-brick, day-by-day fashion seemed to make goals more attainable and less over-whelming. "Day by day…brick by brick…easy. I can do that!" Ideas began to take shape in Jay's mind. He picked up his pen and began to answer the day's question.

6:57 P.M.

"**H**ey, Vic…I kinda' had an epiphany today about how we can get our tax stuff organized. What if right before dinner Monday through Friday, we sit down together for only fifteen minutes at a crack and work on it. We'll throw everything on the floor in the second bedroom and go at it…a little bit at a time…every day. This way, it will stop hanging over our heads and we can feel great knowing we're taking action and getting it done! C'mom…fifteen minutes a day…no big deal at all!"

Jay and Vicki had always been procrastinators when it came to tax season and this year was the worst. Having had to file a late extension, the Garfield's had a shoe box full of unitemized receipts. They were great at throwing everything related to doing the year's taxes in a shoe box or a downstairs drawer, but when it came to finally sitting down and sorting through things…disaster. It was all a mess and neither had an appetite for wading through the "tax stuff" and getting it done.

"Whatcha' think? Fifteen minutes before dinner…both of us working together? Yes? No?"

"Yeah! Great idea, Jay! I like it! We can do that, definitely! What made you think of that?"

Jay shared with Vicki *The Power of One* concept he had been thinking about. He told her that he'd come across it reading something on the computer (true!) and that it was a concept that helped people succeed in achieving goals that initially seemed overwhelming. Vicki was impressed. Of course she loved any idea to get this tax ogre off their backs, but even more, she loved the fact that Jay seemed to have turned the corner and was consistently thinking forward about things. She admitted that it had been a long time since she had felt such consistent and positive energy coming from Jay. He was more animated. He was happier. And she loved it. She silently sent a prayer of thanksgiving into the universe.

10:23 P.M.

As Jay sat down in front of the computer later that night to journal his thoughts, he relived his interaction with Vicki earlier. They had been so jazzed by the simple fifteen minute idea that they had decided to start the project immediately. Despite being a Saturday night and the plan to work on the taxes was a Monday through Friday plan, both felt the motivation to start right away. Feeling much freer now that they had a plan that seemed workable, Jay and Vicki had rummaged through every possible drawer looking for anything related to tax work. It had almost seemed like a game when one of them would call out, "We've got a winner! Here's another one!" After close to forty minutes of looking and throwing receipt after receipt in the middle of the bedroom floor, they declared victory, high-fived each other, and laughed.

"Yeah…cool night! Who'd have thought we'd have had fun starting the dang taxes!" Jay whispered to himself audibly.

He pictured the night in his mind as if he were a third person standing in the room. Again, he saw their laughter. He saw Vicki's face come alive…her expression radiant as she raced around the house. He heard himself expanding on *The Power of One* tax organizational plan…excitement in his voice…arms flailing with enthusiasm. He was speaking at a rapid pace as if each word was in competition with the next to come out of his mouth first. His energy was incredibly high, and he, too, was totally alive. It was unusual for him to picture himself with so much fire, but he loved it.

"No doubt I'm on the right path! Just keep it up, Jay! Day by day…step by step!"

Jay wished that he could talk to Amicus now and share the events of the evening. He wanted to tell Amicus about what it felt like to create a plan…involve Vicki…and take action. He wanted to share with Amicus how totally invigorated and charged up he was now. He wanted to tell Amicus "thank you." As Jay mulled over these thoughts and feelings, he was struck by a peculiar sensation. Jay didn't know who, how or why, but at that exact moment, his subconscious seemed to awaken and a quiet voice cleared its throat and whispered into Jay's mind. The words were simply, "I know, Jay. I know."

Sunday, May 25th

Jay and Vicki slept in that morning until 9:30 A.M. Then, on a whim Vicki suggested that the two of them hustle and make the 11 A.M. church service. In the past, the Garfield's reserved church appearances for Easter and Christmas Eve only, but Jay went with the flow today and said, "Sure...why not?" It wasn't that he didn't like attending church, but Jay had always felt it wasn't the sort of thing he wanted to spend time doing on his day off. Since he had no real work schedule, that argument was out the window. "Maybe I'll even learn something!"

They got dressed in record-setting speed, made seven of the eight traffic lights on the way there, and somewhat sheepishly walked into the service hand-in-hand at exactly 10:59.

Jay was surprised to find he really enjoyed the service. Except for the singing. Jay mouthed the words to the congregational songs, timid that his untrained singing voice would hinder those singing nearby.

On the other hand, the sermon was great. *Bitter Hearts...Bitter Days* was not only enlightening, but it also seemed to fit perfectly with the struggles that he'd gone through after having been fired. Now that he could look back at that emotional period rationally, Jay felt a new peace. He had come to terms with the bitterness that he'd initially felt towards his former employer...and himself. Today's service reinforced that peace. Jay acknowledged in the car on the way home that it had been a great decision to go to church.

"Great idea, Vic; church was good."

"Yeah, it was a good idea...thanks! And, by the way...nice singing, Jay!"

After a few errands and their weekly grocery store visit, Jay and Vicki finally pulled into the driveway shortly after 2:00 P.M. The last four-and-a-half hours had been full, and normally the exhaustion of going, going, going would have caused Jay to head straight for the couch and the remote control, but not today. Instead, after unloading the groceries, Jay anxiously disappeared upstairs to his new classroom. The feeling Jay was experiencing was a good anxious, the kind of anxious that you get when the banana split has been built, and you're now watching the final touches of hot caramel and chocolate being dripped. With mental spoon in hand, Jay was ready to devour today's lesson.

LESSON 6: MAGNETS, PAINTBRUSHES, AND MIRRORS!
(Attitude is the Difference)

Good morning! You woke up feeling energized and ready to go, huh? Great choice, my friend! You always have two distinct choices when you open your eyes in the morning: Take on the challenges of the day with enthusiasm and hope, or let out a groan and start worrying about what's probably going to happen. Those two choices are exactly that...choices. You choose. And each begins with the sort of attitude you have.

The meaning that you give to getting up in the morning determines how you feel. Look at a new day with trepidation... feel negative anxiety. Wake up with a smile and a positive purpose...feel powerfully energized. How we feel starts with how we think. Attitude. Attitude. Attitude.

So what kind of attitude are you bringing to your new day? What kind of attitude do you pack in your lunch bag and carry out the door to face the world? Is it magnetic? Is it colorful? Whatever it is, we know that your attitude will directly reflect how the world sees and responds to you. Magnets, paintbrushes, and mirrors. Attitude is related to all three of these things. Let me show you.

Your attitude is a magnet. Hold a magnet close to a refrigerator and feel it seek out its new home base. The power of attraction between the two is undeniably strong, and once the magnet becomes attached, it will forever cling. Your attitude works much the same way. An attitude committed to succeeding magnetically draws opportunity; it magically attracts people.

A person who wears an attitude that's enthusiastic, confident, and determined will cause people to positively gravitate toward him or her. When this happens, opportunity doors open. On the other hand, a negative attitude bent on whining and complaining will lure like-minded people. Whine and complain enough in life and failure will surely be yours.

Your attitude is a paintbrush. Every morning when you get up, you have a choice to paint your world with the bright colors of hope and positive expectation, or you can choose to paint it with the dark colors of gloom and anxiety. Does your attitude radiate the colors of energy and life, or is it more likely you dipped your attitude brush into the less vibrant colors of gray and black? You are the Matisse of your own world, so look for the positive and paint the bright!

Your attitude is a mirror. Your marriage, your relationships, your career…they are each a mirror reflection of your attitude. The world sees, and then responds, to how you feel and act. If the world sees *success* when it looks at you, it mirrors *success* right back at you. If others see *friendly,* they will shine *friendly.* Reflect out what you want the world to give back and it will come. Smile and be smiled at. It's just that simple.

Napoleon Hill, author of the motivational classic *Think and Grow Rich*, once wrote very wise words about the magical power of attitude: "You search for the magic key that will unlock the door to the source of power; and yet you have the key in your own hands…you may make use of it the moment you learn to control your thoughts." Take control over your attitude and you develop the power to change everything in your world. Transformation is from the inside out.

For the rest of this day…for the rest of this week, this month, this year, your life…develop an awareness of what kind of attitude you are projecting. Be a magnet that draws opportunity. Paint brilliant thoughts and actions. Mirror success. If you do, you will have the chance to not only greatly inspire others, but to also live a life that you will find deeply satisfying and rewarding. Now how is that for a goal?

Question:

Attitude. Are you attracting, painting, and reflecting what you desire?

For the next hour Jay sat at his desk. With pen leaving paper only long enough to get to the next word, Jay answered Amicus' question. In his notebook, he made three columns:

1. Before being fired.   2. Immediately after being fired.   3. Today.

Each of the categories brought different feelings and words as Jay put himself back into the moment each required. The attitude comparisons were dramatic and Jay was absolutely amazed at what he discovered.

"Wow! Sheesh…what a difference! Attitude really is everything!" he reinforced to himself.

Monday, May 26th

"New day…new attitude…new life!"

Jay was sitting at the kitchen table feeling enthusiastic about himself and his world. He had risen early with Vicki and had spent time going through the Help Wanted ads while she got ready for work.

"A few new ones," he shared when asked if he had found anything promising. "I'll throw three to four new resumes out with the Sunday crop." As soon as Vicki kissed Jay on the forehead and walked out the door, Jay headed upstairs to class and Professor Amicus.

Glancing first at the printer to see if Amicus' lesson had again found its way there, Jay then put his sole attention on the computer. His face was anxious and he squirmed in his chair. His seat gyrations and the general feel of his body reminded him of the moment he sat waiting for the curtain to rise when he saw *Phantom of the Opera* for the first time.

"Promising expectations," he thought. It felt good. The screen lit up and in letters that seemed to glow was the seventh lesson in *Bamboo Farming 101*.

LESSON 7: BAMBOO FARMING!
(Be Tenacious)

Ready for a great week, my friend? This week some very exciting things are going to open up for you in life! How do I know this? Because you're looking for them! In life we always find that which we seek. Yes?

Let's start today's lesson using a little story with a big message.

Another day...another week...another year. The farmer trudged out to his field to water and fertilize the root system of his mysterious crop. Again. To many people, this particular farmer seemed crazy. Why? For nearly five years this man kept tending to a field where nothing was happening; nothing was seen growing.

When told that his efforts were fruitless, he would only say, "Be patient. You'll see."

So, the people waited. And waited. They waited five years, and still nothing. They laughed at the farmer's effort. They laughed at his foolish vision. They laughed at his blindness to reality. But the farmer would only smile.

"Be patient. You'll see."

And then it happened. A single shoot emerged from the ground. The people mocked the farmer. "After five years, look at what little you've grown! Perhaps you can trade your little baby shoot for a new packet of magic seeds!"

The farmer smiled. "Be patient. You'll see."

When a crowd of unruly townspeople returned five weeks later, they were shocked. Gazing out onto the once barren ground, they couldn't believe what they saw. Instead of small shoots of modest plant life multiplying across the field, they saw the entire field covered with amazing woody plants. What was truly awe inspiring, however, was that these "tree plants" towered 90 feet above the ground! Humble to the end, the bamboo farmer said nothing. He only smiled.

I think that I can safely assume, Jay, that you've never grown bamboo. I imagine, too, that I'm safe in assuming that you've never met a bamboo farmer either. There is no doubt, however, that you would learn a lot from such a meeting. You see, growing bamboo and achieving goals are similar in their demands. They both require foresight, confidence, and tenacity. Overnight success is not something that can be expected with either.

Like the bamboo farmer, people desiring to achieve unique success require foresight. They need to be able to imagine the future. They need to have a picture of their goal sharply imbedded in their mind. It's that picture that's often the only thing that drives them and keeps them motivated. The bamboo farmer can visualize a towering field of mature bamboo years in advance. He can picture going to market. He's motivated by a payday that's five years down the road. People who desire success in their personal quest envision eventual success just as clearly. The day-to-day monotony of striving for a goal is made worthwhile by a clear vision of the outcome.

Like the bamboo farmer, people desiring to achieve unique success require confidence. There will be those pessimists who fail to see progress and will do their best to discourage bamboo growers. Similar cynics will do their best to discourage people shooting for unique goals. They tell them to be realistic. They do their best to let the dreamer know that his or her aspiration is a fantasy that will never be achieved. Achievers should not listen. Heeding advice from a pessimist is risky business. Achievers need to have one hundred percent confidence in themselves despite the gale forces coming at them. They need to believe that eventual success will come.

Like the bamboo farmer, people desiring to achieve unique success require tenacity. It's not an easy task to keep watering something that never breaks the ground. Similarly, it's difficult to keep pressing towards a specific goal when indifference or, worse, rejection is met at every turn. Being tenacious means aggressively going after a goal. Yes, new strategies might need to be developed in order to succeed, but nothing can ever over-shadow the passion to make that goal a reality.

Bamboo is a member of the grass family grown in the tropics. Success, however, is something that's grown in your heart and mind. Foresight, confidence, and tenacity...these are the qualities that allow the bamboo farmer to succeed; these are the qualities that will help you to achieve. Decide now to model yourself after a bamboo grower and adapt these three character-istics. If you do, I have a distinct feeling that five years from now, like the bamboo farmer, you'll be smiling as well.

Question:
If you adopted the tenacious spirit of a bamboo farmer, how would your world change?

Before Jay considered his answer, he printed out the day's lesson. Ever since Amicus had printed out copies of the first three lessons for him, Jay had made sure to follow suit by printing out each subsequent lesson that followed. As the printer churned out today's printed page, Jay imagined himself bamboo farming.

"Man...those guys really have confidence, don't they? What keeps them going? They must get really frustrated at times. No doubt I'd have a *For Sale* sign up on my farm before the first year ended!" Jay laughed to himself. "I don't know if I could do that...but isn't that Amicus' point? I need to learn to develop that sort of commitment!"

Although Jay knew he'd just learned a very valuable life lesson, the real power of the lesson was to take shape in the future. Every time for the rest of his life that his work failed to bear immediate fruit and he felt like quitting, he would be reminded of the tenacious bamboo farmer. Amicus had planted a very important seed into Jay's conscious mind...the seed of perseverance. Unknowingly to Jay at that moment, it was Jay's unconscious mind where that seed was being nurtured and beginning to take root.

Tuesday, May 27th…5:32 A.M.

Jay's mind had been racing all night long, and he had a hard time sleeping. The first seven lessons of Amicus' course had his brain spinning.

"Where do I begin? How does this all come together? How does this help me now? What am I supposed to do?" The thoughts in Jay's mind moved so rapidly Jay felt like his brain was a New York subway terminal at rush hour. Everything was pouring in-and-out all at once.

Finally, unable to quietly lie in bed any longer, Jay got up. The mega-downpour of information his mind was handling was just too much. He had to move; he had to write; he had to eat; he had to do anything to make his mind slow down. The clock showed a ridiculous hour for Jay to be getting out of bed, but sleep was impossible. Slowly pulling the covers off and quietly tip-toeing out of the room, Jay went downstairs. He started by opening the refrigerator. "What looks good? Nothing. I can't eat."

Jay picked up his job search notebook off the kitchen table and looked through it. All of the jobs he had applied for were either written or taped in it. Many had been crossed off by now and quite a few were circled and marked with notes or a star, but no matter. Starting from day one of the *Find-a-Job* project, Jay again carefully read through each listing.

As he studied each entry on the eight notebook pages of jobs, he listened to himself think. "Could I do that? I have experience here, but it seems so boring. What was I thinking with that one? Yuck!"

Jay noticed one definite pattern developing: he hated them all. Well, he didn't actually "hate" them all, but none of them turned his passion engine on. Not even close. He started to feel a negative anxiety building as he read through them a second time.

"Geez…is this what I'm going to end up doing? Dang…I don't know if I can handle that!"

Sure, there probably were a couple of promising entries that existed on the list, but not a single one struck Jay at that moment as something that he wanted to spend his life doing. None of them motivated Jay with the same overwhelming fire and passion he felt after reading one of Amicus' lessons. And that's what he wanted deep down.

"Is that possible? Is it even realistic to think that I can find a job that inspires me like that?"

It was a long morning. Vicki was up at her usual time, but Jay had been kicking it around the house for much longer. As each minute of the morning passed, he became more anxious…more restless… more irritated.

"What am I going to do? Is this all life is…really? Is this what life is about? Finding a job…paying bills…pretending to have a great life…and then dying? I want more than that! Amicus…where are you? Help…please!"

After sending Vicki off in their morning goodbye ritual, Jay slinked upstairs. Yes, he slinked. He was mentally exhausted. All morning he had spent deliberating his fate, his future, and his destiny.

"I need answers! I'm frustrated, and I have no clue as to what to do. I think I'm going to change my middle name to *Clueless*. It fits. Jay *Clueless* Garfield. C'mon, Amicus…be there. Help a guy out! Point me in a direction! Please…."

Jay was, of course, desperately motivated to find answers to every single question that he had been asking. He wanted to know which path he should take. He wanted someone to tell him, and right now, he wanted that person to be Amicus.

"Make everything come together today…please! I just want a direction! I just want to move forward! Amicus…please…please…let the lesson today point to where I'm supposed to go…."

As anxious as he was for today's secret, direction-determining lesson, Jay thought it best to review the previous lessons just in case he missed something. "The answer is here…c'mon…read closer, Jay…. Think! Think!"

He studied every word of his Amicus notebook. Every lesson was memorized. He read every paragraph a second time. Sometimes when he sensed that he was missing something he was supposed to learn, he read it a third time. "Where? Where is it, Amicus? I know it's here. Show me!"

Jay looked at his answers. "Geez, Jay…nice effort here! How shallow!" Jay was looking at his responses to the first few lessons. He added more written thought and detail to what he had previously answered. Insight and depth seemed to be growing within Jay and the pages of his notebook soon expanded in both. Answers were built-on. Jay was pulling more and more out of himself.

Jay felt a tug within to focus on *Lesson 2*. "The answer…what I'm looking for…it's somewhere in here! Imagination…imagination …stretch yourself, Jay! C'mon…stretch! Find it!" Jay desperately desired to find a job…a life…where he felt the energy and the conviction to show up every day and give it his all. He wanted to make his life count.

"Is it too much to ask?" Jay was pleading for some higher being to hear his 911 distress call. "I want to find something…to do something that's important! I want to find something I really care about! And I'll find it even if I have to create it!"

A shudder ran up Jay's spine. "Even if I have to create it?" he thought. "Where in the world did that come from?" Jay was questioning his own voice. "Starting something on my own? Yeah…right! Like that would ever happen!" But the thought made him hesitate and think. "Hmmm…you think?"

As if he had just been shown a glimpse into what could be, Jay Garfield began to imagine bigger than he ever had before. Awestruck at the possibility? Although that may not describe Jay's mind-set perfectly at that moment…it was close. The thought of maybe creating his own career path didn't just meander through Jay's mind. It rushed through like a mighty torrent.

Fifteen minutes later, Jay brought himself back to the here-and-now. Leaving the entrepreneurial path that he had dared to venture onto in his thinking, he returned to the task at hand…today's lesson. Still feeling exhilarated to the core about the possibility of being a real-life entrepreneur, Jay turned on the computer. Amicus' lesson dominated the small screen.

LESSON 8: DON'T QUIT!
(Avoid the Easy)

Hello! I'm so happy that you've chosen to show up today and go for it! Thank you! So let me ask you, my friend…can you sense it? Are you beginning to see the possibilities? Are you beginning to feel the "What if…?" of life? Exciting, huh?

I find parables fun, Jay. They are simple, understandable, and have immense potential to teach and highlight truly powerful principles. Let me start with one today to illustrate my message.

Desperately desiring to cross the river, the scorpion begged the frog for help. "If I could only ride on your back as you cross, I could make it," the scorpion said.

Of course, the frog knew about the scorpion's deadly reputation and was, therefore, hesitant to honor the scorpion's request. "If I were to let you ride on my back, how can I be sure that you won't sting me?" the frog questioned.

"How could I sting you after you were so kind as to help me cross the river?" the scorpion replied. What the frog lacked in brains, he made up in kindness. He agreed to help his new friend.

Riding securely on the frog's back, the scorpion held on tightly as the adventure began. Halfway across the river, however, the temptation to sting the frog grew too strong. The scorpion succumbed to the pressure and stung his companion.

"How could you sting me?" cried the frog. "Now we're both going to die!"

As the two started to sink to their death, all the scorpion could say is, "I'm sorry. I guess it was just my nature."

People, like the scorpion, also have a tendency to fall back on their nature. Good intentions lead the way when a goal is set, but far too often people become sidetracked by the temptation to do the easy thing and quit when the going gets tough. In quitting early, goals have no chance of being reached. When a dieting person surrenders to that tiny voice that tells them that it's okay to have just one potato chip, human nature then takes over and the temptation to eat a second chip turns into a third…and then a forth. Before long, the whole bag is gone!

When a big goal is set, it often means that someone is trying to achieve something that is currently outside of his or her comfort zone. At first, the individual is thrilled by the thought of how great life will be when the goal is accomplished. But as soon as he or she begins to experience the hard work, countless hours, and major inconveniences that need to be overcome, trouble begins. Focus is then shifted more on the pain associated with working towards the goal rather than with the pleasure that will be felt once it's achieved. Like the scorpion, the individual usually resorts to his or her natural tendency to do the easy thing. In this case, he stings himself and the goal party is over.

Of course, nothing can guarantee that you'll accomplish your goal for certain, but there's one thing that will guarantee that you won't accomplish it…quitting. Yes, temptations and distractions can sidetrack your mission, but you can never stop trying. You must never quit.

One of the most famous jockeys of all-time, Eddie Arcaro, lost his first two hundred and fifty races before he eventually won. Imagine two hundred and fifty failures! Eddie, however, never gave up. He loved riding and he loved the thought of winning, so he persevered through the tough times. Can you honestly say that you would have gotten on the horse after fifty losses? How about a hundred? Two hundred and fifty? Tough call, huh?

If you'd been an incredibly poor speller in school, would you still have dreamed of becoming a great playwright? George Bernard Shaw did. If you'd finished at the bottom of your class, would you ever have dreamed that you had the intelligence to make great scientific and life changing discoveries? Thomas Edison did. Imagine the world without Edison's electric light, phonograph or "moving pictures." That's right, movies. "Mr. Last-in-his-Class" invented all of them.

Very few people, my friend, have ever been born with their ticket to success automatically punched. Certainly not Barak, nor Hillary, nor Oprah. Albert Einstein was labeled *mentally slow*. Abraham Lincoln and Henry Ford were both said to have "no promise." In fact, arguably the greatest basketball player in the history of the world, Michael Jordan, failed to make his high school basketball team. The one thing that distinguishes all of these people from the crowd, however, is the same thing that can distinguish you in finding personal and professional success…never resort to doing the easy thing and quit.

When the journey towards achieving your goal becomes tough, break away from the human tendency to sting yourself and quit. Push past the temptations and distractions that cause you to lose sight of your goal. Choose fortitude. Choose perseverance. Go the extra mile and keep pushing forward. If you do, not only will you find your result different than that of the mythical scorpion, but you might also find yourself soaring like those whose success you admire.

Question:
What does doing the easy thing get you in life?

Jay smiled. Had it been the exact answer he had hoped to find before the lesson? No. Had he been told what direction he should go? No, again. But Jay realized that he had still received an answer to his questions. Jay now recognized that the idea of "never quitting" was probably what he most needed to hear at that moment. Sure, Jay was getting frustrated not knowing what to do. Sure, he was afraid that he might not find a job that he liked. There was no doubt that at this moment he was incredibly vulnerable to taking the easy route. Jay knew that if he didn't catch himself, he could easily let panic push him to accept the very first offer that came along. Amicus' message simply reinforced the notion to hang in there. Jay again quietly vowed to keep pushing until he found something that he really did like.

"I promise to myself…that I will…not…settle! I will find something that I love…and I won't quit until I do!"

Later that afternoon, Jay received two phone calls from companies that were interested in setting-up interviews. Practicing his newly found belief that he should only chase opportunity in a direction that stoked his passion, Jay took a bold step and turned down the first request.

"Thank you so much for calling, but I've decided to go another direction."

The second call, however, was a different story. It was with one of the largest advertising agencies in southern California. Jay was thrilled to get the call and set up an interview for the next day.

Wednesday, May 28th…7:20 A.M.

For the last twenty-four hours, Jay's mind had been occupied with thoughts of becoming an entrepreneur and of going out on his own. It was a thought that scared him, yet at the same time, it invigorated him. Jay had researched the internet and the Business Opportunity section of the classifieds thoroughly. He had even gone so far as to call a few of the available businesses for sale. Unfortunately, Jay found the process entirely intimidating for multiple reasons.

"I don't know the first thing about buying a business…let alone how I would afford to pay for one if I did like it!"

Many of the businesses being sold were represented by business brokers who made Jay even more uncomfortable about the whole situation of buying a business. "I don't understand why you can't just give me information about the business. Why do you need a profile on me first? I'm the buyer…and I'm just looking for more information in order to see how interested I might be."

"Sir, we need a profile on you before we can share any confidential information about our client. We need to make sure that you're qualified and meet our client's buying criteria. After that, I'll be happy to give you whatever information you need. Now please, your name…."

That's how the situations went. Reluctantly, Jay played ball. Not quitting when the process went in a direction he didn't like was exactly what he had just learned in yesterday's lesson. "Don't do it, Jay…don't get mad. Hang in there and just play the game." Jay quietly thought.

Of course, Jay knew that the brokers were salesmen, and although Jay knew the tricks of the sales trade, it didn't make a difference. He still felt uncomfortable on the other end of an aggressive call.

"So tell me, Mr. Garfield…how much are you looking to spend?"

"At this point, I'm not certain. I'm definitely looking for something with less money going in…perhaps owner financed…and certainly a positive cash flow will be important." Jay thought he sounded like he knew what he was talking about.

"Well, Mr. Garfield…my clients are not big on carrying paper. I'm sure you can understand their concern. What if a new owner… I'm not saying you…ran their business into the ground before the note was paid? So let me ask…how do your financials look?"

Jay's hesitancy and vagueness didn't assist in helping him get many specific answers from the brokers, but it had been a start. He knew that if he was going to be serious about really working with a business broker, he'd have to take a crash course on buying, owning, and operating a business so that he would be on less foreign ground in future conversations. Obviously for the moment, Jay was just getting used to the idea of going out on his own; he was simply "tire kicking" and gathering information with no immediate intention of buying. "But who knows…I could," he told himself. Still, Jay felt a sense of pride knowing that he was at least on the business lot looking. It was a big first step.

After his calls, Jay wrote notes on two businesses that seemed the most attractive. "An established community bookstore and a twenty-two year old, mom-and-pop florist shop. Well, that's interesting. Who'd have thought?"

Each opportunity appealed to Jay's desire to do something that made people feel good. The bookstore helped people learn and grow, and the florist shop made people smile. Jay could…just maybe…see himself doing one or the other. Thoughts of stocking bookshelves and creating flower arrangements flipped through his mind as he headed upstairs to visit with Professor Amicus.

Jay opened his Amicus notebook and flipped through each of the previous eight lessons committing the title of each to memory:

1. AWAKEN YOUR GENIE! (Dream Again)
2. JUST IMAGINE! (Dream without Limits)
3. BLOCK OUT NAYSAYERS! (Believe in Your Dreams)
4. 5,110 DAYS! (Visualize Long Term)
5. THE POWER OF ONE! (Focus Short Term)
6. MAGNETS, PAINTBRUSHES, AND MIRRORS!
  (Attitude is the Difference)
7. BAMBOO FARMING! (Be Tenacious)
8. DON'T QUIT! (Avoid the Easy)

As he read the titles, visual images of each lesson popped back into his mind. "A genie and a magical lamp…Jules Verne and using your imagination…a time machine and visits to people who said it couldn't be done…seeing the big picture of a Mt. Rushmore…building a great life day-by-day…being a magnet and attracting opportunity…having the tenacity of a bamboo farmer…avoiding the easy and never quitting…. Wow!" Jay took a deep breath. "That's a lot to take in…but I want to remember as much as I can about all of these!"

Satisfied with his brief review, Jay turned his attention to the next available blank page in his notebook. On the top of the new page, Jay wrote *Lesson 9*. Amicus' next lesson was now shining from the screen.

LESSON 9: THREE MORNING QUESTIONS!
(Start the Day Right)

Greetings, Jay! Undoubtedly, the lessons from previous days have started to spark a wide range of motivating ideas. Knowing that your success intensity is now up, my friend, I want to hit on a couple of points that will help you keep it there! Ready? Let's start with a little story….

The two college students were enjoying their weekend get-away so much that they decided to stay an extra day. Of course, that's not what they told the professor in explaining why they missed his mid-term exam.

Standing before the professor the day after the exam, the two students speaking with one voice said, "We're really sorry,

Professor! We wanted to get out of town in order to avoid study distractions, but on the way back home we got a flat tire. Unfortunately, we didn't have a spare, and since we were so far out in the boonies, it took forever for a tow truck to come and tow us! Stuff just happens, you know?"

With a knowing grin, the professor shifted his glasses on his face and stared back and forth between the two for what seemed like a minute before he answered. "Okay. I will give you two the benefit of the doubt. I will allow you to take the test tomorrow with no penalty." The two students left the professor's office elated at their success in pulling one over on him.

Seated in separate rooms the next day, the two students opened their test booklets and each was thrilled to find that the test was only one question. Thrilled until they read the question: "Which tire?"

As the rather sly professor proved, asking the right question can surely make a difference. Asking yourself the right questions, my friend, also can make a difference in your life. The professor's question helped him determine the truth regarding the flat tire. The questions that you ask yourself can help you determine the quality of your day...and the success of your life.

For many, getting up in the morning to trudge off to work isn't something that's looked forward to with great anticipation. In fact, the unspoken sentiment for a huge majority goes something like this: "It's Monday morning...yuck! Just let me get my coffee...and don't talk to me until lunch!" Sound familiar? I thought it might.

The truth is, Jay, you can determine the quality and success of your day by simply adjusting your strategy in the morning. You can give yourself more energy, more passion, and a brighter outlook by doing one thing: change the first questions that you ask yourself.

You may not have realized this, but every morning when you get up, you ask yourself a series of questions that determine how your day will progress. The answers to those questions more than likely will set the tone for the rest of the day. Your questions in the past have usually gone something like this: "What do I have to do today?" and "What projects are hanging over my head that need to get done?" *What do I have to do* questions aren't conducive to helping you build any morning momentum. They aren't helpful in allowing you to live with power. Instead, they're questions that drain your spirit and energy right from the start.

Let me prove my point. Think about Christmas and the holiday season. Recall how excited you were as a kid to wake up on that special day and open all those fantastic presents you found under the tree. The first questions running through your mind that morning were solely focused on exciting and motivating thoughts: "Wow! I wonder what I'm going to get?" Do you remember that morning's excitement? Quite a bit different than how you start your days now, wasn't it?

You know, you can feel the same excitement today if you choose. It's really very simple. When you wake up in the morning re-direct your thinking so that you ask yourself three essential questions:

Question 1: What am I excited about doing today? (Think about how great you will feel when you do it!)

Question 2: Whom can I serve or encourage today? (What can you do that will make someone else feel great?)

Question 3: What am I most grateful for in my life right now? (Think about something specific that makes you feel fortunate, and yes, there will always be something!)

Do this exercise first thing in the morning while you are in bed waking up, or do it while you are brushing your teeth or taking a shower. You might even write the questions down and tape them to your bathroom mirror or to your steering wheel as a reminder. Do whatever it takes. Just ask them.

My friend, your ability to live with passion, purpose and power depend on what you put into that amazing computer perched on your shoulders. **Start your mornings off right and affect the direction of your day…and future…by simply taking a page out of the professor's handbook. Ask the right questions.**

Question:
What can you do to make sure that you start your day by asking the right questions?

Jay knew exactly how he'd be certain to remember the questions. He pulled a three-by-five index card from inside his desk and wrote them down. Tearing two pieces of clear tape from the dispenser, Jay took his newly created *Morning Questions* card and headed for his bathroom mirror. Right above the sink where he brushed his teeth every day, he taped the card.

"There! That's cool! I can't miss reading it now!"

With great inner confidence, Jay strolled back into his office in order to shut down the computer for the morning. Before he did, however, he had a thought to do one more thing. Pulling another three-by-five card out of his desk, Jay wrote down the list one more time. This time, Jay headed to Vicki's bathroom and taped it above her sink as well.

Wednesday, May 28th…10:35 A.M.

A few hours later, wearing a charcoal suit, bright red tie, and white Oxford, button-down shirt, Jay pulled opened the huge oak door that marked the entrance to Brown & Bigelow Creative. "Impressive!" Jay immediately thought. "These guys know how to make an impact! I like it!" Admiring the elegance of the entry's surroundings, Jay walked up to the receptionist desk, made eye contact, smiled, and gave his name. "Jay Garfield. I'm here to see Ms. Walston for a 10:45 appointment." Jay's smile earned one in return.

"Please have a seat, Mr. Garfield, and I'll let Ms. Walston know that you're here. Can I offer you some coffee? It's pretty good this morning. Surprising how good coffee tastes from a new coffee pot." She smiled again.

Jay laughed. "You're so right! It does! But no thank you, Erin. Thanks though for asking. That's very nice of you." Jay had noted Erin Thomas's desk nameplate. He was impressed with her gracious courtesy and professionalism. He made a mental note to share his positive experience with Ms. Walston. "Ole Shirls could learn a thing or two from Erin… no doubt!" Jay thought to himself.

As he waited, Jay found himself making comparisons between his original advertising home and Brown & Bigelow Creative. He'd felt proud to have been a part of JLJ Advertising, but this was a whole different level of success. Jay could feel the difference. Heck, he could see the difference! On the walls around him hung the plaques and awards that Brown & Bigelow Creative had won. Jay had attended enough advertising award dinners to know that these guys were great, but seeing the fruits of victory from those evening dinners hanging on the walls now was impressive. "Now I know why I felt like the dog's tail when bidding against these guys!"

Erin put down the receiver. "Ms. Walston will be out shortly. Just give her a few minutes."

"No worries. Thank you."

Jay opened his folder and reviewed for the fourth time the information that he'd written down about Brown & Bigelow. He had looked at their web site extensively. He thought he had known about them before, but being here now put everything into place for Jay mentally.

"Best business web site I've ever seen, awesome client list, amazing offices, friendly staff, awards up the kazoo…unbelievable! These guys walk on water!" Jay felt a crack in his adrenaline dam as nervousness started to kick in. "Now, Jay…don't start psyching yourself out! You're good…you deserve to be sitting here! Breathe…breathe…breathe."

Jay attempted to calm his nerves through reciting by memory the client names he'd written down. He memorized the yearly billing dollars and other growth statistics he'd discovered in his web search. He wanted to use all of these retained facts in his interview to show that he was the sort of guy who came prepared; he was a salesman who did his homework. Jay was determined to make a solid first impression.

"Those who prepare for success…experience success!" Jay had remembered these words for what seemed like practically forever…or at least since high school. Jay's basketball coach would yell out the declaration every time he lined his team up on the court baseline for running drills. Again and again he would snap at his players to quit bending over and hacking and get back on the line to run. Then the whistle would blow again and they would be off and sprinting for the seventh time.

A new sort of whistle was blowing for Jay now. It was 10:43, and a very impressive looking woman in her mid-forties wearing a white business suit had just said his name out loud.

"Jay Garfield? I'm Laura Walston. Nice to meet you!" She extended her hand.

Jay stood up. Temporarily out of sorts from still being on the running line, Jay shook the hand of Bigelow & Brown's Vice President of Operations. "Ms. Walston. It's a pleasure to meet you. It's also a pleasure to be interviewing with Brown & Bigelow Creative."

12:27 P.M.

Ninety minutes later, Jay handed the parking lot attendant his validated ticket. He was smiling confidently on the outside, but on the inside his unbridled elation was jumping up and down like a kid in a rented jump house at a birthday party.

"Wow! Never could I have imagined this! Not in my wildest dreams!" Jay congratulated himself aloud as he pulled his car out of the underground parking structure. "Amazing! Jaybo! You nailed it! Way to go, buddy! You might have landed a job today!"

Soon after leaving the bumper-to-bumper pace of downtown L.A.'s lunch traffic, Jay steered onto the 101 North and headed home. His inside celebration now shifted to overflow status escaping to his exterior. Other drivers couldn't help but smile at the animated man driving alongside of them who appeared to be singing at full lung capacity. A few drivers even scanned their radio dials in search of the same great station to which they thought Jay must be tuned. It was hard not to want the freedom that Jay was exuding….even in congested traffic that was moving less than thirty-five miles an hour.

Although Vicki had called Jay during her work break, he wanted to give her the specifics of the morning interview after she'd gotten home. "It went fantastic, Vic, but let me fill you in on the details tonight. We're going out to dinner!"

Later that evening, Jay whisked Vicki away to their favorite Thai restaurant. He replayed the interview blow-by-blow through most of their dinner. "It was all perfect! The place is so classy…the best! And Laura Walston? There's no one at JLJ like her! Talk about an 'A' player…she's it!"

Jay shared with Vicki that his comfort level remained a "10" from the moment he first sat down in front of Laura's desk. "To begin with, I think I was probably smiling the whole interview! I noticed my mouth was even tired when I left the office from being in the smile position so long!" They both laughed.

"Everything just seemed to flow! I felt so relaxed that it didn't even seem like an interview! We discussed the two accounts that I'd edged them out on at JLJ…and it felt so great to be recognized as a top performer!"

"However, the big rush came when, after close to forty minutes, Laura asked me about setting-up a second interview…but for another job! Let me see if I can remember exactly how she put it…ummm… it went something like, 'Jay, I know that you've come in to interview for an opening as an area account executive, but I have to tell you, maybe fate had you walk through the door today for another position entirely.' I couldn't believe it!"

"She told me that my presentation skills were so impressive that she wanted to talk to me about an unadvertised position that they'd hired a search firm to help with. It will be a brand new position for them…a national job so that they can compete aggressively with the advertising big boys. They want to showcase their talent in places outside the western region. When she told me that I have many of the qualities they're looking for, I was blown away!"

"So...for the next thirty minutes, the tone of the interview changed. Here I was in Brown & Bigelow Creative and the Vice President was selling me on a job! I loved it! This has to be one of the best days I've ever had in my professional life!"

Vicki and Jay laughed over their plates of curry while Jay told his story. They both knew there was no guarantee. He hadn't been offered anything except the chance to interview for a pretty great sounding job. "But you know what, Vic? I think that I have a chance at this job! I really, really do!" Together, they toasted the future...and a second interview at Brown & Bigelow Creative.

Thursday, May 29th...6:30 A.M.

Upon waking, Jay splashed water on his face and then sat down in the middle of the bedroom floor. He started stretching. "I feel like going out for a run this morning. I think I'll get some fresh air and stretch these lungs a bit."

Vicki laughed. "Just make sure that you don't overdo it, Superman! You might look awfully funny showing up at your next interview being pushed in a wheelchair."

Despite not being much of a runner, Jay certainly looked the part. Clad in new Nike shoes, multi-colored running shorts, and an old *No Fear* T-shirt, he headed out the door and started running in the direction of the park, four blocks away. After about a hundred paces, he realized that he was going to be worn out before he even got to the park. He adjusted his stride from world-record setting marathon speed to a more normal Jay Garfield pace.

He hadn't jogged much over the years and could feel every cell of his body shouting out that painful truth now: "Oh man...this hurts big time!" Jay slowed down even more, not out of choice, but necessity. Jogging at walking speed, Jay felt like his lungs were going to explode and his legs were melting into the sidewalk. Struggling to make it to the edge of the park, he turned around and ran back in the direction from which he'd come.

Day one of Jay's running endeavor had ended with far less victory than he had originally and unrealistically expected. Standing bent over in the driveway wheezing, Jay muttered out loud for no one other than himself, "Nice, Jay. Real nice, superstar."

He hobbled to the door preparing for the ultimate in ribbing from Vicki. Luckily, she just grinned and didn't say a word when she saw him come back into the house. Jay groaned and collapsed onto the same floor where his hopeful morning stretching had taken place less than thirty minutes prior.

8:45 A.M.

Freshly showered, but with muscles still trembling from exertion, Jay sat in front of his computer. He was still thinking about how far out of shape he had let himself get. "Less than a mile…that's pretty ridiculous, dude. But tomorrow, I'm going to tackle that run again."

Having been a high school athlete, Jay was not new to developing a workout plan. In his Amicus notebook, he turned to the last page of the book and wrote out a four week running plan. "I can do this!" Jay thought. With Olympic hope reborn, Jay started reading the new lesson that appeared on his computer screen.

LESSON 10: SHARPEN YOUR AX!
(Avoid Dullness)

Great morning, isn't it! You really can create a great day when you focus on exercises that invigorate the body as well as the spirit and the mind, can't you? In all three areas…mind, spirit, and body…keep up the effort! If you do, you'll be rewarded with the ability to run further and faster than you've ever imagined!

Remember our last lesson on asking the right questions in order to create positive morning momentum? This lesson is designed to continue the momentum theme…but for more than a day. This lesson is about how to keep life momentum.

After a number of preliminary contests, the two finalists in *The Great Wood Splitting Challenge* stood shoulder-to-

shoulder. Well, sort of. You see, there was a rather large difference in the size of the two men. The first contestant was a giant of a man. A towering, burly individual, contestant #1 looked as if he was taken right out of the pages of lumberjack lore. His beard was heavy, his laugh hearty, and his muscles were gigantic.

The second contestant was much smaller. Contestant #2 stood ten inches shorter and weighed over a hundred pounds less than his Paul Bunyan-like opponent. Although this fine woodchopper had easily defeated his three previous challengers, he was given little chance of knocking off the *Giant of the Forest.*

As the contest began, fifty tree rounds were lined up in front of each contestant. The log splitting giant began to whip the mighty ax over his head and back down with awesome force. He easily split his first twenty tree rounds while the underdog favorite, contestant #2, had split only seventeen. Then thirty-six versus twenty-eight. With the giant's lead building, the smaller man picked up his ax and walked away. The giant laughed his hearty lumberjack laugh and kept bringing his ax down on the tree rounds in front of him. He mocked his opponent for seeming to be tired and taking a break.

When the smaller man returned, he trailed by twelve logs. What's more, the vocal giant needed to split only ten more rounds in order to claim the title. There was no doubt that every person witnessing this great log chopping contest agreed that it would be the giant who was soon to be lifting his ax triumphantly over his head in victory. That is, all agreed except for one person…the giant's opponent.

Amazingly, the underdog began splitting logs with astonishing speed. The giant's lead was quickly cut in half…and then in half again. As the smaller man brought down his final blow on log fifty, the giant stood in shock…log forty-nine still in front of him.

"How could you beat me!" the giant bellowed. "I never even stopped to take a rest like you!"

"Ah! But there's your mistake, sir! I never took a rest!" declared the smaller man. "I merely stopped to sharpen my ax!"

Ax sharpening is one of the most important things that you could ever do to keep momentum going in your life. Regular *ax sharpening* of the self-improvement kind is what will allow you to achieve your lifetime goals.

What is *ax sharpening*? It's staying sharp! It's consistently and routinely taking the time to sharpen your motivation, your confidence, and your determination. It's pursuing a regularly structured personal development plan. It's about self-awareness and keeping focused. It's about investing in motivational materials, books, CD's, and magazines. It's about spending regular time with successful, driven people who inspire you.

Why do people become dull and lose their life momentum? Why do people give up on goals and become permanently down, never to get up again? The answer is that diesel truck called everyday life. Money worries, relationship problems, long days at work, what to fix for dinner…all of these begin to add up and take their toll. People become so intent on just handling the everyday tasks and problems thrown at them that they lose sight of their own big picture. Life simply wears away at them and dullness and mediocrity set in.

If you're going to avoid traveling down that same road, the bottom line is that you need to develop a conscious plan to combat the natural grind of life. You need to avoid being dull and complacent by consistently filling your mind with thoughts that refresh and empower you. Don't think for a second that you can succeed without working on yourself consistently. Maybe in the short term you'll get by, but in the long run your spirit will become tired of striving without being fed. You spend time maintaining your car to keep it running smoothly; how much more time should you be spending maintaining yourself?

Great athletes, musicians, leaders…they all sharpen their ax to stay on top of their game. If you want to reach your own life pinnacle, you need to as well. **Never, never, never stop the process of *ax sharpening*! Make a lifetime commitment to read, learn, and grow! If you do, you could find yourself to be a winning log chopper in your own life!**

Question:
What routines can you build into your life to make sure that you keep your ax sharpened?

"Wow! I'm right on with my thinking!" Jay was pleased that even before he had read today's lesson, he'd taken the time to write out a four week exercise plan for getting back into shape. Amicus' lesson, however, did three things for him today: 1) it stimulated the idea that personal accountability—and maybe even daily monitoring—was necessary to produce results, 2) it made clear that a long-term exercise plan was necessary if he was to continue to stay in shape after the four weeks, and 3) it highlighted the fact that he needed to create an *ax sharpening* plan for himself mentally and spiritually, too.

"I need to develop a routine...something consistent! Now let's see...what do I need? Hmmm...let's start with the whole idea of staying mentally and emotionally sharp. I need to create regular time to read and learn...and maybe journal my thoughts and progress."

On the left hand side of a notebook page, Jay wrote the days of the week. "I need something that will work for me...that I can be consistent with. What if I start with Tuesday, Thursday, and Sunday as my *ax sharpening* days. But when...what time?"

Jay contemplated the times of the day, trying to be as specific as possible. He considered the natural breaks of the day in the morning, afternoon, and evening. He eliminated the afternoons first.

"Since I'll be working soon, it'll be tough to be consistent in the afternoons. How about evenings? Hmmm...before bed perhaps? That seems good...but wait. I'm usually tired and my emotional energy is lower. How about mornings? Well, that used to be a tough time for me, but I've done well getting up lately. Why not? Let's do it! That'll certainly help me get my days off to a good start!"

At first, Jay thought dedicating thirty minutes three days a week would be a great goal. He soon changed his mind and threw himself completely into the idea. "C'mon, Jay! If you're really going to do this… then really go for it! Do a little every day! First thing in the morning… let's say only ten minutes. If I want more…great! But ten minutes to start!"

With total conviction of heart and mind, Jay committed to his new self-improvement direction. "Success! I feel it! I now have an exercise plan and an *ax sharpening* plan! Sharp mind…sharp body! I love it! Now I just have to follow through!"

Loving his accomplishment and his new plans, Jay felt totally exhilarated from his morning effort. Taking what seemed like a disappointing morning run and a bad start to the day, he had turned everything around quickly with positive action.

Feeling empowered now by his newly created *ax sharpening* plan, Jay knew he needed to add a few books to his motivational library. He had an interview scheduled later that afternoon, but there was plenty of time to do some internet shopping with online bookstores. After performing a few applicable keyword searches, he started by ordering a couple of motivational classics: W. Clement Stone's *Success Through a Positive Mental Attitude* and *Benjamin Franklin's Autobiography*.

"Hmmm…what else," Jay pondered. "Let me work on some vocabulary building, too. What can I listen to while I drive?" Scanning the possibilities, he decided on a CD called *Vocabulary Building for the Person on the Go…and Grow*. "Goofy title, but this sounds good! Go for it!" Pulling out his credit card, Jay filled out his order. "These will be great! I can't wait for these babies to get here!"

The rest of the morning, Jay fell into his daily routine: job hunting, calls to prospective employers and agencies, and sending out resumes. His late afternoon job interview served as a mini-sabbatical and gave Jay reason to leave the house.

Already having had a taste of what he might love to do with Brown & Bigelow, Jay wasn't going into today's interview with much enthusiasm. Originally, he had been thrilled to get the phone call for the interview with this new company. In fact, initially, he had been happy to get a phone call for any interview! However, things changed now. He felt he had a new mission…a mission for which he was slowing growing faith.

"I want to love what I do…and do what I love!" He had read the expression in an internet job article and decided to commit the philosophy to heart. Today's interview selling a niche medical magazine didn't quite fit in with Jay's new found goal and he had a much different energy about him walking into the interview.

Instead of cancelling the appointment altogether, however, Jay rationalized that he should honor his commitment and go.

"Plus, it will give me a chance to practice this darn interviewing game!"

2:57 P.M.

Half-heartedly, Jay left the afternoon interview feeling disconnected. The flow of the interview had gone poorly and there had been no real connection made with either the company or the interviewer. Jay wondered how much of that lack of connection was because he had programmed himself to have low expectations before even walking into the appointment. His attitude towards the job had been nonchalant from the very beginning.

"What did I expect? Of course I'm going to feel like this when I set my sights low and don't bring my 'A' game! I won't do that again! No more lackadaisical effort! If I'm going to be a first round draft choice, I need to act like one!"

Friday, May 30th

The sound of the morning alarm came too early, but like a good soldier, Jay didn't hesitate and popped out of bed. Going to the sink first, Jay turned on the faucet and splashed his face. Cold water signaled to his still sleepy mind that there was no hope of sending Jay back under the cozy covers. The day had started.

Dropping to the middle of the room to stretch, Jay was ready for another go-at-it on Day Two of his get-back-in-shape exercise plan.

"Oh wait! I need to do some *ax sharpening* first!" He scrambled back to his feet. "Okay…let's see. Where should I start?" Sorting through the small book shelves in the area designated as the "library," Jay looked over the limited reading choices. "Grisham…Rowling…C.S. Lewis …nope. Hmmm…gosh, not a big selection! *Sherlock Holmes and the Hounds of the Baskervilles*? Not quite! Oh wait! Here I go!" Pulling a tattered, old copy of *How to Win Friends and Influence People* off the shelf, he made his first choice.

Jay had read the book years before when he graduated from college and, unlike most other books that came before and after it, Norman Vincent Peale's paperback had avoided the fate of most that came into the Garfield house. Jay had a philosophy that if something hadn't been read or used over the last two years, it wasn't needed.

Put it in the donation pile! were words Jay loved calling out during spring cleaning sessions. Vicki disagreed with most of Jay's choices, especially when it came to asking about clothes that she hadn't worn for a long time.

"But this might come back in style! You never know! I like it!" Vicki would argue back. The article of clothing in question never failed to make it back into her closet.

Books, on the other hand, were another story. There was never any argument over what books made the donation box. This was Jay's domain. He crowned himself the *Sole Decider* of all books. Of course, no college textbook remained in the house. They were all done away with years ago. The last bunch of book lottery winners were small paperbacks that were just serving time on the shelf before their number was up, too. Peale's book, though, seemed to have won the book lottery a number of times and had probably won a permanent life stay by being chosen now. It had made an impact earlier in Jay's life; he remembered at least that much about it. And now, it was to make the starting line-up of Jay's new morning book club.

"Perfect! I remember you!" Jay said out loud to the book in his hands. "When the student is ready, the teacher will appear! So what do you have to teach me?" Jay sat down on the old futon couch and began to read.

Ten minutes of reading turned into seventeen before he laced up his running shoes and headed out the door. "Okay…take it easy today,

Jay. Just work into this. Slow and steady…limited pain." The last part about limited pain was the easiest to follow as his muscles were still stiff from yesterday's run.

With a day's wisdom under his invisible running belt, Jay started out at a snail's pace. "I probably look silly at this speed!" he said to himself, well aware of the countless times he had pointed out fifteen-minute-mile joggers to Vicki. "Why doesn't that guy just walk? He looks ridiculous!" Jay's arrogant running commentary on other runners was coming back to haunt him. "I'm now one of them! Great, Jay…great!"

Making it to the park without his muscles fully rebelling, Jay continued once around the half-mile park before heading home. Although he still collapsed at the driveway finish line, he was proud that he'd succeeded in pushing himself a little further than the day before. "Victory!" With limited energy, Jay pumped his fist affirming his exercise survival triumph.

After collapsing on the floor for fifteen minutes, Jay managed to push himself into the bathroom and clean up. Then, hobbling to his classroom, he eased himself into his chair. "Late…but present, Professor Amicus." Opening his spiral notebook, Jay noted that he had filled up almost forty percent of the pages. Impressed with what he was creating, Jay wrote down the words *Lesson 11*. He then steadied his eyes on the screen and began to read.

LESSON 11: THE MULTIPLIER EFFECT!
(Multiply Success)

Congratulations! You're at the halfway point, Jay! I'm pleased with your stick-to-it perseverance! Can you feel the transformation beginning? Can you sense that your life is starting to change direction and head down a more passionate and purposeful path? Keep up the good work!

In thinking about today's lesson, I believe that this message has come at a perfect time to remind you of the "multiplying" power of daily successes. Read on and see what I mean.…

One day, on *official business*, I happened to be at the race track and came across a pair of interesting old-timers who were leaning out over the rail near the track. With quiet amusement, I watched the two scream and holler at the horses as they sped by only to watch each of the first four races end in the exact same way…one of the old-timers would shake his head in bewilderment while the other would pump his fist in the air triumphantly. After the fourth race had finished, the slightly bewildered old-timer turned to his enthusiastic friend and said, "You've picked the winners of the first four races, and I'm still trying to chase just one horse into the Winner's Circle. How do you do it?"

The ecstatic winner looked at his unlucky fellow bettor and hesitated for a brief second, wondering if he should share what to him was potentially the greatest secret in the world. His face softened, then he whispered his answer so it was not heard by anybody else, "Well, usually I stick a pin into the race sheet without looking. Wherever the pin lands, that's my horse!"

The disbelieving listener said, "So, every race all you do is stick a silly pin in the race sheet? That's how you do it?"

"Not exactly. The pin only works for the first race each day. It helps me pick one winner only."

"Then how do you explain having won four races in a row?"

"Well, I was making my first bet today, and found that I had forgotten to bring a pin. Of course, no one else standing in line had a pin, so I just took the fork out of my lunch bag and…well…there you have it!"

I'm sure that you'd agree that this lucky bettor had a peculiar way of multiplying his success! Peculiar or not, however, people always listen to a proven results producer. Some desperate, unsuccessful race bettor might even run off to a nearby track restaurant in search of his own four-pronged utensil after hearing this story!

What about you though, Jay? Would you be interested in learning a secret that's a sure-fire way to multiply your *winnings* on life's racetrack? Would you be interested in learning a secret that multiplies your own success? Yes? Then I'm going to share another success secret with you that is not based on luck; I call it the *Multiplier Effect*.

Look at the numbers *3* and *4*. There's a very small difference between the two numbers actually...just one number in fact. But what happens to those same two numbers when you multiply them five times with themselves? Well, that very small difference between *3* and *4* turns into an incredibly large and dramatic difference! Let me show you:

$$3 \times 3 \times 3 \times 3 \times 3 = 243 \text{ and } 4 \times 4 \times 4 \times 4 \times 4 = 1,024.$$

Now that's called multiplying power! That's a big difference! And you know what? You can multiply that kind of power into your own life! Again, let me show you.

Imagine right now that your average current day's effort on a scale of 1-5 (poor-great) is a *3*. Your effort and production is right in the middle...average. But imagine if you change your average effort each day from a *3* to a *4*. What does this mean? It means doing twenty-five more sit-ups. It means fifteen more minutes writing the book that you want to write. It means making ten additional sales calls. It means connecting with your spouse for an extra five minutes a day.

The results? Well, you tell me. What would happen to your production if you made ten additional business calls each day? How would key relationships in your life respond if you made it a priority to do just a little bit more for them each day? Now remember, we're not talking about doing a lot. Just a little. Just the difference between a *3* and *4*. Forget even taking your performance up to a *5*! Who would want that much success in life? Sarcastically speaking, of course.

By maximizing your performance just a little bit each day, my friend, you create a situation where positive things start multiplying fast. You get closer to finishing that book. You make one additional sale this month over last. You lose an extra couple of pounds. You create momentum.

The power of the *Multiplier Effect* is put into full force by your willingness to do just a little extra towards the achievement of your goal each day...every day. There is really nothing magical about it! It's just taking the art of success and turning it into a mathematical science. More calls...more contacts... more leads...more sales! Applying this principle to how you live every day will multiply your success into something much bigger! Faster!

Ten more calls every day for a month equals 220 extra calls. Ten more calls every day for a year? 2640 extra calls! If you were to close only one percent of those 2,640 extra calls, that would still be twenty-six more sales! Now that's multiplying success!

Whether or not the horse picker found a sure-fire way to multiply his good fortune at the track is debatable. The secret that I am sharing with you, however, is not debatable. A little extra push or effort on your part every day will most definitely multiply the number of trips that you make into life's Winner's Circle! Commit to raising your performance from a *3* to *4* daily and watch the *Multiplier Effect* change your world faster than you could've ever believed!

Question:
In what specific ways can you change your daily performance from a *3* to a *4*?

Reading the five times 3 compared to five times 4 multiplication example again, Jay thought, "243...1024. Hmmm...that's a big difference!" I'm glad Amicus also put the example in terms of sales calls because now I can easily see what he means. I wonder if in other areas the results would be as dramatic?"

Jay opened his notebook and began listing areas where improvement was important to him and where he could benefit by the power of the *Multiplier Effect*: career, finances, spouse, learning/ growth, health. "That's a good start. How would I rate myself in each area right now? Okay...think, Jay...think...think. One is low...five is high...so how do I rate?" Jay's scorecard read:

Where I am now:
1. *Career: Score 1…I have no job! Of course, it's a "1" and that's only because that's the bottom of the scale!*
2. *Finances: Score 2…Thank goodness for the unemployment check so we're okay for a while.*
3. *Vicki: Score 4…We're close right now! Big improvement! Good communication! Great support!*
4. *Learning/growth: Score 5…Right now I'm doing great! I'm growing every day! Thank you, Amicus!*
5. *Health: Score 2…I'm having trouble running to the park and back, but I have a good foundation and a plan to improve!*

It was weird seeing his life measured in numbers on paper, but it gave him a very strong self-awareness of where he actually was and how he was doing in his life. "Man! I'm blowing it! Look at a couple of these scores! Embarrassing! I need to get things together big time!"

Disappointed but encouraged with the thought that he could improve, Jay continued the exercise. "Now…how do I take my score in each area up a notch, or two or three? What do I need to do?"

Jay was digging deep. He was taking on a very tough task, one for which people rarely muster the mental courage: personal evaluation. He was looking at his life and asking himself the tough questions. "I want to make the 'Multiplier Effect' work for me. I want to change and change big!" Jay was thinking hard. "Awareness…that's a great start. Realizing where I am is good…but I don't want to be where I am! I want more! I want to be able to come back here in three months and feel like my life has changed significantly! Hmmm…what can I do to raise my scores?"

Now Jay was talking out loud to himself. "Career? That's easy! I need to find a darn job! That will take me to at least a '2' even if I hate whatever I find!" Jay went over each category individually, wrote it out again, and then wrote goals next to each major topic. When he was finished, he looked at his updated list.

Where I want to be:

1. Career: Score 4….Find a job I like! (Something that inspires me, helps others, and that I don't have to bust my tail doing for 60 hours a week!)

2. Finances: Score 4…Live comfortably and invest 10% a month.

3. Vicki: Score 5…Maintain current relationship level, plus add small gestures like notes and cards. Maybe a weekly date night? Plan vacations more often.

4. Learning/growth: Score 5…Maintain regular reading and learning pattern. Work consistent plan!

5. Health: Score 5…Consistent workouts (minimum 4 days a week)…watch diet. (No junk food!)

Jay felt proud of his effort. It was easy to feel optimistic about the future when you had a plan and the passion to follow through with it. Jay had a growing sense of personal power that he hadn't had in a long time. He was feeling in control. Just a simple awareness of what he was doing well and what he was not doing well heightened his confidence that his world was going to turn out for the best. Now that he believed it was up to him to make good things happen…well, that was all the magic he really needed.

Saturday, May 31st

With sweat beading his forehead, Jay immediately proceeded upstairs after finishing his morning run. Grabbing a towel off the rack to dab the dripping perspiration, Jay rubbed the towel over his face. The run had felt good. Sure, struggling with a two-mile run wasn't going to get him thinking about running a marathon anytime soon, but he was doing it. He was working his exercise plan. "Day-by-day, Jay…just be patient and work the plan. You're doing it. You succeeded for the day!"

Over the last couple of days, Jay had noted how much better he was already feeling and how much further he had been able to run since day one, and that was reason to celebrate. Still feeling the adrenalin of the jog, he bypassed the shower and proceeded straight to class. He knew there would be another lesson waiting for him and he wanted to get to it. "Well, Amicus, my teacher friend, let me hear what you have to say today!"

LESSON 12: DIRT OR GOLD?
(Expect the Best)

Do you feel it, Jay? Can you sense it's going to be a great day? Believing that it will be is the first step in making it happen! Expectations in life make a huge difference in the quality of our lives. Expect great…realize great. Today's lesson will reinforce this principle. So, are you ready for a great lesson?

As the traveler stood by the gas pump watching the dollar indicator continue to click higher, he hollered to the old service station attendant sitting nearby, "So tell me, Mister. What are the people like in this town?"

The old-timer paused, then looked up from his whittling project. "Well, let me ask you, partner, what were the people like in the last town that you just came through?"

The tourist didn't hesitate for even a second in responding. "The people in the last town were terrible! They were mean, rude, and completely negative!"

The wise graybeard smiled slightly, nodded his head, and said, "You'll find people here much the same."

No sooner had the first traveler pulled out of the station when a second tourist pulled up to the pumps. Again the old man was asked what the people were like in this town. Again the old-timer asked the visitor what he had found in the last town. The traveler enthusiastically replied, "The people were great! They were helpful and gracious, and I wish that I could have stayed longer!"

The old sage smiled slightly and said, "You'll find people here much the same."

Revealing? Let's assume for a moment, Jay, that there's a third traveler. You. Now suppose that the old-timer asked you, "What were the people like in the last town that you came through?" Would your response be more like traveler #1 or traveler #2?

For the sake of making this easier, I'm going to venture that your answer is as positive as traveler #2's. However, this answer leads itself to follow-up with a very interesting second question. Would those who know you best...your family, friends, and coworkers...agree with you? Would they say that you look for the positive? Or would they say you look for the negative?

A reporter once asked Andrew Carnegie how forty-three of the people that worked for him became millionaires. Carnegie responded to the question by saying, "You develop people the same way you mine gold. When you mine gold, you have to move tons of dirt to find one ounce of gold. But you don't go in there looking for the dirt. You go in there looking for the gold."

So, back to you, Jay. Do you look for the dirt or the gold in life?

In every aspect of life, you find that which you seek. Whether it's your relationship with your boss, the customer service representative on the phone, or a new job, you will find what you look for... good or bad.

So what does this mean? It means simply that you need to be sure that you're mining for gold and not for dirt. If you think failure is inevitable, it is. If you think your job is dull, it will be. If you tell a child that he's average, chances are he'll perform that way. You have the ability to turn a situation into exactly what you predict. Richard Bach in his book *Illusions* wrote, "Argue for your limitations and they will be yours."

So, knowing that if you look for the dirt in life, you'll find it ...why look for it? Life is so much more rewarding and feels so much better to your spirit when you look for the excellent... the positive...the gold. The epitaph on the pessimist's head stone read: "I expected this." Be careful for what you expect, Jay, because as the old-timer working at the gas station knew, you'll probably find it.

Question:
Are your expectations leading you to find the gold or the dirt in life?

"That's laying it down at my feet!" Jay thought. "Good question. Do I expect the best from myself, or do I accept whatever happens? Do I look for the gold in my life, or do I look for the dirt?"

Jay reflected back on his effort yesterday outlining five areas of his life that were important for him to do well in: career, finances, Vicki, learning/growing, and health. "Heck...did I even have any expectations before? It seems as if until recently I wasn't looking for the gold or the dirt...and instead just existing. How sad."

"Gold or dirt?" Jay let the question root itself in his mind. "In a way, isn't that the center of everything...my expectations...what I look for in my life? I mean...geez...I have kinda' been coasting with no real purpose or direction and my results are definitely reflecting that. I don't really look for the good...or the bad. I just coast. And that's why I got fired. Bottom line. I really was dispensable. I made myself that way." Jay's self-awareness was growing at a rapid pace. "What I expect out of my life, I will get. What I seek, I will find. So, c'mon Jay, get off your butt and seek something great!"

It was 10:45 A.M. by the time Jay had finished the day's lesson and cleaned up from his morning run. His body felt that *good* tired after having exercised hard. His brain, however, was still grinding away. Thoughts from not only the day's lesson but the previous eleven lessons sat at the forefront of Jay's mind. For the last twelve days, Jay had been undergoing a dramatic shift in his entire thought pattern. He had entered his own version of *The Twilight Zone* where everything in life now looked different to him. It looked better...more promising for sure...but so different. He was different.

Knowledge is always a powerful tool; self-knowledge can be life-changing. Jay Garfield would have to forever ignore a bunch of newly uncovered personal truths if his life was to ever slide back into the mediocre existence where he once lived.

Downstairs in the kitchen, Vicki was putting the finishing touches on what looked to be an incredible picnic. The two had decided to take advantage of a gorgeous day by driving up the coast and heading to a quiet beach they knew. Enjoying the perfect gift of the Pacific Ocean and accompanied by an overflowing picnic basket, they had all the makings for an ideal day. The cherry on top, however, was a nearby beach bike rental shop. Jay and Vicki thought that they would give a tandem bike another shot considering that the first time they'd rode on the same two wheels together they laughingly fell over almost every time they went from stop-to-go.

The lunch had been perfect. The ocean perfect. The relaxation perfect. Lying stretched out on a beach blanket and completely stuffed, the two played a game of alternating questions. Like many married couples who thought they knew almost everything about each other… but didn't…Jay and Vicki found this spontaneous game to be eye-opening for learning things that they hadn't previously known.

Vicki had no clue that Jay's dream job was to spend a year doing social work in Africa, or that the trait he admired most about her was her friendliness to strangers. He complimented her, "You can talk to anybody. At the store…in a restaurant…in an elevator…you just aren't afraid to talk to people. I think that's so wonderful! I wish I had more of that in me."

Vicki hadn't known Jay's biggest regret was not getting involved in theatre in school. He explained, "With sports and everything, I never had the time. I went to an audition once, but left before it was my turn to go on stage. I was afraid of what some of the guys on the team would say. Crummy, huh? I think it would have been so fun to be an actor. Imagine, going to a movie and seeing yourself on the screen!"

Jay jumped off the blanket and, in his best Rocky Balboa imitation, started boxing in the air as he hummed the memorable sound track tune, and then said, "Yo, Adrian…whatcha' say you and me go rent a bike and go work off some of this picnic?"

Laughing, the two gathered up the bits and pieces of their picnic and trudged up the hill to load the car. With *Round 2* of the rented tandem bike event still to look forward to, Jay and Vicki were having a great time. Although they would prove later that they were still rookies on the tandem, it didn't matter. Everything else about the day…and them…was in perfect sync. When they pulled into the driveway at 8:20 that night, Jay and Vicki felt as if this had been one of the most edifying and fun days that they had shared together in a long time.

Sunday, June 1st

Jay decided to give himself a present and take the day off from his morning run. It wasn't in his original written plan, but his body felt tired and he needed to let his weary muscles recuperate. Counting yesterday's two hour tandem ride, Jay had exercised four straight days and he was pleased with that accomplishment.

He could have let himself get angry for not working his plan one hundred percent, but Jay realized the original plan had been a bit too optimistic and needed to be tweaked slightly in order to be of long term value. Four days in a row was more than the total number of days he had exercised in the last six months! Jay chose the *celebration* route instead of the *beat-myself-up* path.

"Accountable flexibility…that's what I call it!" Jay reassuringly proclaimed.

Neither Jay nor Vicki was eager to jump out of bed and get the day started, so together they resolved to take the morning slow and easy. "Hey…sometimes just relaxing can be a goal, too!" Jay half-jokingly teased.

Jay's motionless body lay resting, but his mind was doing anything but relaxing. He was reflecting back on yesterday's picnic conversation with Vicki. Jay had shared his recent thoughts and actions about the possibility of buying or starting his own business. He had hesitated telling her about the idea initially for fear of seeming too whimsical, but after letting it ruminate for a couple of days, Jay decided that the picnic was a perfect time to talk about it. Of course once she heard the idea, Vicki was totally interested and went with the conversation flow.

"That's an exciting idea, Jay. What are you thinking?"

"Well, Vickers, I'm not sure exactly. I'm a little nervous about the whole idea really…I mean I've never done anything so aggressive and bold. I do know that I'd like the business to be relevant and to help people, but that's really all I have on my wish list right now. Oh… besides making lots of money! What do you think?"

Like Jay, Vicki found the idea appealing, but scary. Like Jay again, she too had no idea what kind of business to pursue. "Geez…off the top of my head, I really don't know either. I mean where do we even start?"

Jay continued. "I actually took the step to call a broker last Wednesday regarding a couple of opportunities that seemed possible. One was a florist shop and the other a community bookstore. In the end, I don't know if I could do either, but I felt like putting myself out there a bit and looking into it."

"The florist shop sounds fun! Being surrounded by beautiful flowers all day and helping people share a beautiful gift with others sounds great! Seeing you arrange flowers in a vase, however…well, that I have more trouble visualizing!" Vicki laughingly teased her husband.

She continued, "As for a bookstore? Competing against mammoth stores and the internet could be hazardous to our financial health. Plus, it seems like the investment of inventory would be pretty high, too."

Lying in bed now, Jay sensed deep down that neither possibility would be a choice that they would eventually pursue. The bigger question, however, still lingered: was running his own business…any business…even for him?

"What really would I do? Could I do it? Could I be successful? Gosh…what am I going to do with my life, period?"

The gigantic question of "What to do with my life?" was beginning to haunt Jay's thinking every hour of the day. Sometimes the thought showed up as a quick, mental-flash reminder to his unconscious to solve the dilemma. At other times, the question loomed in Jay's conscious and he became completely lost and overwhelmed while brainstorming his life's possibilities. Ever since Amicus had planted the seed of carving his own Mt. JAYmore, Jay frustratingly asked himself over and over what that great legacy and masterpiece might be.

Jay reached over from his side of the bed to the night stand and grabbed the phone book lying in the drawer. Leaning on one elbow, he thumbed through the Yellow Pages to see if one of the business headings at the top of a page could be something that interested him. Like a kid scanning an ice cream menu of over fifty flavors to determine the merits of each, Jay scanned the listings of the phone book quickly calculating the pros and cons of the different choices.

"So many choices! So many things to consider!"

The process of looking for the perfect business and asking himself question after question soon became too overwhelming. Jay closed the book, set it back in the drawer, and crashed back onto his pillow.

"There are so many things to learn! How do I run a business? What do I need to know? What about training? How do I grow it? There's licensing and taxes and…wow…so much!"

Abruptly sitting up in bed, Jay took a long, deep breath…the kind that you might take when you realize that the campground is three hiking miles away instead of two. Was it fear he felt? Was it nervous adrenalin? Whatever it was, Jay knew that buying or opening any business was going to be like climbing Yosemite's Half Dome. He wasn't ready yet, but if it was something he really, really, really wanted…it could be done. He just needed to psyche himself up in a big way first.

9:55 am

Jay stood in front of the stove whipping up a quick batch of morning pancakes. "This one's a survivor…this one isn't. These two are passable if I turn them on their good side…" Jay wasn't great at pancake duty, but with lots of butter and syrup, his cakes were palatable.

For her part, Vicki was stirring a pitcher of orange juice that had been sitting frozen in a can five minutes before. The two sat down and ate together, but both were more interested in silence and reading their sections of the paper. Jay had always been a Sports-section-first type of guy while Vicki loved to flip through the Sunday ad inserts.

Eventually, they both eased their way through the paper. Finally, fed and up-to-date on all news valuable to each of them, they got dressed for church.

An hour later, the Garfield's found themselves squeezing past other churchgoers in the row and joining in singing *How Great Thou Art*. As hard as Jay tried this morning, his mind wasn't doing a good job of focusing on any part of the pastor's sermon. Jay might have been staring at the outline of the day's message in front of him, but his attention was fully targeted on the phone book exercise that had taken place ninety minutes prior.

"Is there a business for me? Am I better off working for someone else in the long run? What's my calling? How do I know? How does anybody know? Is everybody sitting here in church thinking the same as me?"

Jay couldn't get his brain to stop. The staccato of self-interrogation continued like firecrackers going off on the Fourth of July…one after another, after another. Jay's nervous agitation was building to a crescendo. It became a monumental effort of his control and discipline just to sit in his chair.

"I have found a temporary mission at least….just trying to sit here patiently without exploding!"

In the final prayer before the end of the sermon, Jay sent up his own SOS into the spiritual universe with the hope of being thrown a life preserver in the form of one very big answered prayer. He also thanked God for allowing him to get through the day's service.

The ride home from church was noticeably quiet. Each was hardly saying a word to the other, but saying much to themselves. Vicki, too, was more deliberate in her own personal thinking this morning. She was deep in thought and reflective about life's sometimes dramatic and life-altering events. Jay's firing had been one of those events for them, and although many aspects the event were turning out positive, there was still so much worry involved for her.

"What does our future hold, God?" Although the words of Vicki's prayer were silent to the ear, they carried a loud message from her heart.

Upon returning home, Vicki went outside to enjoy the great

weather and work in the yard. Gardening and planting flowers were a favorite pastime when time permitted and today would be one of those special occasions for her. Jay, on the other hand, headed upstairs for his favorite new pastime…*Bamboo Farming 101*.

"Amicus, Amicus, Amicus…I feel so alive, yet I'm still so confused. Please…tell me something that would point the way I should go."

Jay was talking to himself, but a part of him held out the strangest hope that Amicus could hear. Feeling an unsettling blend of frustration and anticipation, Jay turned on the computer. Amicus' lesson was there.

LESSON 13: PUT WOOD ON THE FIRE!
(Action Produces Rewards)

Hello, dear friend. I sense today that you might be struggling a bit. So many new and mind-opening thoughts have besieged you lately that it makes total sense you could be fighting through some important issues. Everything you're going through now, however, is a part of the positive change and growth process. Mixed waves of certainty and uncertainty are swimming together for sure, but this is natural. For growth to happen, it's necessary and important.

What is also important is for you to keep reinforcing and feeding your mind positive thoughts and ideas. You're establishing momentum and creating change, but you've got to keep your foot on the gas. It's easy to quit when you don't see yourself producing results, but don't do it! Your life will successfully heat up only if you keep taking action! Today's lesson reinforces this cause and effect necessity.

"What kind of stove are you anyway! You couldn't give off enough heat to melt an ice cube!" The bitter, old man sat in front of the jet-black stove cursing the inanimate object as if it could respond.

"I bet that a match could throw off more warmth than you could! If I stood next to the refrigerator, I would feel more heat!" The man continued his barrage of negativity. For its part,

the stove sat apparently immune to the sharp criticism because it threw off no more heat.

But the truth was, it wasn't immune. Actually, it had heard every biting word. The stove with its mystical human-like character had heard the vicious slander.

Being able to contain itself no longer, the target of the bitter man's relentless attack spoke. With a deep rumbling from inside, the stove bellowed out, "If you ever considered putting more wood into me, I might possibly consider putting more heat out to you!"

Of course, you've yet to come across a talking stove with a personality. (Wait for the future!) However, the truth that this imaginary persona roared out is undeniable: If you want more heat, you need to toss on more wood.

It's a very rare event in life where a person is able to receive a reward without putting in the effort. Although Sir Isaac Newton didn't come up with this cause and effect principle, the wood-for-heat axiom stands almost as pure as his law of gravity. We can surely count on it happening.

The rewards that you receive in life, whether they're tangible (a nice big paycheck) or intangible (a feeling of pride), are directly related to the effort or service that you provide to other people. Cause and effect in its most simple form is this: throw in wood…get back heat.

Whenever you find yourself unhappy and questioning your results, Jay, don't even begin to think about packing it in! Instead, boldly throw even more action and effort into your world! Don't question others as to why you aren't succeeding, but begin to question yourself. If you're dissatisfied with the rewards you're receiving, start focusing on the effort that you're giving. If you want more success, give more service. If your life isn't everything that you would like it to be, look in the mirror…and start causing. Cause something better. Cause more heat. Don't just complain and wonder, but rather take action and perform.

I remember there was once a woman who month-after-month would fall onto her knees each day and pray to win the lottery. Over time, her prayers became more ardent and more desperate until one day, I clued her in. I told her that if she wanted to win the lottery, first she needed to buy a lottery ticket.

With the exception of winning the lottery, rewards very seldom simply fall into people's laps. Rewards need to be coaxed. Mr. Lincoln wrote, "Things may come to those who wait, but only the things left by those who hustle."

Learn to quit waiting and expecting rewards to naturally appear. Start hustling, Jay! March outside, grab an armful of firewood, haul it in, and throw it on the fire! And when the fire burns down and your passion starts to get cold…more wood, more wood, more wood! If you do this, the principle of cause and effect will eventually take over and you will be reaping the warm feelings and great rewards that you desire.

Question:
In key areas of your life, what can you specifically do to throw more wood on the fire?

Jay turned back a few pages in his notebook and looked at the two lists that he had created a few days prior: *Where I am now* and *Where I want to be.*

"I'm gonna' go with Amicus' analogy. I'm going to imagine that each of the categories that I've listed is sorta' like a stove whose ability to put off heat…or success…depends on the amount of wood…or effort…that I throw into it. So, if I want a bigger bank account…I need to throw on more wood. If I want better health…more wood. If I want a job…more wood again. Now let me think…what is the wood for each?"

As Jay examined his previous five self-improvement sections closely (*Career, Finances, Vicki, Learning,* and *Health*), he decided that something was missing. "What about my son? What about my friends? What about relationships with other people in general? Hmmm…let me add all of those under the same category as *Vicki.* I'll change that section title to *Relationships.*"

Jay wrote the list down a third time in his notebook and began to brainstorm ways that he could add "wood" to each category. His list looked like this:

MORE Wood on the Fire:
1. Career:
   A. Send out more resumes and make more calls.
   B. Read books and do internet research about starting and
      owning a business.
2. Finances:
   A. Make monthly budget and see where current spending
      is actually taking place.
   B. Put first ten percent of everything we make into an
      investment account.
3. Relationships:
   A. Vicki…
      1. Set a weekly date night.
      2. Set a date and plan to take a vacation together.
   B. Josh…
      1. Call more often.
      2. Schedule time for him to come out and visit.
      3. Find ways to be more a part of his life when
         he's not here.
   C. Friends…
      1. Plan regular activities to get together.
      2. Come up with ideas to make new friends
         (a jogging partner?).
4. Learning/growth:
   A. Daily reading or audio in the morning
      (a book a month?).
   B. Learn hobbies/take up new activity.
      1. Ocean kayaking?
      2. Gourmet cooking class?
      3. Book club?
5. Health:
   A. Eliminate junk food and watch diet.
   B. Don't eat so late.

C. *Follow regular work-out plan.*
D. *Don't stay up late.*
E. *Take vitamin supplements daily.*

As Jay brainstormed, he was struck with a three-word thought: "Awareness. Attitude. Action. In a way, it all comes down to that. Be self-aware of my thinking and my actions. Choose an attitude that is positive and purposeful. Take daily action on my goals. Awareness. Attitude. Action. Awareness. Attitude. Action. Awareness. Attitude. Action." Jay repeated the *three As* over and over in order to cement the newly discovered power words into his brain.

"I can do this, man! I can! I have the power every single day to make things happen in my life! No one can make these changes for me…but that's the great thing! I'm in control! Me! I choose my attitude. I choose my thoughts. I choose my actions. I own my life!"

As Jay continued his dramatic look into himself, his internal dialogue occasionally shifted into the third person. "You want a great tomorrow, Jay? Then get off your tail and make today count! That's the secret! That's what Amicus is trying to teach you! All the actions you take in the moment…in the now…will determine all the results of your tomorrows! Put forth great actions and you will achieve great results!

"I mean, if you think about it, you already are producing results! You might not have found a job yet, but you can feel the change internally! Look how much hungrier you have become in the last couple of weeks! Look how much more focused you are! It's all about putting wood on the fire. Awareness…attitude…action…that's the wood! That's the wood! That's the cause that leads to the effect!"

Monday, June 2nd…9:03 A.M.

After finishing his early morning run, Jay noticed that the answering machine was blinking. There was a message. It was from Laura Walston.

"Hello, Jay, this is Laura Walston from Brown & Bigelow Creative. Sorry I missed you. Hope all is well in your world. Jay, this is rather short notice, but we would love to see you again this afternoon at four if that's possible. Again, sorry for such short notice, but we only finalized the job details last night and would like to see you. Please call me as soon as possible to confirm this message. You have my direct number already I believe, but let me give it to you one more time. 495...72...27. Thanks, Jay, and I really hope that we can see you later today."

Jay felt an amazing adrenaline rush. The feeling was incredible! "A second interview with B & B? Wow! It's happening!"

Jay knew that he had slammed his first interview out-of-the-park and, although it was true that he had been expecting a second interview, Laura's call proved that everything was coming together. Jay knew that it was probably a good idea to wait a few minutes before calling and confirming the appointment, but he had to share his great news with someone. Of course, Vicki was the lucky, call-winning recipient.

"Vic! Call home and listen to the voice mail on the machine! It's from Brown & Bigelow and I'm going back in today for a second! Go ahead and call now; I'll let your call go through and won't pick up!"

After adequately letting his excited spirit settle, Jay made the big confirmation call. Jay was happy that the call went straight to Laura's voice mail. While her voice recording was leaving message instructions, Jay cleared his throat in order to present his clearest and most professional sounding speaking voice.

"Laura...this is Jay Garfield. Please know that it will be my privilege to see you again today. I look forward to seeing you at four. Thank you so much for calling. Have a great day!"

Concerned about making his second impression even better than the first, Jay scurried off to the closet and picked out a combination suit, shirt, and tie that looked like something that a national account executive from Brown & Bigelow Creative would wear. He would hit them with the best he had today...in performance and wardrobe.

With the morning's interview excitement dominating Jay's thoughts, he temporarily forgot about his classroom lesson with

121

Amicus. Fortunately, the three questions he had taped to the bathroom mirror reminded him to get to class. Before venturing off to read *Lesson 14*, however, Jay answered the daily three.

Question 1: What am I excited about achieving today?

"Heck…is there any doubt! Brown & Bigelow all the way, baby! This could be the one!"

Question 2: Whom can I serve today?

"Let's see…what can I do today? Ummm…hmmm. Oh, I know! I will mow the Moser's lawn next door after I mow our yard! That would be cool! Rod will love the gesture!"

Question 3: What am I most grateful for in my life right now?

"Wow! Where do I begin? I'm grateful for having such a supportive wife…for my interview with Brown & Bigelow…and for the amazing blessing of having met Amicus!"

With his answers to Questions 1 through 3 now decided, Jay walked the few steps from one room to another while whistling the theme song from the television classic *Gilligan's Island*. He had a gut feeling that today was going to be his day, and maybe…just maybe …he knew where he soon would be hanging his work hat. Maybe today was the day he would be rescued from the uncertain world of the unemployed.

"C'mon, Jaybo…don't get too excited. This isn't even close to being a done deal. All you've accomplished is landing a second interview. Nothing more. Control…show some control."

Holding two big, deep breaths back-to-back took some of the edge off Jay's nervousness. Turning on the computer, he put any thoughts of the afternoon Brown & Bigelow meeting on the back burner. Now he focused his attention solely on Amicus' lesson, hoping to find some unique insight that might even help him land today's exciting new opportunity.

LESSON 14: PREPARE TO HIT .367!
(Prepare to Succeed)

Big things do seem to be happening, don't they, my friend?

Jay wondered how Amicus always seemed to know what was going on in his life, but the thought only made him smile. Actually, it was comforting.

It's key to remember that any success you experience is not because of random luck. It's because you created it!

Let's follow this theme of *creating success* by learning about a man who also knew a thing-or-two about making things happen…except he did it by waving a baseball bat at pitchers!

One of the greatest baseball players of all time was a color ful character named Ty Cobb. Some avid fans of sports history will remember Mr. Cobb as one of the meanest and most disliked players to ever put on a uniform and cleats. Likewise, they'll also remember him as arguably the greatest hitter who ever stepped up to the plate. Ty Cobb faced pitchers with a ferocious confidence that caused the men on the pitcher's mound to greatly fear him. Sporting a lifetime batting average of .367 when .300 is a magic mark that few players ever attain, Cobb was simply an awesome player. And he knew it.

At the age of seventy, the star player from the past was asked by a reporter, "So Mr. Cobb, what do you think you would hit if you were still playing these days?"

Without missing a beat, the confident Cobb said, "About .290, maybe .300."

The reporter shot back, "That's because of the travel, the night games, the artificial turf, and all the new pitches like the slider, right?"

"No," Cobb said. "It's because I'm seventy."

With an incredible self-assurance in his ability to produce results, Ty Cobb joins the legions of history's other peak

performers in sharing a common trait: great confidence. When Cobb dug into the batter's box, he expected to win his one-on-one battle with the pitcher. He expected to knock the cover off the ball and send it screaming on a line drive trajectory over second base and into center field.

Confidence is a state of mind that brings with it amazing power. It's an attitude that consistently produces line drive hits past outstretched gloves. But how do you develop that kind of self-assurance? How do you acquire the confidence that allows you to swing with home run power in your life? There is an answer, Jay. It's called preparation.

Being one hundred percent prepared and game ready is the foundation of confident thinking. Preparation is what allows the greats to be great. Preparation is what allows the top salesperson to routinely make the sale. She knows her goal. She pictures what she's going to say. She knows how to overcome every objection as soon as it comes up. She knows her product inside and out. She knows that the greatest enemy of *excellence* is *good* so she is willing to commit whatever preparation is necessary to be excellent.

Preparation is what allows the teacher to truly inspire. Preparation is in knowing exactly how the lesson plan will flow. It's in knowing what questions to ask and what answers to give. Being one hundred percent comfortable with the teaching material allows the teacher to focus on meeting the fluctuating needs of her students while maintaining an engaging presentation. Preparation allows the teacher's eyes to communicate that special magic that can only be communicated when she's feeling entirely confident with her lesson.

Larry Bird, the legendary Boston Celtic basketball player, understood greatly the concept of preparation. Preparation is what made him the best. It went much further than shooting for hours before and after practice or perfecting every shot and move. Preparation to Larry meant getting down on his hands and knees before a Boston Garden home game to examine the floor to look for loose bolts. He would then dribble the ball over every spot on the hardwood finding the areas where the ball bounced just a bit differently. Whenever an opponent would dribble the ball in the game over a dead spot, Larry would go for the steal. He knew that his opponent would not expect the odd bounce and that it would be easier for him to lose control of the ball.

That's preparation, Jay. That's how confidence is developed.

How about you? Have you gotten down on your hands and knees to examine the hardwood floors on the Boston Garden of your own professional playing ground? Do you stand at the plate in your meetings and presentations with the same confidence and boldness that Ty Cobb had when he glared down at opposing pitchers? Talent is important, however, very little can stop the professional who puts in the extra hours, days, weeks, months and years preparing to succeed. World champion performers know this. And now you know this.

There's a saying: *Luck is the crossroad where opportunity and preparation meet.* If you want huge opportunity to develop in your life, Jay...prepare. Then prepare some more. Discover the incredible power of knowing your stuff. Like Ty Cobb and Larry Bird, you'll discover what it means to get that special glimmer in your eye which others read as pure confidence.

Question:
What can you do to build bold confidence into your life?

Jay paused and reflected. "What do I need more confidence in? Lots actually! Where do I even begin? Well, for one, I hate talking in front of groups! Presentations are the worst!"

Of course, very few people thrive on public speaking, and Jay was no different. He dreaded those very important occasions at JLJ, when he would be required to stand and speak before a group of decision makers. Most observers might have said that Jay was an effective presenter, but he never thought so. Before an upcoming presentation, Jay was reliably a nervous wreck. Afterwards, he would beat himself up internally for being what he felt was "sloppy, uptight, and mediocre."

Jay couldn't identify what it was about those moments that made him so uneasy. He could know every person in the room, yet still dreaded opening his mouth and speaking. Of course, fear of public speaking is considered a detriment to any salesperson's success. The stress of actually speaking was one thing, but the worry that preceded it was even more intense.

The instant Jay learned that he was expected to speak before the group, he would hit the stress alarm. The longer the interval between learning about the presentation and actually giving it, the worse the stress would grow. If an event was scheduled to take place in two weeks, Jay would carry a sickening knot in his stomach every day until the day of delivery. Yes, developing confidence in the area of public speaking was a good place for Jay to start.

In his notebook under *Lesson 14*, Jay wrote a few notes about why he needed to build his confidence when speaking to groups. He let his pen capture the emotion of those horrible-feeling moments. He wrote about shaky nerves, a dry voice, and an overwhelming fear of blowing it. He put himself in a perfect mind set as he did the exercise, even feeling the ugly stomach knot naturally begin to grow.

"I need to get over this fear…and soon! If I ever do get offered the Brown & Bigelow position, group presentations will probably be my bread and butter!"

Jay asked himself Amicus' question again, this time personalizing it. "What else can I do to build bold confidence in my life?"

Health-wise, Jay knew he was on the right track. He already felt better about himself just from following his recent exercise plan. Jay knew it was only a matter of time before the fruits of his new regimen would begin to kick in; soon he would feel and look more fit.

"I've got some areas I'm doin' okay in, I guess. I'm definitely gaining confidence daily." He hesitated, "But still…the reason I really need a kick-in-the-butt is my fear of failing! I hate being mediocre… and I want to do big things…but I just need more confidence to go for them!"

"Why am I so afraid to dream big? Why am I afraid to take action? What makes me so different from a millionaire? Why can't I be him? Am I afraid of being rich? Yeah, right, Jay, you're afraid of having lots of money!" Jay rolled his eyes.

Angry, and getting angrier by the moment, Jay couldn't sit still any longer. The hard hitting realization of his current inadequacies began to make Jay's insides boil. "I'm so sick and tired of being sick and tired!" Jay remembered having read and memorized this line, and now he'd found a great reason to use it. "I need to put some more freakin' wood on the fire because I'm tired of failure! I'm tired of worrying about money! I'm tired of worrying period!"

Jay knew that he wasn't going to find an immediate magical elixir to turn his world around. With less than six hours remaining before his big interview at Brown & Bigelow, he decided to burn off some tension and complete a few things on his *To Do* list. Jay headed to the garage, opened the door, pulled out the loud, noisy mower, and spent the next seventy-five minutes following through with his morning plan. In between dodging sprinkler heads, Jay prepared mentally for his afternoon interview.

Taking action on a plan…especially the physical act of mowing the lawn…helped Jay simmer down and start to focus in a positive way again. Today's lesson, and all of the previous lessons, slowly had been raising a deep, personal dissatisfaction within Jay, as well as a craving for much more in his life. Jay knew that creating the positive change that he wanted in his world would not come from the action of others, but rather from his own personal action.

Jay knew, too, that big results weren't going to happen overnight; it would take time. Jay's emotions raged as he realized how he had been blowing it for such a long time by first letting his actions slide and then allowing his efforts to reside so comfortably in a place of mediocrity. He was aware that his years of second-rate performance and weak thinking weren't about to be changed by a few days of hopeful thinking and positive action. Unfortunately, he was going to have to pay the price of creating new habits and working hard in order to arrive where he felt he should already be.

Having cooled down emotionally and physically after mowing the lawn, Jay spent the next two hours thoroughly reviewing recent online issues of *The Advertising Professional*. He studied current trends and paid particular attention to the industries that were aggressively spending advertising dollars. Jay wanted to commit a few numbers and names to memory so he could use them to his best advantage later during the interview. Jay's goal was to showcase his professionalism and be as prepared as possible. He was not going to let this chance to make a solid second impression slip by without his ultimate effort.

3:54 P.M.

Jay stood outside the giant Brown & Bigelow Creative doors. "Okay...*Round 2*! Here we go!"

Jay hesitated slightly before opening the door. He took an extra deep breath, and whispered to himself like a coach talking to his young prodigy, "Nail it, Jay! Go in there and smoke it! You're the man!"

Jay's adrenaline pumped hard. Surprisingly, it wasn't nervous anxiety he felt, but rather an excited energy capable of being reshaped into something powerful. Jay was ready. And he knew it.

Today, Jay didn't have to tell the receptionist who he was. Erin already knew. She greeted him pleasantly and immediately informed Laura Walston that he had arrived. For the second time in as many visits, Jay was impressed. Erin's efficiency and recall served to further add to the first class impression that Brown & Bigelow was continually making on him. "Visiting clients would be blown away by this!" Jay thought.

Laura came out wearing a very tasteful dark blue suit with a brilliant scarf draped around her neck. Her easily recognized Rolex, expensive hairstyle, and perfect make-up gave off the aura of incredible success; she was the epitome of taste and style. Laura greeted Jay warmly. A small voice inside his head told him that this was going to be a very good meeting.

"So, Jay, how's interviewing been going?"

"It's going really well, Laura! I've been very pleased with what my effort has been producing, and I'm confident that the perfect opportunity will soon present itself."

The two continued to talk about the interview process. Jay knew she was fishing for him to share what other opportunities were opening up, but he didn't bite. Of course Jay currently had no offers on the table and was very eager to land something soon, but he didn't want Laura to sense his need. He wanted to convey an attitude of sturdy confidence and let Laura assume that his services were in demand. It was a part of the cat-and-mouse interview game.

Another idea that Jay wasn't willing to share was that he was seriously contemplating the notion of being his own employer. He still wasn't sure if that was really the direction he wanted to go, but hopefully today's meeting would help nudge him one direction or another.

Jay noticed that, as he spoke, Laura seemed to carefully measure his every word and gesture. He knew that she was studying him and deciding whether her initial impression of him had been correct or not. But no worry. Today, Jay loved being the star of the show. Like the talented actor he once wished to have been, he was giving his audience a charismatic performance and was shining brightly.

"This is your moment, Jay! It's your time!" Very aware of what he was thinking and feeling, and how he was responding to Laura, Jay was definitely in the zone. Today was his day and he knew it. Jay felt like a potential first-round draft choice whose name was about to be called.

Before the day was over, Jay also had the chance to meet and spend time talking with Mr. Bigelow. They discussed college football (both were big USC fans), golf (Bigelow had a putter behind his desk), and, of course, they dabbled briefly on advertising philosophies. Except for the two questions at the end of their conversation: "What are you hoping to bring to Brown & Bigelow?" and "Why does Brown & Bigelow appeal to you?" the meeting could have reasonably taken place at a sports bar between two new buddies over a couple of beers. Their first meeting was very relaxed and it flowed well.

When Laura came back to retrieve Jay, she led him back into her office. Before she sat down with him, she excused herself for a few minutes to no doubt confer with the company's namesake about his opinion. When she returned, Laura took a seat behind her desk. Although still friendly, she shifted gears and became much more matter-of-fact.

"Jay, obviously you know that we're interested in you. You have a number of qualities that we feel fit very well with Brown & Bigelow. We think you're a strong candidate. Nonetheless, I'm sure you can appreciate how careful we need to be in hiring the person who will be our National Account Executive."

She handed him a piece of paper. "Here is an outline of the job description, including salary, commission, benefits, and anticipated travel days per month. I hope that you find everything on the sheet to meet your requirements." She hesitated in her spiel to watch Jay respond to what he had been handed.

Of course, the first thing that Jay's eyes floated to was the compensation figures. Although the base was somewhat moderate, the commission structure was incredible! Doing some quick calculations in his head, he concluded that the earning potential in this job was nearly triple what he had made previously. Jay tried not to let on to what he was thinking. Limiting his eyes to quick glances back and forth across the paper, Jay appeared to barely read it. Playing his best poker hand, Jay smiled back at Laura and said, "This appears to address a number of questions that I have. I'll definitely take the time to review it closely."

Reading nothing in Jay's reaction, Laura continued. "One more thing before you leave, Jay. Your resume lists two references that are very much appreciated. Before you leave, however, could you leave three more references with Erin? Preferably, we would appreciate it if you could leave references from past clients."

With her Hollywood-type smile once again coming forth, she continued. "Actually, I guess there are two more things. Don't make any big career decisions until you hear from us again. Okay?"

Jay laughed. "Laura, it was a great pleasure to have had this time to talk with you again. It's easy to see why your company is the best in the business. I'd love to work with you!" With that, Jay headed out to the reception desk and began racking his brain for three past clients whom he felt would sing his praises.

Tuesday, June 3rd... 7:37 A.M.

Jay dusted off his bike. Instead of running this morning, Jay decided to do some pedaling. While stretching in the middle of the bedroom floor (which had become an early morning ritual), he and Vicki rehashed their conversation from the previous evening.

"What if I got offered the Brown & Bigelow position? Would I accept it? Wouldn't I be a fool not to?"

Again, like the night before, the two of them batted the idea back and forth and dissected it from every possible angle. No new light was shed on the subject this morning that hadn't been illuminated the night before. The answers to so many career questions for Jay were still just as unclear. Somewhere in the back of Jay's mind, he couldn't altogether commit to working for Brown & Bigelow. He wasn't sure if it was a safety mechanism to protect him from possible rejection, or if his instinct was telling him that there was something else that he was destined to do instead. This morning, Vicki was throwing out possible ideas as to what that might be, but none of them one hundred percent resonated.

Jay followed Vicki's car out the driveway on his bike. He playfully raced her to the end of the street, and then waved good-bye as she turned left and he turned right. Jay rode for about twenty minutes before turning around and heading back to the neighborhood park. Leaning his bike up against the ball diamond fence, Jay pushed his legs to climb the bleacher steps two at a time. He took a seat alone at the top.

Of course there was nobody on the field playing at this early hour, but still Jay looked out onto the field as if watching an imaginary game. Pulling a breakfast banana out of his fanny pack, Jay peeled back the skin and took a bite. His mind turned to the Garfield family financial situation.

Although money was still okay and they were under no immediate financial crunch, Jay knew that they would have to start dipping into their savings in larger chunks soon. The six-month car insurance premium was due the next week. After that the pressure would slowly mount. Vicki's monthly check covered about seventy percent of their regular bills, and Jay's unemployment check certainly helped, yet funds in the checking account were starting to dwindle. He knew that withdrawing money from their savings account would be inevitable soon. Jay realized that he would simply have to accept that fact and not worry about it so much.

"Good things are beginning to happen and everything will work out. We'll be okay."

Jay sat alone in the stands, appreciating the bright, morning sun glistening on the playing field grass. He noticed brilliant sunrays shining like mirrors on the trees behind the third base dugout. Overhead, feathery white clouds lazily floated through a crisp blue sky. Nature's art gallery had temporarily captivated him and it felt good to be sitting in the bleachers breathing it all in. Jay was truly enjoying the moment. Far too often in his life, he had neglected taking the time to enjoy one of life's most precious gifts…nature's unmatched and ceaseless creativity.

Soaking in everything about the dazzling images around him, Jay began to wonder. "How many times have I failed to notice this perfect picture? Probably a million. How often have I been so preoccupied with my little world that I failed to see how beautiful everything around me really is? Every day."

Feeling rich in everything that he was seeing, Jay was struck by a profound realization: *Good things really can grow out of bad events.*

At that moment, he pictured himself as a mythical phoenix bird rising from the ashes and experiencing a new life. Having gone through one of the most dramatic experiences of his life—being fired—Jay now realized if it hadn't been for that single event, he wouldn't be growing, changing, and appreciating life as much as he was now. Jay knew that if he had never lost his job, he would never have come to a place in his life where he could so wholeheartedly welcome such simple wealth.

Jay had never been a devoted fan of reflection and prayer, but these last few weeks had opened his mind and spirit to a more conscious level of existence. He now saw tremendous value in having a more defined purpose, and in making the most of every moment and experience that life offered. Sure he was out of work, but this wilderness period was teaching him valuable lessons about what was important and how to live. With this new perspective, Jay Garfield would be forever enriched.

While he sat taking in the park with new eyes and counting his blessings, Jay noticed that he was no longer sitting alone. He had no clue when the other man had arrived or how it was possible he slipped in next to Jay unnoticed. But there he was. The instant Jay recognized the man's presence, the stranger spoke, "What a glorious, glorious day! Don't you think?"

Caught completely off guard, first by the gentleman's sudden appearance, and then by the beautiful deep tone of the stranger's voice, Jay could think of nothing more exceptional to say than a simple, "Yes, it is."

Somewhat embarrassed by the brevity of his answer, Jay chuckled under his breath at his temporary lack of composure. His brain tried to come up with something else to say, but he was at a loss for words.

The stranger continued, "I love the mornings. They bring with them a chance for a do over. New day…new hope. Are you a golfer by chance? If so, then you'll understand when I say that a new morning offers us a chance for a Mulligan. We get to disregard the fact that yesterday was full of 3 putts and bad shots; we get the chance to pull a new ball out of our bag and do it right today."

"Yep…a new morning offers us the chance to think about how we'd like our world to be different. Then we have the rest of the day to do our best to make those early morning wishes come true! Yep… just like golf…a new hole…a new day…a new chance in which to do something really good."

Jay listened intently. "Every day we have the opportunity to fix what went wrong the day before, you know. Every day we have the chance to pursue living our best day ever. That's pretty fantastic. What's more, if we consistently take the time to learn from our previous days, our ability to live our best day increases."

After a lengthy pause, he continued, "You can tell I'm a thinker, a philosophizer. It helps me in several ways. First, it prompts me to appreciate everything I have. It's always easy to want more, so it's wise to remind myself how much I already have. Second, taking time to reflect on the past, teaches me how to achieve what I want in the future; it reveals why I've had failures in the past. I'm able to see open doors that were hidden from me before. I'm enabled to proceed in a new direction and to avoid making the same mistakes."

The stranger kept talking, "That's why I come out here and sit at the park. Maybe you've discovered this secret, too; take the time to stop and think…you'll see the world, and your life, with new eyes. To me reflecting on life is kinda' like looking at my life through the camera lens rather than always at the camera lens. Do you know what I mean? When I look at myself with a photographer's eye, I see my life objectively, in a detached manner, and a new world of understanding and possibility opens up."

Curious, Jay just stared and took in everything that was being said. He still wasn't quite certain what to make of the situation. First he had been shocked by the man's appearance out of nowhere; now he was somewhat mystified by this philosophical monologue on Mulligans and camera lenses. Still, Jay said nothing. Although Jay's mouth was completely zipped, the nerve endings in his brain were firing at a machine gun type pace.

"This is weird to think, but this guy reminds me a bit of…no way! Maybe?"

Jay squinted, trying to bring the stranger's face into better focus; it was hard to see what he looked like in detail. The man's position in the bleachers forced Jay to look straight towards the extremely bright sun in order to see him. "There's no way that's him…no way! Is there?" Jay knew it was a preposterous idea. He squinted his eyes, blinked, and squinted again, trying to observe the figure in the royal blue sweat suit with greater clarity.

Suddenly leaning back on the bleacher step behind him, the stranger turned towards Jay and made eye contact for the first time, "Well, what do you think, my friend?"

Jay wasn't sure what to say. "Ummm…yeah…I guess so. Holding the camera always gives us a different perspective on what's in the picture…yeah." Jay could now see the stranger's hair was a handsome silver color.

Ignoring Jay's uneasiness, the persistent conversationalist continued, "I thought that you'd understand. You seem like the sorta' person who would. I'm pretty good at spotting people who are sharp; I don't start rambling on to just anybody," he laughed.

After a moment, he continued, "Do you know who Oliver Wendell Holmes is?" A response seemed irrelevant. There was barely a pause before he went on, "Mr. Holmes was at one time a Supreme Court Justice; he is well-quoted. Observing this glorious morning, I'm reminded of a statement he made: 'A mind once stretched by a new idea can never go back to its original dimension.'"

Interpreting the meaning of this quote for Jay, the silver-haired man proceeded, "Once you've felt the adrenalin rush and the excitement of *What if?* it's hard to imagine living the same old life. When people take the time to be quiet and to meditate and reflect, they give themselves the opportunity to answer life's grand questions. You know, the big ones, like: *What do I want to do with my life? What is truly important? What is the purpose of life?*

For me, today is certainly a *What if?* sort of day."

Jay wasn't sure what he was seeing or hearing, but he was hesitant to break the man's flow.

"Now, each of us has a completely different mission to fulfill, and I believe that it's when we give ourselves a time-out that we begin to hear the voice of possibility inside of us pointing the way. Certainly, not everybody's mission in life is to walk on the moon...although that, too, was someone's mission once...but I believe each of us has a hero-like purpose, a purpose that can bring out the best in us. I think my hero-like purpose today is to show the other guys in my foursome that we all don't have to hit our ball into the lake on #14!"

With that, the elderly muse let out a brief belly laugh, then he stopped talking and appeared to reflect on his own words.

A chorus of birds in a nearby tree seemed to pick up on the silence; they began to chirp more clearly and beautifully than Jay could ever remember hearing. He turned his head to find the birds. "Where are they?" Jay asked aloud.

Jay was amazed at the incredibly enchanting sound he was hearing. He stood up in the bleachers, turned toward the trees, and studied each one closely. Looking for movement in the branches, he saw nothing. Yet, the avian melody grew in intensity. It was absolutely captivating! Jay didn't know how long the song had lasted, but for seemingly no reason at all, it stopped as abruptly as it had started. Jay turned to see what his companion might have thought of the brilliant chorus, but he had vanished.

Jay looked everywhere for the man. He pushed his bike through the park for a half an hour searching for any sign of the mysterious stranger in the royal blue sweat suit, but he found nothing.

"Just how long had the birds been singing? How could I have missed his departure? How could I have let him slip away without responding to him?"

Jay found fault with himself for losing the opportunity to continue talking, or at least listening, to the man. All the while, nagging in the back of Jay's mind, was a feeling that there was something very familiar about the man. Already having disregarded the notion that this could have been Amicus, Jay wondered why Aristotle-like mentors gravitated towards him.

"I must have a sticker on my head that says, 'Wanted: life advice!'" He laughed at the image as he got back on his bike to pedal home.

Having parked his bike in the garage, Jay checked to see if there were any phone messages—there were none. He took a shower, and reviewed his daily three questions. Try as he might, he could not move his thoughts along to what needed to be done for the day. Jay was still preoccupied with the mystery man at the park.

Entering his office, he turned on the computer. Thoughts of reading another lesson took over. Amicus' lesson radiated from the screen.

LESSON 15: HEAD INTO THE JUNGLE!
(Go the Extra Mile)

Hello, Jay! I sense that all the previous lessons have contributed mightily to your having a lot on your mind today. Rest assured, this lesson is not meant to add more weight to heavy thoughts, but rather to give encouragement and to keep lifting and pushing those thoughts forward! Don't give up, my friend! Keep working through challenging trials and you'll eventually find the results you seek. Here's a story to help illustrate.

Standing in a straight row with their backs against the wall, the kindergartners chatted away. As they did, their harried teacher moved along the line examining each one of her students to make sure that they were prepared to head into the snow. Adjusting caps, straightening jackets, and finding lost mittens, the teacher was moving as quickly as she could to help each of her twenty little people get ready to face the cold.

Having solved the dilemmas of the first nineteen, Miss Baker approached the last student. Sitting on the floor, the little

boy was furiously trying to pull on his boots. He was having limited success. The teacher noticed that the boots looked quite small, but, undaunted, she helped him force each foot into its matching boot. All the while, the boy rattled on about how his dad had been late for work because he couldn't find an ironed shirt and how his mom had said that she was going to sign up his dad for ironing lessons. Johnny was starting another story about how the hamster got loose when Miss Baker interrupted him, "There! You're now ready!"

Looking down at his feet, Johnny said, "You know, teacher, these aren't even my boots." Miss Baker could do nothing but laugh. Then she went about pulling each of the boots off, which proved to be a more difficult challenge than putting them on had been.

After the second boot was removed, the child interrupted his story about the hamster hiding under his bed long enough to say, "They're really my brother's boots, but my mom makes me wear them anyway."

Sometimes, my friend, even your best effort will fail to bear fruit. And if it does, it will be easy to want to take your bag of marbles and go home. You might go so far as to concede, "I tried," thinking this is an acceptable reason not to try again. But it isn't an acceptable reason. There isn't one.

The day you give up trying to accomplish something that's important to you is the day you allow yourself to be pushed to the passenger side of the car and let someone else, actually everybody else, take the steering wheel. When you give up trying, you no longer have control of your own life. Your destiny is no longer in your own hands.

When you reach the point of frustration where you feel like giving up, I want you to remember a very special Avon Sales Representative named Sonia Pinheiro. In fact, Sonia was one of over thirty-six thousand Avon sales representatives in the Amazonian region of Brazil who were competing for business. The competition to get new clients, as you can imagine, was fierce. Most gave up.

But Sonia didn't. Neither failure nor the difficult derailed her. The potential exhilaration of succeeding and the pain of not accomplishing her goal were a motivating combination that made it impossible to quit. So what did she do? Sonia took all of her Avon products and headed into the jungle.

Disappearing into a remote part of the Amazonian region, Sonia took her bag of goodies to the Tembe Indians in Tenetehara. The Indians had no clue as to what Avon even was, but Sonia, with her tubes of lipstick, mascara and men's bikini briefs, showed no sign of worry. She sold her product anyway. Accepting fish and almost any other item worthy of being bartered, Sonia developed a new and untapped market.

But, she could have quit. Temporary failure and rejection is a simple fact of life for those who choose unique paths, Jay. Rejection is a guarantee for anybody who wants to step out of his or her comfort zone and create, build, or develop a new idea...book...company...or project. There's no way to avoid rejection, and there's no way to succeed and achieve great things without it. Don't become stymied by the rejections that you receive. Instead, become driven by the dreams that you hold.

When failure is knocking and rejection has you pinned down, cast your thoughts towards the resilient example of our friend, Mr. Lincoln. His life is an inspiring reminder of how much willpower can be mustered even under the darkest of circumstances. Abe stands as a remarkable example of what the human spirit is capable of overcoming when faced with the much easier option of quitting.

It's easy to forget that this remarkable legend of a man is more than a mythological hero. He was a flesh-and-blood person who experienced the same challenging emotions, struggles, and trials that you have...except on an even larger scale. He had both a fiancé and a son die. He experienced financially devastating business losses, endless public embarrassments, and multiple crushing election defeats. He anguished over career decisions.

He knew ultimate despair. But through it all, Abraham Lincoln persevered and proved victorious. And you can, too, Jay!

A favorite storyteller of mine, Mark Twain, once told of a man who had died and gone to Heaven. Being shown around in Heaven by Saint Peter, the man realized that Peter knew the answer to almost everything. Being a devoted student of military history while on earth, the man asked Peter, "Who was the greatest general of all time?"

Peter pointed to an obscure man in the corner. "He was the greatest general of all."

"But you must be mistaken, Saint Peter. He couldn't have been the greatest general. I knew him on earth, and he was a shoe maker." Peter looked at the cobbler with a bit of sadness. Peter answered sadly, "You're right. He *would have* been the greatest general of all time…if he had followed his dream and become a general."

So, my friend, if you find it difficult to slip on that pair of boots again because of failure, do it anyway. Don't let yourself put on conformity or mediocrity. Sure, getting knocked down is tough, but remember that a person who is knocked down by life can get up again. A person knocked down by conformity never does. Re-think your strategy, re-equip yourself with the right tools, and learn from Sonia Pinheiro and our not-so-fortunate shoe cobbler. Go the extra mile. Head into that jungle if necessary; just make sure you keep pushing forward. One extra step and who knows? You could find yourself walking the path of generals…or at the least, one very famous Avon representative.

Question:
What past failures await another attempt?

Jay opened his notebook. Amicus' lesson had struck gold once again. As Jay stared blankly at the screen, his mind was a couple thousand miles away…playing catch with his son. He vowed to call Josh that night and set a date to fly him out west.

Wednesday, June 4th

During his morning bike ride, Jay circled the park a couple of times in search of the man in the royal blue sweat suit. Although it was the same time and location, he couldn't find him. The birds were quiet. Jay couldn't help but wonder if he had imagined the whole event; it now seemed so strangely obscure.

Fifty minutes later, at home, Jay saw that the answering machine light was flashing red. There were two messages. The first message was from a company which he had crossed off his interest list long ago. The second was from Laura Walston.

"Good morning, Jay…this is Laura from Brown & Bigelow. I'm sorry I missed you. Can you please call me back as soon as you get this message? Again, my direct number is 495…72…27. If I'm not at my desk, please have Erin page me. I look forward to talking with you soon, Jay. Thank you so much!"

"Oh, wow! Could this be it? I think I'm about to be offered a job!"

Jay took a deep breath. Message one could wait. Returning Laura's call couldn't. He dialed her number only to hear voice mail answer. Instead of pushing the one button, Jay pushed two and was transferred to Erin at the receptionist's desk.

"Hello, Erin. This is Jay Garfield. I'm returning Laura's call. Is she available?"

"Hello, Mr. Garfield! Laura said you'd be calling and that I was to track her down when you did. Please hold for a moment and let me find her for you." Jay waited anxiously for Laura to come to the phone.

"Jay, good morning! Thank you for returning my call! Jay, we would like to fly you up to our office in San Francisco for the day to meet and interview with Peter Brown, the other principal in the firm. We were hoping to book a flight for you tomorrow morning. Is that possible?"

Laura's question caught Jay off guard. He hadn't expected there would be a third interview. He had assumed that Brown & Bigelow would be making a decision based on his first two interviews and his final three references. In addition, Jay was surprised to learn that for his next interview he would have to fly to another city.

After receiving Laura's call, Jay's initial excitement slipped a notch as his brain quickly processed this new request. He wasn't sure if he should feel disappointed at having to interview one more time, or if he should feel elated that he was still in the running for this job. Emotionally, both options were miles away from what he had really wanted: a job offer.

Displaying no outward signs of feeling either disappointment or elation, Jay simply said, "Laura, I will definitely rearrange my schedule in order to make this work. Why don't you give me the logistics. Then, let's catch a plane!"

Jay wrote down the flight information, and the interview was a go. *Round 3* with Brown & Bigelow had been scheduled, and Jay would be hitting the road.

Jay gave the surprising news of having to sit for a third interview new meaning in his head. Playfully, he announced to himself: "Congratulations, Jay Garfield! You're still in the game! And now they're investing in you! You've won a flight to San Francisco!"

Next, Jay made two quick phone calls. First, he returned the job call requesting an interview. "I'm sorry, but I'm not going to be able to interview for your position. I've decided to go in another direction, but thank you so much for considering me."

Jay couldn't see himself getting excited about working for this niche manufacturing company. It wasn't that the product was bad or that there was anything negative about the business; it just wasn't for him. Turning down the interview was a bold action that reinforced his resolve to find a job that inspired him.

Jay's second phone call was to Vicki. "I'm flyin' out to San Francisco tomorrow morning to meet Peter Brown…the Brown part of Brown & Bigelow. Pretty cool, huh?"

Vicki hit Jay with a barrage of questions regarding his conversation with Laura and about the trip. "Are you excited?" "Are you nervous?" "Are you spending the night?" "Do you have a pressed shirt to wear?" "Do you want me to take you to the airport?" "Are you flying out by yourself?" "Did you think that they had already made a decision when she called?"

Jay answered all of Vicki's questions in sequence. "Yes...." "Yes...." "No...." "Yes...." "No...." "I think so...." "Yes."

After the second interview, Jay had failed to ask what the remainder of the interview process was going to be. Laura had not shared with him the fact that Brown & Bigelow's plan all along was to host three rounds of interviews and complete a thorough background check on each top candidate. Jay had felt so darn positive after his first two meetings. When those feelings were added to the fact that Laura had asked him to interview for the job initially, Jay wrongly assumed today's call would be a job offer.

Jay reminded himself that one more interview didn't mean failure. It simply meant that Brown & Bigelow Creative was making certain they pick the right horse. Jay was still in the running.

Jay focused on tomorrow. "Okay...that's good," Jay affirmed to himself. "Just one more interview, then maybe...maybe...I'll be working in a dream job for a dream company!" Jay conducted this positive self-talk workshop in order to get totally onto the right emotional track.

"The funny thing is, now that I've realized that it isn't going to be as easy to get this job as I had tricked myself into thinking, I want it even more. Despite my increasing urge to go out on my own, all I want right now is to join the Brown & Bigelow team."

Jay had ignored a huge wild card throughout the whole Brown & Bigelow process; there were other exceptional candidates being considered for the position. Peter Brown's personal Day Planner indicated that it was going to be a long day for him on June 5th. He had scheduled separate three-hour blocks to accommodate each of the three final candidates. In one of those blocks was written "Jay Garfield/ Los Angeles."

9:39 *A.M.*

It took about fifteen minutes for Jay to stop agonizing about the latest development in the Brown & Bigelow saga. For a brief moment, Jay had fallen back into his old pattern of worry.

"Oh, c'mon, Jay! Don't go and over-think this and certainly don't worry about it! What will happen…will happen! All you can do is be prepared…show up on time…and do your thing! The rest is up to them. If they want to hire you, they will. If not, you'll find something else you like!" With that Jay put thoughts of the Brown & Bigelow interview aside.

At 3 P.M., Jay had scheduled a job interview with a local non-profit. He grabbed his notebook to jot down a few thoughts and focus his brain on the immediate task at hand. "Okay, so these guys need someone who can do what?"

The doorbell rang. Jay leaped up and ran down the stairs to answer it.

"Hello. Jay Garfield?" It was a package delivery person holding a carton.

"Yes? What do you have for me?"

"If you'll just sign right here, it's all yours."

Jay signed the form and was handed the box. He looked at the label. "Oh, fantastic! The books I ordered!"

Success Through a Positive Mental Attitude, *Think and Grow Rich*, and the vocabulary-building CD series had arrived. Jay quickly opened the carton and pulled out the first members of his new educational library…the keepers…the ones he would come back to again and again. Just flipping through these books and randomly scanning their pages sparked Jay's motivation. They also reminded him of Amicus.

"Oh, man! How could I forget?" Feeling energized, Jay sprinted up the stairs, taking two at a time. He slid into his classroom seat.

Before focusing on Amicus' lesson, Jay took a moment to reflect on how vulnerable he still was in dealing with minor setbacks. Jay's mental dialogue shifted back and forth between the voice of a third person internal coach and that of himself. "Heck, Jay…the B & B thing wasn't even a big disappointment and it still threw you!

Jay continued, "I need to keep working on controlling my emotions. The good news is that I regrouped, and that's what's important!"

Jay was beginning to understand that creating opportunity took time…and so did learning and applying many of the tools he was acquiring from Amicus. Self-mastery is not something one develops overnight…if ever. But Jay was also discovering that once a foundation of positive thinking is in place, it is always available as a refuge for grounding one's thoughts and recharging one's energy, no matter what emotional event was happening in his life. He was now living proof that this was true.

He had lost his job...but, as a consequence, had found his life. He might not have a career direction yet, but he did have a new and deeper appreciation of work, health, relationships, and the importance of setting aside time daily for personal battery recharging.

"I still need to find that place of steadiness and balance where I'm not so easily affected by everything that happens to me. I'm happy that I'm moving forward and growing. I need to realize that my life is going one hundred percent in the right direction, with or without Brown & Bigelow!"

Now Jay turned his attention again to the one responsible for his newly inspired life momentum...Amicus. Amicus had introduced Jay to a completely different way of thinking. He presented familiar principles to him in a way that connected with his brain, like a special three-pronged chord connects into the wall. With Amicus' help, success and life principles came to life. They generated real energy. Furthermore, they had helped turn around Jay's attitude and expectations one hundred and eighty degrees. With a new lesson waiting on the screen, Jay quieted his mind one more time and began to read.

LESSON 16: 1,440 MINUTES!
(Develop Time Mastery)

It's good to see you, my faithful student! I sense that your days are becoming fuller. This often happens when positive momentum enters a person's life; there doesn't seem to be enough time in the day to accomplish everything. It is said, "When you want something done, ask a busy person," because the busy person is learning to master time. And that's what today's lesson addresses...the value of time. Let me start with a simple story.

A vacationing couple was enjoying a picnic in the warm California weather. They noticed the birds singing, the sun glowing, and an old man sitting patiently by the river's edge with his fishing pole cast lazily in the gently flowing water. After

a couple hours of relaxation, the couple decided it was time to get going to their next destination.

While packing up, they noticed that the fisherman hadn't moved an inch during the last two hours. Before heading to the car, the visitors strolled over to the old man. "It doesn't look as though you've had much luck. There don't seem to be many hungry fish today."

"Nope," said the old fellow. "There ain't. Rarely is. The object of fishing here isn't to catch anything. It's to show my wife I have no time to peel potatoes."

Henry David Thoreau, the enlightened Nineteenth century author whose pen contained ink that has lasted through the ages, wrote: "It is not enough to be busy…the question is: what are we busy about?"

Time. Each person has as much time as Edison when he invented the light bulb…as much as Sylvester Stallone when he wrote the motivational script *Rocky*…as much as Mother Teresa when her humanitarian efforts changed the world. In fact, this is one area in which the most successful people and the least successful people stand as equals; they are each given 1,440 minutes of time every day. The clock ticks at the same speed for both. The major difference between the two groups is how they use this gift.

How do you use your time, my friend? Are you making the most of your precious 1,440 daily minutes? Or, like the fisherman, have you found ways to squander valuable time at the expense of doing something that would be far more productive, valuable, and empowering?

Think about how many times you've wound up in front of the TV spending imaginary money buying vowels and watching the *Wheel of Fortune*, knowing that there was something else you had planned to do, but didn't. Think about how many times you've slept late on the weekend only to ask yourself Sunday night, "Where did the weekend go?"

At one time or another, each of us has succumbed to the urge to put off something important in order to pursue something a bit less strenuous or less mentally taxing. Everybody has had occasion to meet that ugly, time-sapping, life-wasting monster known as "procrastination."

The problem is, however, that achievement of goals and great success in life requires that you move past procrastination. It requires that you make productive use of your time. You cannot throw away your most valuable resource yet hope to become a star in life. Success doesn't work that way. Sure, you might be tired and feel like not doing something that you otherwise want to see accomplished. The key is to push past the tiredness. Learn to play life with great energy! Be productive! Focus first on the big things you'd like to achieve each day, then tackle the smaller things!

The writing of Ralph Waldo Emerson, a rather colorful poet and philosopher, comes to my mind. He wrote: "The right performance of this hour's duties will be the best preparation for the hours or ages that follow it." Ah!! So very true, Jay! What you do today will determine what you say to yourself thirty years from now when you are sitting in a rocking chair reflecting upon your life and your experiences. Make that future conversation something incredible! Develop mastery over your schedule, and use your 1,440 minutes wisely every day.

Question:
What changes do you need to make in order to maximize your daily 1,440 minutes?

Jay opened his notebook to the next available page and wrote *Lesson 16*. Under it, he began to make a list of ways in which he could maximize his time. He added an asterisk next to the two that really stood out: 1) outlining a *To Do* list for the next day before going to bed, and 2) breaking his day down into constructive four-hour time blocks: 8:00 A.M. - Noon, Noon - 4:00 P.M. and 4:00 P.M. - 8:00 P.M.

"Yeah! I like it! This is good! This should help me stay organized and really kick me in the butt every day to be more productive!"

As Jay printed out Amicus' lesson from the screen and inserted the pages into his notebook, he was thinking about why he failed so often to get as much done as he wanted. "Do I set my expectations too high for what I want to accomplish? Or am I really just a giant time waster? Hmmm…."

He continued, "Why exactly do I procrastinate so much anyway? What does wasting time do for me besides raising my guilt level three notches? Afterwards, the chore still hangs over my head! It's never going anywhere until I do it, so why do I wait?" Jay was thinking about yard projects, monthly reports at work, paying the bills, doing taxes. Areas for procrastinating came in all sorts of different packages.

Mentally reviewing his list of questions, Jay paraphrased them again: "Why did I used to procrastinate so much? Was it laziness or just a fear of succeeding?"

He thought a bit about the possible reasons before answering: "Who knows exactly; but I'm done with it! No more!"

Unfortunately, Jay had been a procrastinator of legendary proportions. Asking Jay to help with the household chores was like asking a congressman to eradicate political party gridlock in Washington. Sure, the head would nod up and down, most likely accompanied by an *I'll do it now!* thrown in for good measure. However, it wasn't going to actually happen.

Vicki liked to playfully tease her husband about his enthusiastic energy in beginning a project that would soon dissipate into taking an afternoon nap, or watching an *important* game that was a *must win* for his team. "Feel like taking a snooze in the hammock today, Jay? Then why don't you go out and think about pulling some weeds!"

Procrastinating at JLJ had been common practice for Jay as well. Putting things off made work much more stressful than it needed to be, but Jay still did it. Whether it was a client proposal or an end-of-the-month report, Jay was always pushing it right up to the time limit. The ironic thing was that he knew that continuing to be a procrastinator would forever keep him one step behind fulfilling his full potential. Although the realization struck a sensitive nerve, he still found creative ways to perfect the art of procrastinating.

Now he told himself: "No more! Enough is enough! I'm no longer gonna' do it! I'm through with procrastinating! I do things when I schedule them…not when I'm in emergency mode to get them done! I will develop self-mastery over how I use my 1,440 minutes!"

11:03 A.M.

Jay marked his place in the W. Clement Stone book he was reading and took a seat in the stylist's chair. He had decided that a quick trip for a hair cut was necessary before tomorrow's big interview in San Francisco. Only two miles from home, The Haircut Store was fast, convenient, and offered a fairly decent haircut. This was Jay's third visit, and each of the two previous times the stylist had given Jay a cut that he liked.

Today Jay was sitting in front of a new stylist. "Clean on the sides…a little longer on top…rounded in the back." These had been his usual instructions. This time, however, Jay felt a little more daring. "How about something with a bit more style than I'm currently wearing, Carmen. Nothing outrageous…just a cool cut for a business guy. What do you say? Think you can add a pinch of creativity up top for me?"

Jay got to know his stylist as he sat staring into the mirror. In fact, over the next twenty-five minutes, Jay learned more about Carmen than he ever could have imagined was possible in such a short period of time. Maybe it was because she had a lot on her mind, or maybe it was because she sensed that Jay was sincerely interested in her life. Whatever the reason, she described her life history and current situation in detail.

Carmen was a working, single mother of two kids. She shared how her twelve-year-old daughter was now much more interested in make-up and boys than in school, resulting in an *F* on her last math test. Carmen angrily talked about smelling cigarette smoke on her fifteen-year-old son's clothes when he had come home yesterday. She labored on about how at home each of them either sat in front of the TV or walked around with headphones, only occasionally coming up for air and finding time to yell at her or their sibling.

"If it's not one thing, it's another when you're a parent. It's just so hard knowing what to do all of the time, and I get so frustrated. I try my best, but having to work two jobs makes it impossible to give my kids the attention they need."

Jay felt discouragement in her words. He saw in her face how the worry of life had begun to take its toll. She didn't smile. As she talked, Jay was met by the realization that life is tough at times for everybody.

"Life's never a piece-of-cake. We all have our unique struggles that weigh us down, don't we?" Jay thought to himself.

"So what do you think?" Carmen was holding a mirror behind Jay's head so he could look at his haircut from behind.

"Well, except for that little bald spot I see creeping in, I like it! It looks great!"

No doubt the cut was edgier than anything Jay ever tried before. Carmen had left it longer on top and added some jell to give his hair a more tossed, Hollywood look. Jay liked the new image. He even thought he looked younger!

"Fantastic, Carmen! Nice job! That's just what I wanted! Thank you!"

Jay rose from his chair. As he opened his wallet to leave a tip, Jay was struck with the idea to leave Carmen two additional gifts rarely given to her by a customer…a hug and an encouraging word.

"Carmen, life is hard, for sure…but you keep hanging in there and doing your best! You have great talent as a stylist and any salon would be happy to have you! Plus, your kids are lucky you care so much about them! Maybe set a family night each week where the three of you do things together. I don't know…just an idea. You never know what will come out of it!"

Carmen's eyes grew teary and she smiled for the first time. "Thank you for saying that…and that's a good idea. I think I'll try it."

Jay put a ten-dollar bill on her counter in addition to the eighteen dollars for his haircut. Carmen's smile widened.

Jay walked out of the shop, never having felt so good about leaving a tip. "Life can be hard, but it sure feels good to help others."

At home once again, Jay immersed himself in reading *Success Through a Positive Mental Attitude*. He knew it was a classic on self-help, and he was anxious to start *Chapter 2: You Can Change Your World*. He loved this inspiring material and found it to be a perfect complement to Amicus' writings. Jay spent an hour reading before he looked on the internet to see if there were any new and appealing job opportunities. He found one.

It was 1:15 P.M. by the time Jay got dressed and ready for an afternoon interview. Admiring his new hairstyle in the mirror again, he ran his hand through it to spruce it up. "Awesome! I love it!"

Today, there had been no procrastination in getting ready. Jay was all set to walk out the door for his interview, with plenty of time to spare. He chuckled to himself, remembering the countless previous occasions when he had to run out the door and was late to work. A couple of those times, he had been in such a hurry that he forgot his belt or accidentally had put his socks on inside out. One time Jay had even matched the wrong suit jacket and slacks together. They were almost a match, but all day he had felt silly wearing two shades of black. His confidence definitely wasn't at peak levels on any of those days.

Today, however, was different. Jay was on his *A game* and he felt confident. He double-checked his readiness, imagining he was an airplane pilot checking the status of his plane before take-off. "All systems go! Let's fly!" He was ready to perform.

It was a hot day. The car's air conditioner was set on high, sending a continuous cool draft onto Jay's face. With driving directions having been clearly imprinted on his mind, Jay turned his focus onto his earlier interaction with Carmen.

"I wish I could have said more to encourage her!" Jay was down on himself, thinking he hadn't done enough. If anybody knew overwhelming discouragement, Jay certainly had. He knew that feeling defeated by life was a terribly dark place to be.

Even though Jay was now feeling that his effort with Carmen had been less than perfect, it was far from the truth. What Jay had yet to realize was that sometimes even the smallest of encouragements can help in a big way. His attentive ear, supportive words, and generous tip had hit their mark, making a significant difference. Jay continued to think about Carmen, imagining other positive ideas he might be able to share with her the next time she cut his hair. He made a mental note: *Be certain to set an appointment specifically with her.*

"Vermont Ave. 1 mile," Jay noticed the exit sign. It brought him back to the present moment and to this afternoon's interview. Originally, Vicki had found today's opportunity on an internet job site. Jay considered it appealing enough to respond with a cover letter and resume attachment. The position was with a non-profit business called Families with Friends.

Vicki had enthusiastically played up the organization when she first showed Jay the posting. She remembered an employee who had utilized the group's assistance previously; he raved about the value of Families with Friends. Jay's research revealed that the organization provided a variety of services to families that needed financial, legal, and counseling assistance. In essence, they were an organization whose name completely matched their mission: caring people who helped families through life's hard times. At this point in his life, Jay found any organization with a positive, life-affecting mission to be exceptionally appealing.

Jay pulled into the parking lot of a very professional, yet modest, two-story building. The receptionist had given him perfect directions. Jay had made excellent time in getting to the interview and had twenty minutes to spare. Instead of going straight into the office and waiting, Jay decided to stretch his legs by walking around the block.

So far it had been an interesting day with a couple of twists. First, there was the Brown & Bigelow interview surprise, then the conversation with Carmen. Together, these experiences served to remind Jay that he never knew what life had in store for him on any given day. He had to admit, chances were that every day had the potential to be interesting.

Of course, Jay had choices. He could have chosen to see the day's events in a less optimistic way, thus turning a good day into a bad one. He could have let the call from Laura turn his day upside-down. Instead of flowing with the change, realizing the positive aspect of continuing to be a candidate for a great job, he might have been put off because the position wasn't being offered to him yet. He could have chosen to be upset over receiving one day's notice to catch a plane and fly out of town for a company with whom he'd already interviewed twice. Likewise, mentally he could have spun Carmen's monologue into his stylist venting about how crummy her kids were, when he was simply trying to get a haircut. But in regard to all the day's unplanned events, Jay chose to think and feel the opposite. He chose to respond positively to everything that had happened instead of choosing to react to it negatively.

"Overall…I don't know if I've ever felt this much peace in my life. I'm really enjoying my journey…and the process of just experiencing life. I'm starting to feel like a more complete person…and I like it. The ultimate…really…is not just in striving every day…but instead it's in enjoying a purpose for which to strive. Gee, I sound like a Buddhist monk now, don't I?" Jay laughed as he finished his walk and approached the office door.

Jay was free of expectations going into this interview. Before entering the business, he took a few of his customary deep breaths to help ease himself into a more relaxed and positive state of mind. He had learned this breathing technique at JLJ, and sometimes it worked to reduce the crazy, nervous tension he felt before big client meetings. It wasn't that he was nervous now, but the rush of the day had caused him to feel like he needed to slow down on the inside. Jay straightened his tie, then walked into Families with Friends.

Immediately, he felt this was a very calming and warm environment. Half-a-dozen beautiful plants lined the area around the reception desk. On the walls hung very large pictures of people playing and laughing together. Directly behind the receptionist was a sign that read: "Families with Friends…supporting the health and growth of the entire family." Jay approached the receptionist, giving her his name. She handed him a clipboard on which there was a detailed application. Diligently, Jay filled out the application. Carefully, he clipped a resume onto it. After a moment's review, to be certain he had completed all questions on the application, Jay handed everything to the receptionist.

Ninety minutes later, Jay's interview was finished. Feeling elated as he walked out of the building, Jay realized he had just completed one of the best interview experiences he ever could have imagined. Furthermore, he would have been hard pressed to remember having had a more satisfying conversation with someone whom he had just met. One more surprise had been added to Jay's day. This one was the best.

The Executive Director of Families with Friends, Jennifer Malone, was a person who proved to be a perfect match for her position, and also a person with whom Jay connected perfectly. She was a charismatic leader with a big vision for her organization's role in the community.

Furthermore, she had a heart for serving people that was pure gold. When she spoke of her organization, she exuded a passion that Jay found exhilarating. She was deeply committed to her work, and there was no doubt that the phenomenal growth the organization had experienced over the last three years was due largely to her leadership.

The accelerated growth of the company had sparked the need for a new major staff position. The opening Jennifer sought to fill was for a public relations and fund raising pro. The case load of the organization had increased ten-fold over the last few years, and the organization needed someone to go out into the community not only to spread the great news of what was being accomplished by Families with Friends, but also to raise much needed funds to help meet a growing demand for services. The position required someone who could wear multiple hats: writer, literature designer, presenter, and donation rainmaker.

Jennifer had conceded, "I know, it's a lot of things to ask of one person. But we're optimistic that we can find a person who fits the bill."

On the drive home, Jay thought of all the exciting opportunities that the job offered. "Wow! There's just so much challenge in this position…and so much potential for the organization! There are so many opportunities and needs to fill! What a potentially great job!"

Jay wasn't sure if the position was right for him, or even if he was qualified to do everything that would be required. "I'm an okay writer, and I have a good sense of design. I can throw together attractive printed pieces quickly, so in those two areas…I can do it. The speaking and raising money part…well, that's scary!"

In overdrive, Jay's brain continued to spin: "The organization is no doubt very, very special. And Jennifer…she's flat out fantastic! The big issue though, is that the job just doesn't pay beans!"

And that was the reality. Little pay for a job that was motivating, challenging, and had great societal value. Compared to the Brown & Bigelow position, the compensation package was worth about one quarter as much. No matter how much Jay loved the new opportunity, bills still needed to be paid. Right? The hard, cold financial realization left him feeling deeply frustrated.

Thursday, June 5th

Jay hadn't slept well at all. He and Vicki had stayed up until nearly one in the morning talking about Families with Friends, Brown & Bigelow, starting a business, life, goals, and a wide variety of topics directly related to these important issues. Options were definitely starting to reveal themselves, and although no decision was immediately pending, some decisions about personal values were beginning to loom. Value choices relating to money, life purpose, personal time, and family were coming to the forefront. The future was turning into the present rapidly and upcoming Garfield decisions were going to have a lasting and dramatic effect. Jay felt the enormous weight of those decisions.

"Let's say I was offered both positions…hypothetically…which one would I accept? Would I take the money and glamour, or the chance to really do something that could make a huge difference in other people's lives? It's not that the advertising gig doesn't make a difference…it can…it just depends on how I go about doing the job, I suppose. But the Families with Friends job…well, that's hitting at the heart of helping people. Right?"

"Then there's the whole wildcard option to become an entrepreneur. Buying a business…starting a business…who knows? But the idea is definitely super appealing!"

"Do I just base everything on our financial needs? Josh will be going to college someday and that will cost big bucks. We've always survived because we've learned to tighten our financial belt so darn much, but it would sure be nice to really enjoy life and do some fun things like travel and stuff. Wouldn't it?"

The questions were all rhetorical. Were there any correct answers? Jay wanted there to be at least a couple. He wanted to know the right path so he could proceed in that direction, and although Jay's gut constantly pushed him to favor the position with the money, Vicki favored pursuit of a career that served others. She was pleased that Jay was so drawn to a job working for a non-profit like Families with Friends, and far less reluctant to throw the opportunity out just because of the size of the paycheck. Vicki strongly pushed the idea that the decision shouldn't be based on money, but that the biggest consideration should be what job really excited him.

Which job thrilled him when he thought about it? Which job would make him look forward to getting up in the morning? At this point, Jay didn't truly know those answers. Both opportunities had strong appeal on two entirely different levels.

"Could I work part-time for both I wonder?" he had teased.

With the big trip to San Francisco planned for later that morning, Jay should have been sleeping, but he couldn't. The interview yesterday had thrown a huge wrench into everything. This was a life-changing and important time in Jay's life, and he correctly felt that this decision was a biggie. He had loved Families with Friends. He had connected with the people at Brown & Bigelow. Both jobs were right there in front of him. What happened if he was offered them both? But wait…what happened if he was offered neither? Angles…angles…angles. The issue was so much more complex than just two possible job opportunities. The two options almost seemed to represent a crossroad in life, and Jay was standing in the middle of the intersection.

"Which way? Which direction?" He imagined looking left…then right…then left again, considering the two polar directions.

"If I land neither, that could be the sign to go at it on my own… you think?"

Totally exhausted, mentally and physically, Jay bypassed his early morning ritual of stretching and exercising. He lay in bed while Vicki got ready for work. With arms folded behind his head, Jay continued to stare at the very same ceiling that had occupied his attention since 1:00 A.M. When Vicki finished getting ready for work, Jay finally allowed his feet to find the floor. He met Vicki downstairs and they chatted a bit about his 10:20 A.M. flight to San Francisco. He wasn't sure what time he would return home; since the flight was a full-fare ticket, he had some flexibility in which flight to catch back.

Before she scurried out the door, Vicki gave Jay a big hug and a quick *I know you're going to knock 'em dead!* speech. She was rushing faster than normal this morning because she planned to stop at the post office before work and drop off a handful of mail that included Jay's thank-you note to Jennifer Malone.

"Call me and tell me how it goes when you finish! Love ya!"

With his physical energy waning from limited sleep, Jay slowly hiked back up the stairs and into his office. "Let's see what Professor Amicus has to say today." The screen lit up. Amicus' lesson was there.

LESSON 17: WHACK THE WORRY WEED!
(Eliminate Worry)

Decisions…decisions…decisions! They can be tough sometimes, can't they? I strongly sense that the time is drawing near for you to make a few very important decisions in your life, my friend. Let me briefly remind you, however, that this isn't a time to let your thinking gravitate to and get bogged down in the fateful. Rather, your mind should be directed more toward the hopeful. You'll find this to be a much more energizing and empowered way to live. Perhaps today's lesson will have great value in helping you focus on the positive.

Without a doubt, Jay, worry is one of the most debilitating emotions to ever strike the human spirit. Its power can be overwhelming. Once worry has crept into the mind, it acts as a construction crew of sorts by building a huge roadblock that prevents a person from moving forward positively in life. Then, once worry has stopped a person in his tracks, it changes form and becomes a quicksand that slowly swallows him. Not a pretty picture.

Worry is definitely not an attractive or beneficial emotion. It saps you of your personal power; it sends you spinning into such a negative spiral that you can make yourself sick. High blood pressure, ulcers and, in some cases, heart disease…each have been known to have their origin in worry. This is not just opinion, Jay. This is the cold, hard medical truth.

Think of all the things…big and small…that people worry about. They worry about their health and if the bills are going to get paid. They worry about how long the car will keep running. They worry about whether the soccer coach knows that their kid is really meant to be a forward. They worry that they're going to lose their job. They worry if the birds are going to eat all the fruit on the backyard trees. They worry about what the world

thinks of them. The funny thing is that the world really isn't even paying attention. Everybody is too busy worrying about their own lives.

People worry about things to the point that they become ineffective in so many areas of their life. Worry takes the steam out of their goals. It steals their joy. Worry strangles the very life out of them. In fact, the word *worry* is actually derived from an old Anglo-Saxon word meaning *to choke*.

Worrying is usually about people losing their perspective and allowing themselves to fall into the role of victim. The vast majority of people, at one time or another, have proven their mountain climbing skills on molehills. A very entertaining character whom I enjoyed greatly, Mark Twain, summed it up best when he said, "I have known a great many troubles, but most of them never happened."

But, Jay, you don't have to be powerless when you become inflicted with the worry bug. By putting your worry into perspective, you can still keep moving forward. You can get yourself out of the quicksand that drags your feet down, and you can jump right over the roadblock that impedes your progress. You just need to change your perspective. By changing your perspective, you can deal with worry in a positive, new way. You can make whatever, at the moment, seems unbearable… bearable. Take a close look at the problem over which you find yourself worrying, and ask yourself a very important question: "What can I do to turn this problem into something positive?"

As scary and unsettling as they might be at times, problems are really nothing more than challenges wearing masks. You can begin to regain control over your emotions by asking yourself: "What can I do to turn this into a positive?" By asking this simple question, you take that crucial first step in getting out of your pity chair. Worry is simply a weed that grows when you do nothing. Worry gets snipped at its base when you take action.

The next time you begin to see worry weeds taking over your mental garden, don't just sit there and watch them grow! Don't lay powerless, saturate your mind with doubt, or throw up your hands and say, "This is a disaster!" Instead, look at the problem in a bright and shining new light that can invigorate your spirit and evaporate your despair. Look at the problem as a chance to whack the heck out of the worry weed!

Change your perspective, jump out of your chair with snipers in hand, and start doing something positive about your problem. Ask, "What can I do to turn this problem into something positive?" By doing so, you will have taken the first step to learning a very rare and lost art form…the art of not worrying.

Question:
What positive steps can you take to whack a current worry weed out of your mind?

Leaning back in his chair and chuckling, Jay asked himself, "How does he seem to always know what I'm thinking?" He had no clue how Amicus knew to throw the perfect lesson at him each time.

"Perfect begets perfect, I guess. No doubt the right lesson in life shows up when I need to hear it the most."

It was true. This was the lesson Jay needed to absorb, and immediately. Ever since last night, Jay's insides were feeling very tied up. He felt as though he was suffocating. The positive energy that had been building inside him seemed now to be slowly dissipating. Jay needed to regroup, and filling his mind with Amicus' teaching had been the perfect solution.

"Reading Amicus' words…reading anything empowering…is crucial to helping me stay on the right course. I need to keep learning and charging my own battery every single darn day. It gives me balance and perspective. It reminds me that the world is bigger than me. I don't need to worry! I don't! It's silly…it's stupid…and it leads me nowhere productive."

Jay had again stopped the negative thought patrol from taking over any further. He had had enough and he realized that it was time to adopt a pro-active solution for stopping the incessant need to worry. On the top of his notebook page, Jay wrote:

LESSON 17: WHACK THE WORRY WEED!

Underneath it, he wrote for emphasis: *Make it happen! Now!*

"What are the areas that I need to stop worrying about?" Jay started to write his thoughts down.

I worry about:
1. Career: What should I do? I want to make my job count for something. I want to feel as if I have a mission in life and not just an 8-5 to pay the bills. I'm afraid I won't find it.
2. Money: What happens if we can't pay the bills? We can't live on Vicki's check forever. I don't want to always have to worry about how I'm going to pay the mortgage and car payments. What if we never have more than we do now? That would really suck.
3. Josh: I know I've already screwed up in so many ways with him, and I worry that Josh will be hurt by my mistakes as a father. I haven't been there for him like I should have been…not even close…and that really bothers me.
4. Being mediocre: I don't want to live a mediocre life. I want to feel as if I've really lived, traveled, done things, and experienced life. I'm afraid that I won't do it. I'm afraid that I'm destined to be forever average and live an unfulfilled life! That's a very ugly feeling.

Looking at his written answers, it was easy for Jay to ask himself what he really gained from worrying about any of these things. "What does worry really get me? Does it make me feel better? Do I get any closer to solving any of the issues I worry about? Worrying is absolutely pathetic! It gets me nowhere!"

Next, he turned his attention to things that might possibly help take the sting out of his worry. "Okay…using Amicus' words…what do I need to do to whack the worry weed?"

Jay wrote the four main worry items again.

To stop worrying I need to:

1. *Career: I need to understand that it's all going to work out if I just keep at it like I'm doing. I will find the right job for me. I need to keep looking and sending my resume out every single day. I need to have faith in myself and my talent and know that I will eventually be hired and the job will be great!*

2. *Money: I need to quit imagining the worst is going to happen. It's not! There are so many different options before we ever begin to lose our home. Long term? Just follow a regular monthly investment plan. Read money-type magazines and information on internet sites in order to grow in what I know. My big goal? Make it a priority to budget and learn about investing rather than to worry about not being able to pay the bills!*

3. *Josh: Realize that there's nothing I can do to alleviate past mistakes, but I can start being a great dad and getting involved in my son's life today! Instead of worrying about it, call him and talk!*

4. *Being mediocre: Worry about it and I will become it! Plan to live a great life! Plan! Plan! And then work my plan.*

Just addressing the topic of worry with a written plan felt better. Jay reaffirmed his thoughts verbally: "Action...taking enormous, vibrant, make-it-happen action will get rid of your worry, Jay. Do it. And do it every day. Action over worry...and then worry no more! With strong, positive action everything will work out."

10:37 A.M.

Nearly two hours later, Jay was on board Flight 707 bound for San Francisco and his meeting with the Northern California team of Brown & Bigelow. The plane ride from the Burbank airport had been quick, and to Jay's surprise, Laura Walston was at the airport in San Francisco to greet him. Laura had flown in the night before for an industry awards dinner and was planning on walking Jay through the day.

As usual, Jay felt completely comfortable in Laura's presence. The thirty-five-minute car ride to the downtown office of Brown & Bigelow was relaxed and conversation flowed easily. The two of them talked about Los Angeles, San Francisco, exercise, hobbies, crazy drivers, and billboards. Because both were in the advertising business, they had an increased awareness not only of billboard locations, but also of the messages posted on them.

Laura was pointing out the car window, "That's our client over there. It's a new campaign we're working on and with which we're very pleased. That company over there...we're working on them. We have a new pitch scheduled next week that we think will blow their socks off."

When Jay and Laura arrived at the office, they headed straight to the Brown & Bigelow conference room. Lunch had been ordered for Jay, Laura, and George Brown, the first half of the Brown & Bigelow name. Jay found Mr. Brown to be a guarded man who spoke softly, but listened well. Brown's answers to Jay's questions were short and succinct, and always followed by a question from Brown.

"Our strength is in branding. We can quickly turn a relative unknown into a name. Tell me, Jay, is there any specific advertising campaigns that you really like? And secondly, share with me some of the big clients that you have landed previously."

At one time, George Brown's style would have made Jay uncomfortable. But not today. The worry exercise Jay had walked himself through earlier was paying dividends. Jay answered each question the best he could. He was calm, relaxed, and friendly. Laura's presence at the table definitely helped, too. Although she was contributing little verbally, Laura offered Jay continual support with her constant smile and friendly face throughout the entire Brown grilling.

Unwavering from his own game plan to learn more about the company, Jay was unabashed in firing away with his own questions.

"What markets do you hope to break into first? What kind of support will your national account people receive? What is your philosophy in lead generation? What kind of numbers are you looking for this position to produce?"

Again, Brown's answers were brief. "Dallas and New York...we always provide whatever support is necessary to help our sales staff... we're big on direct mail and, of course, picking up the phone and dialing...five times our quota for local sales people."

It was Brown's turn to hit Jay with more questions. "What do you think, Jay? What kind of numbers do you think you would deliver in twelve months? What do you think a reasonable quota would be?"

"Brown is good," Jay thought. "He certainly doesn't give much away, does he?"

How Jay did, he couldn't be sure. It most certainly had been a challenging day. George Brown had been a tough guy to get to know. It was hard to read his face or make any strong assumptions from his energy level. He was cool-headed and unshakable.

Jay hadn't realized it during the interview, but later on the plane ride back to LA, he knew Brown had been testing him. He had wanted to see how Jay would hold-up and respond if the pressure was applied. Brown was giving Jay much the same heat as a potential national client would be giving him. Neither the potential client, nor George Brown, had any intention of making it easy. They both would be causing Jay to scramble for every edge he could find.

Altogether, the lunch interview had lasted ninety minutes, and Jay had given the meeting the very best of his heart and mind. Realizing now what a masterful interviewer Brown had been to squeeze so much out of him, Jay slumped in seat 14-A totally exhausted.

The rest of the afternoon at Brown & Bigelow had been spent meeting other members of the San Francisco team. Jay also had the opportunity to sit quietly observing an ad development meeting for a prospective clothing client. Jay was pleased that the company trusted him enough to observe the B & B team in action. Even more, Jay thought the creative talent that had surrounded the five-person table was truly superior.

With the San Francisco meeting now in the history books, everything about Brown & Bigelow had fallen into place for Jay. Meeting the players, seeing the creative team at work and walking through the corporate halls had fully enabled Jay to see why JLJ had lost so many potential clients to Brown & Bigelow. These people just weren't good...they were phenomenal.

Jay collapsed into bed that night uncertain how to grade the day. He knew his performance had been solid, but had he performed up to Brown & Bigelow's standards. Had George Brown found him effective? Had Jay made the sale? Before the worry weed even had a chance to rear its head, Jay cut it off.

"Just see what happens…no worries." Jay reflected on his morning lesson regarding worry. Like a light bulb that had just been turned on in a very dark room, Amicus' morning question lit up in Jay's mind: "What positive steps can you take to whack a current worry weed out of your mind?" Jay knew the answer: laugh at himself and go to sleep.

Friday, June 6th

Jay's first reaction to the morning alarm clock was to turn it off and go back to sleep. But he knew that was old-school thinking. "When the going gets tough…the tough get going!" Jay purposefully dragged himself out of bed.

He was tired. Two nights in a row, the Garfield's had stayed up late talking. Upon arriving home from the airport, Jay discovered Vicki had dipped into her magic Italian cooking bag and pulled out an amazing lasagna. Over dinner, he shared how the day had gone from beginning to end.

"What's my gut say? Hmmm. I honestly don't have a feeling one way or another anymore, Vic. Maybe *yes*…maybe *no*. I did the best I could. It's now out of my hands. One thing I do know is that starting tomorrow I'm going to be focused on finding other opportunities. I have to assume the Brown & Bigelow opportunity could be something from the past. I'm going to move ahead aggressively looking for another great possibility."

Yesterday's travel had supplanted Jay's morning exercise. He knew it was very important to get out there this morning to reaffirm this new habit. A pesky, nay-saying voice in his head was already screaming loudly, "No…don't go! Lay here!" Jay was wise enough not to succumb to that little, no-good voice, and thereby preserve his long-term exercise plan.

Amicus 101

It would be painful to get out the door and move his legs this morning, but it was more painful to think of jeopardizing the exercise momentum he had been slowly building. Jay knew that even the slightest mental slip—to not push and exercise now...in the early going—would be absolutely hazardous to his long-term success. Willing himself to get up and take action prompted two things to happen: the screaming *don't exercise* voice was muted, and a fresh, invigorating voice took center stage shouting, "Way to go, Jay!"

He had finally fallen asleep the previous night after deciding to throw sandbags around the worry that was seeping into his mind. Still, he knew he needed to develop skill at stopping the act of worrying in its tracks earlier, before it had a chance to overflow and effect his emotions.

While going through his morning stretches, Jay took time to reinforce a recent Amicus lesson. He pulled his Amicus notebook off the dresser, then sat down in the middle of the room to stretch his hamstrings...and his mind...again.

As he stretched, he reviewed Amicus' previous message:

> **The next time you begin to see worry weeds start to take over your mental garden, don't just sit there and watch them grow! Don't act powerless, saturate your mind with doubt, or throw up your hands and say, "This is a disaster!" Instead, look at the problem in a bright and shining new light that invigorates your spirit and evaporates your despair. Look at the problem as a chance to whack the heck out of the worry weed!**

A smile graced Jay's lips as he read the passage. He felt a wave of confidence shoot through his mind as he realized that he had just demonstrated the power to control the limiting thoughts that would try to hold him back. Moments ago, he was feeling the burden of having to exercise. Now Jay celebrated the small victory he felt in learning to control the computer that rested on his shoulders.

Jay finished stretching and reviewed his *Morning Momentum* questions before he headed out the door. His body might have shuddered from the cold morning air, but that didn't stop Jay from

164

putting in his fastest run to date. In total, Jay had jogged five miles in just under fifty minutes. He had sprinted the last hundred yards, and as he crossed an imaginary finish line, Jay lifted his hands in the air as if he were an Olympic athlete breaking the tape.

Physically he felt exhausted, but mentally and emotionally he was as energized and proud of himself as he had ever been. Hands on his hips and sweat dripping from his face, Jay slowly cooled down by walking back and forth in front of his driveway.

"Great job, man! Great job! You got out here…and you ran superbly! Way…to…go!"

Back in the house, he found no messages on the voice-mail. Wishful thinking might have hoped for something from Brown & Bigelow, or even Families with Friends since this was the last day before a weekend …but not today. No worries.

Jay bounded up the stairs with such enthusiasm and purpose that no one ever would have known that his legs were entirely fatigued and weak. He turned on the bathroom radio, jumped into the shower, and began singing backup to the ten-year-old pop hit that was currently playing.

Showered and re-charged, Jay sat down at the computer swaying in the chair and snapping his fingers to the imaginary music beat he still heard in his head. Any curious onlooker would have wondered if he could share in the same magical elixir Jay must be taking in order to feel his obvious, natural zest for life. Jay's mind…his body…his spirit…felt great. He had succeeded in doing something that had been hard this morning. Though his physical energy was spent…overall he felt flat out charged up. He felt alive. This was the kind of alive you feel after succeeding in an act of sheer will, after overcoming inertia and achieving a dream.

The real lesson being absorbed by Jay's subconscious was: "Do good…then feel good." For far too long, Jay had been operating under the exact opposite premise: "Feel good…then do good." Jay's future success and happiness would be so much richer with his new course of motivation and action. He was on the right track now.

"Here I am, unemployed and not sure what I'm going to do, but I feel happier than I have for years. Does that even make sense? How weird! I'm not sure if I even get it!"

Jay was sitting there alone, grinning from ear to ear as if he had just walked into a surprise birthday party. He was finding balance in his life, and his attitude had never been so consistently positive. His personal awareness was hovering at a *level 10*. With great enthusiasm, Jay was pleased with his present life…and most of all…where he felt he was going. He started to read his next lesson.

LESSON 18: BE A BATTERY CHARGER OF THE HUMAN SPIRIT! (Encourage Others)

Well, my friend, we're heading into the home stretch now. We're approaching your twenty-first and final lesson. But before we get there, you still have a few things to learn and remember. I want to stress right now that although these lessons are coming to an end, they will always be yours. Review them often. Cement their power into your heart, and most of all, share them. You're destined for great things, Jay…if you choose. Now for today's lesson.

Intense rejection met the great American poet, Walt Whitman, when he tried to get his most famous book, *Leaves of Grass*, published. Critics clobbered him with their words. One detractor called his work "nonsense." Another said: "We can conceive of no better reward than the lash." At that point, deep frustration and a severe lack of confidence were beginning to permeate Walt's mind. He questioned his own talent, and often found himself asking, "Am I good enough?"

Then, a note arrived. A seemingly insignificant piece of paper carried a message that changed Walt Whitman's attitude, that changed his world. In a crowd of negativity, there appeared a true hero. That hero, a fellow writer, extended to Walt the most precious of all gifts… encouragement.

Ralph Waldo Emerson, known as one of American literature's all-time superstars, had the sensitivity and foresight to drop Walt a simple forty-three word note:

Dear Sir:

I am not blind to the worth of the wonderful gift, Leaves of Grass. *I find it the most extraordinary piece of wit and wisdom that an American has yet contributed. I greet you at the beginning of a great career.*

Ah! The great gift of encouragement! With one simple note, Walt Whitman was empowered with the courage to continue. He was given the courage to persevere in sharing his message of inspirational prose with his fellow man. Finally knowing that his words could really stir the passions of others, Walt Whitman changed his state of mind. In doing so, he also changed his world and his destiny. Mr. Emerson's gracious act gave Walt power. It gave Walt a second wind.

Do you know what I call people like Ralph Waldo Emerson, my friend? I call them Battery Chargers of the Human Spirit. A Battery Charger of the Human Spirit encourages and motivates others to excel and be their best. A Battery Charger of the Human Spirit charges the confidence battery of someone who is down, reinforces the confidence level of someone who is uncertain, and applauds the success of someone who is doing well. A Battery Charger of the Human Spirit gives encouragement, is a builder, a motivator, and a person who strives to help others maximize their full potential.

Like Emerson, our friend Mr. Lincoln was also a Battery Charger of the Human Spirit. History recorded one example of this immediately after the battle of Gettysburg. The President had sensed that there was an opportunity to end the war by pushing hard against General Lee's retreating forces. As Commander-in-Chief of the Army, Lincoln ordered General Meade to pursue. Along with this order, he sent a note that read:

The order I enclose is not of record. If you succeed, you need not publish the order. If you fail, publish it. Then if you succeed, you will have all the credit of the movement. If not, I will take all the responsibility.

Newspapers had constantly published blistering reports about the President, and some good publicity would have served him well. Nevertheless, Abe was not swayed by a desire to find lasting popularity and fame. He was moved to serve his fellow man.

Tabloids had called him a "third-rate country lawyer," stated that he had "looks resembling that of a gorilla," and that he was "good for nothing but splitting rails." Did it hurt him? Certainly! But none of what was written moved him to glamorize his actions in the hope of winning favor in print.

Lincoln saw the bigger picture. He chose to give others credit for his own daring. In this case, he empowered General Meade with the courage to take a risk without the fear of failure or blame. No doubt, General Meade found that to be a powerful incentive.

So, Jay, are you like Emerson and Lincoln, a Battery Charger of the Human Spirit? Do you encourage people to be their best? Do you recognize people's talents and empower them to shoot for their dreams? Are you known as a person who helps others win in life? Please know, my friend, that your enthusiasm, interest, and positive affirmation can make an incredible difference in the lives of those around you.

A little girl, desiring the attention of her father, asked if she could sing and dance for him. "I'll sing and dance, Daddy, and you clap your hands and say, *Wonderful!*"

Make it your mission, Jay, to be the one who says "wonderful." Make it your mission to become the lifetime teammate of others and a self-proclaimed Battery Charger of the Human Spirit for all those whom you meet and know.

One more thing, my friend. An amazing aspect of being a Battery Charger is that others are not the only ones to reap the benefits of your generous spirit. You will, as well.

Centuries ago, Solomon, one of my favorite philosophers, wrote, "He who refreshes others will himself be refreshed." It's true, Jay. Charge the battery of others and you will recharge yourself at the same time. Give encouragement and you will be encouraged. Motivate and you will be motivated. Can you imagine anything more perfect?

So get out there and start giving people a second *life wind*. Start handing out mega-doses of courage. Encouragement literally means *to put courage into* someone. Malcolm Forbes once said, "Diamonds are nothing more than chunks of coal that stuck to their job." Your job as an encourager, a giver of courage, is to keep those potential diamonds around you inspired to the point that their dreams begin to shine in reality!

Continue your journey, Jay, by understanding and sharing the power of encouragement. Presented in the written form, this fabulous gift can be read over and over. Forever. Who knows? Maybe you'll be the one who opens the door to a future American superstar.

Question:
What five people in your life can benefit right now from you becoming a Battery Charger of the Human Spirit?

Jay took one of his famous deep breaths, the type that signaled either something big was about to happen or that his brain was engaged in extra-deep thinking. He let it out slowly. Amicus' question brought to the forefront a principle that highlighted so much of what positive living was all about: live life with a spirit of giving.

Jay grimaced as he thought about the past few weeks. So often he'd been looking for someone to pat him on the back when he should have been out there doing the patting. He'd been looking for someone else to offer him a letter of encouragement, when he should have been creating his own *Atta' boy!* masterpieces to send to others.

For a moment, Jay felt guilty. But just for a moment. Then he smiled. Like a light turning on in his head, Jay clearly saw what was important in life. It wasn't money, possessions, achievements, or results. It was people. It was connecting with and recharging all those whom his life touched. Jay closed his eyes and began to visualize. He saw himself as a Battery Charger for others. He saw himself as a motivator for those whose spirit needed lifting. He envisioned himself as an inspirer for those needing hope. He pictured himself as a Battery Charger of the Human Spirit.

Jay opened his notebook. At the top of a new page, he wrote down the question: *What five people in my life can benefit from me becoming a Battery Charger of the Human Spirit?*

He started writing down the names of those closest to him, but didn't stop at just five. His pen kept writing. And writing. Ten names turned into fifteen, then twenty-five. There were many people in Jay's life who could benefit from him playing the role of a Mr. Emerson. Next to each name, Jay wrote specifically how he could encourage that particular person.

"I'm going to do it, too! I'm going to be a Battery Charger of the Human Spirit and contact each of these people!"

Today was turning out to be a great day. Jay sent off a number of encouraging e-mails to individuals on the list. He made calls to a few, and even sent traditional letters to two others. His words to all were encouraging and motivating. It felt great to be a motivator. It felt great being a Battery Charger of the Human Spirit. And in doing so, Jay's personal level of inspiration soared.

3:15 P.M.

That afternoon, Jay spent time working on two creative advertising ideas that he had for a Families with Friends public relations campaign. Jay was definitely going the extra-mile. He hadn't been asked to offer any suggestions or proposals; he just wanted to do whatever he could to stand out amidst any other strong job prospects. Everything about Jennifer Malone and the Families with Friends mission exuded total effort. Jay wanted to show he was like-minded. Words are easy; actions are hard. Jay wanted to let his actions speak for him.

When Jay was finished, he liked what he had put together. Whether or not Jennifer would like it he was unsure, but he knew it had received his best effort. The first piece was designed to outline the extensive list of services the organization offered. It clearly highlighted the fact that Families with Friends had the capacity to serve families more completely and extensively than any other local community-based business. The second piece was a hard-hitting and pressing appeal to the community for financial support. Well-written and utilizing pictures from a current organizational brochure, the ads were a testament to Jay's talent for putting a message on paper. Years spent brainstorming with JLJ teammates and watching the design experts work their magic had rubbed off on Jay. His finished product definitely accomplished the goal of appealing to both heart and mind. Jay was proud of his work.

"It's time to surprise Jennifer and tell her I have a little gift for her," Jay thought. He picked up the phone and called her.

Realizing it was a Friday and late in the day, Jay wasn't sure if he would be able to reach the organization's Executive Director. Additionally, he conjectured that since he was only a candidate interviewing for a position, she might just let his call go straight to voice mail. He was greatly surprised when the receptionist transferred his call and Jennifer came on the phone in person:

"Hello, Jay Garfield! How are you doing today?"

"I'm doing great, Jennifer Malone! How are you today?" Jay teased her right back using her last name, too.

"I'm busy-as-a-bee, but besides that, doing very well." She laughed. "What can I do for you, Jay? Did you have additional questions about the job?"

"Actually, no. The reason I'm calling is to let you know that I was so impressed with you and your organization's purpose, that I took the liberty to put together a couple of ad ideas. I know you hadn't asked me to do it, and I certainly hope I am not out of line, but I just felt motivated to help…already." Jay laughed hoping she would catch his presumptive joke.

"Although they're not finalized for print, they are ready to be seen. Would you like me to e-mail them or drop them by?" The habit of closing for an either/or action came naturally to Jay from having done it hundreds of times before in his sales position at JLJ.

"You've got to be kidding, Jay! Really? You used your personal time to put something together for us? I love it! I want to see it very much; in fact, you may be a life-saver! It was on my agenda this weekend to create a new piece, so you may have saved me some time! Now I know this might be a huge imposition, but I would love for you to bring it over this afternoon! If you can, I mean."

In Jay's mind, the call couldn't have gone more perfectly. Not only was Jennifer happy, she wanted to see it now! Ecstatic after Jennifer's amazingly appreciative response, Jay agreed to meet her at 6:00. He hurriedly added a couple of polishing touches to his job, got dressed in casual professional attire, wrote Vicki a quick note, and raced to his car.

"Crazy fun!" he thought as he drove out of his driveway... adrenalin pumping full force.

Soon afterward, Jay and the Executive Director of Families with Friends were going over his ad designs. Jennifer was thrilled and showed her appreciation by repeatedly praising Jay for not only his professional creation, but also his extra-mile effort. Incredibly humble, but happy, Jay only smiled a lot and said, "Thank you. I'm so happy to have helped."

Jennifer suddenly turned very serious. "You know, Jay, you're a person who truly stands out, and I think...no, I know...you're the best person to fill our job. I may be jumping the gun just a bit, but after your effort today, I think I have all the information I need to make a decision. I interviewed four other strong candidates that were gleaned from the resumes, yet your background was a perfect match for what we're looking for from the beginning. I thought your interview was great, and your references, as expected, were fantastic. And finally, what you did today really closes the deal in my mind."

She continued. "Jay, how would you like to work for Families with Friends? I know that this position offers a salary that is a far cry from what you could earn elsewhere, but I hope you'll seriously consider accepting. We do a lot of good here and you would be a superbly valuable addition to our team."

Jay was blown away. His intention in running the ad designs over to her was simply to nudge himself up a notch or two in Jennifer's mind as she considered the candidates. He never dreamed this trip was going to result in a job offer. Sure, he'd hoped to stand out with this effort, but to be offered the job right then and there? Wow!

How do you remain calm, showing limited emotion on the outside, when inside you are celebrating as if your name was just drawn for the grand prize in a raffle? It's hard, but as Jay Garfield proved, not impossible. From the split second that the thrill of this announcement had started to run up his spine, Jay somehow managed to let nothing more than a slight grin cross his lips. The sparkle in Jay's eyes, however, contradicted the coolness that his expression reflected.

"Well, to say that I'm pleased would be an understatement, Jennifer. Thank you very much. It feels great knowing you appreciated my effort."

For the next twenty minutes, Jay and Jennifer went over details of compensation and benefit specifics for the Communications Director position. Jay left the Families with Friends office with a soaring spirit. He had just been offered an amazing job! It would utilize all of his talents and give him the opportunity to be creative, resourceful, and most of all, he would be doing something that made a significant impact on people's lives.

The adrenalin that still pumped through Jay's body was totally invigorating. What a fantastic, amazing, incredible feeling! His extra mile effort had produced amazing fruit, and now the decision was his. Jay had to decide whether or not to accept the offer. Jennifer had given him six days to decide. He was to get back to her before the end of the day next Thursday.

Later that night, Jay lay stretched out across the living room carpet while Vicki curled up on the couch sipping a cup of green tea. In the background, soft jazz played on the radio. For the last hour, Jay and Vicki had celebrated the victory of Jay's job offer. It was a team victory. The two also revisited *What if?* and a possible offer from Brown & Bigelow. It, too, could be coming. The two opportunities were remarkably different, but each so appealing. Anxious words and heavy sighs pervaded the Garfield living room. A decision would soon need to be made.

During a moment of quiet, Jay closed his eyes and lost himself in the soft wail of a muted saxophone. He realized how tense he had become after experiencing a few hours of such an amazing emotional high. He let the music enter deeper into his spirit as he focused on his breathing. He breathed in deeply, held the breath, then released it slowly, only to repeat this, stretching his lung capacity one more time. Holding a deep breath longer than normal calmed his nerves. Jay felt his fingers loosen as he shut the door to the noises of future decisions that clamored around in his brain.

In this newly relaxed state, a picture of a man filled his mind. It was the man in the royal blue sweat suit whom he had met in the bleachers at the park. The man was smiling at him. This picture story continued to play itself out as the man turned and walked through a door. The door remained open. Jay followed him through. Behind this door, Jay found himself in a room unlike any in which he had ever been. He looked around the room, but saw nothing tangible; it was empty, as if it waited to be filled. Yet in this room, Jay felt waves of different emotions. Depending on where in the room he directed his gaze, a different emotion struck his senses: peace…frustration…happiness…sadness. When he walked towards a specific corner, the intensity of a particular feeling deepened. It did not take him long to understand that the areas representing peace and happiness were far more comfortable. He was drawn to these areas. It was there that he stayed and soaked in a positive energy that renewed his whole being.

Then, seemingly from out of nowhere, the man at the park reappeared in the center of the room. He opened his mouth and spoke. "Jay, my friend…you now realize the power of choice. It is always yours." With that said, he disappeared.

"Jay, whatcha' thinkin' for dinner?" Vicki's words broke into Jay's conscious dream state. At the moment, however, food was not on Jay's mind. Instead, his mind was focused on the letters of a single word… A-M-I-C-U-S.

Saturday, June 7th…

"You know, Vicki…think about it." Jay was on the floor of the bedroom stretching while Vicki slipped out of bed and into her robe. His mind had been turning in a very different direction ever since the previous night when the mysterious man in the royal blue sweat suit had visited his thoughts. Now Jay was attempting to verbalize his thoughts and feelings for Vicki. Sensing that his tone was serious, Vicki sat back down on the bed to give Jay her full attention.

"My focus on this whole job decision issue is completely off base. What's important is not really which job I end up taking, but rather the fact that I created the opportunity for each. You know what I mean?"

Without waiting for a reply, Jay continued. "Brown & Bigelow, Families with Friends…both opportunities were created because of my effort and my attitude. That's what is truly exciting to realize! That's what I should be focusing on! The worst thing that can happen is that I'll choose a job that doesn't pan out exactly the way I envisioned, and then I have to find something else. Would I be disappointed if that happened? Of course. But you know what? The thing to remember is that I now know that I have the ability to go out and create new opportunities that are great!"

Vicki leaned back on her elbows as she continued listening. "The thing that I see so clearly now, Vic, is this: losing my job was not the end of the world until I made it the end of the world. I'm the one that thought disaster had struck…but it never really had. Things changed, but the problem was my reaction to the change. I made the situation far more desperate than it needed to be…or should've been."

"Jay, that's so positive!" Vicki smiled. "That's really insightful and inspired thinking. I'm so proud of you!"

He smiled back. "I just gave too much power to that moment I was fired…and I lost control of my ability to make anything happen. I was like a giant negative snowball rolling down the mountain. The negative circumstances and events that affect my life don't have to determine the quality of my life. But I had let them. And what's so ironic is that something I gave so much negative power to is turning out to be one of the most positive experiences of my life."

Jay hesitated as his mind wandered back to the dream-like experience of the night before. "We always have the choice of how to feel and what to think. We have the power to choose!"

He continued. "Attitude means so darn much! I can see that so clearly now! It's so obvious! A few weeks ago I was mentally slumming around, feeling sorry for myself, and today, right now, I'm in the position to head in one of many amazing directions. It all boils down to me. It all comes down to my attitude and my effort!"

Vicki chimed in, "What a fantastic revelation, Jay! That is so great! When you say 'many amazing directions' though…don't you mean a couple directions?" Being the positive pragmatist, Vicki was bringing Jay back to the here-and-now.

"Well...no...actually...there is another choice that is making itself crystal clear now, too. Remember how we were thinking of potential businesses that we could start or buy into? I know what it is now. I could start my own work-from-home advertising agency. Before you say anything...think about it. First, I like doing it. Second, I am good at it. And third, I know I can draw customers. In fact, maybe Families and Friends will be my first client! I could really do this, Vic! I can!"

With eyes popping wide open in an exaggeration of surprise, Vicki laughed at Jay's enthusiasm. "Well, you're right, Jay! I guess you do have many amazing directions!"

The two of them considered the possible merits and pitfalls of creating such an opportunity. It would no doubt be hard work, but it could be a lot of fun, too. And just maybe...just maybe...highly profitable. Another hat had officially been thrown into the ring. Now Jay actually needed to decide which one to wear. He had until June 12th to decide.

Jay stood up and walked to the bathroom sink. Smiling, he read out loud the three morning questions taped to the bathroom mirror:

1. What am I excited about achieving today?
2. Who can I serve today?
3. What am I most grateful for in my life right now?

Jay knew that he was building accountability into his life... the morning questions, reading positive books, exercising regularly, reviewing his Amicus notebook...had been crucial determinants in helping him maintain positive momentum and growth. It wasn't always easy to be consistent and follow on a daily basis, but it was always valuable. Time restraints and the resistance of *I don't feel like it* plagued him often, but up to this point, he had prevailed victoriously. Daily accountability was the railroad tracks that kept Jay steadily moving in the right direction without becoming derailed by the ever-changing events and circumstances of life.

11:37 A.M.

After a morning bike ride with Vicki, Jay found himself in front of his computer looking at the nineteenth of Amicus' lessons. "I can't believe it! Only three more!" Jay mused. Amicus had become a significant, energizing, life-affirming part of his day. The lessons were oxygen to Jay's soul; they were power to his mind.

For a brief moment, Jay was struck by a feeling of melancholy. "What happens after the final lesson? Will Amicus be gone? Oh, man…." Shaking himself back to the moment at hand, Jay dove into the next lesson.

LESSON 19: CREATE A GREAT DAY!
(Take Daily Ownership of Your Life)

I sense that your growth, my friend, is multiplying by the day! Isn't it exciting? Isn't it thrilling to know YOU are responsible for the amazing things that are happening in your life? Never lose sight of what you now know, Jay. Never lose sight of your ability to make exciting things transpire. Be always conscious of the fact that you have the ability to create a great day.

"Have a nice day!" You hear it all the time. Family members, bank tellers, grocery store checkers, phone conversations… rarely a day passes in which those simple four well-wishing words aren't heard or said. Unfortunately, this phrase has become so commonplace that people hardly recognize its sentiment. Because of their frequent, unemotional familiarity, the words often lack inspiration; people are left with little impetus to actually make something of their day.

Instead, how about stirring up people's thought processes by bringing new meaning to conversational goodbyes? How about ending conversations with a slightly different, more self-determining version of this farewell wish? How about: "Create a great day!"

Trite? Meaningless? I don't think so. Look at what this expression has the power to do for the mind of the receiver. First,

it causes the listener to consider this rather different remark. Perhaps a smile and a comment will follow. Anytime we can inspire a smile in another, that's a good thing. Second, it gives people a reason to stop and consider a remarkable truth: they have the power to create any sort of day they want...good, bad, or indifferent. So much of your enjoyment of life is determined by how much you choose to be happy! You know this eternal truth, my friend, because you are now living it!

As for you, the broadcaster of these new "Create a great day!" power words, it puts you in a position to share goodwill, plant seeds, and wake up your neighbor. Those are three very gratifying benefits. Would you like to know another fantastic benefit? By throwing a spark out there, you can't help but stoke the fire of enthusiasm that burns inside you. Awaken others, and you awaken yourself.

When you create, you bring to form what wasn't there before. Like the artist adding color to a blank canvas, the writer adding words to an empty page, or the actor adding personality to an emotionless script, you add positive emotion and action to your world. When you encourage others to create, you invite them to do something uniquely brilliant with their day.

Think about it; you have the opportunity to shape the events, experiences, feelings, and thoughts of each of your days! That's powerful! That's awesome! What's more, you can encourage others...those whom you know and those whom you don't know...to shape their days! That's what I call empowered, self-directed living!

Anybody who has ever struggled to plant his feet onto the floor in the morning knows that life can be hard; it can be stressful; it can be overwhelming. But each of those negative, less than optimal feelings immediately takes a back seat to the radiant light of hope. Knowing that you have the authority and the power in your life to actually create a great day is the most potent type of life-affirming hope that you could ever possess. Pass on that hope!

This is your life, my friend! Don't spend it mindlessly, assuming that you have another one in the bank! Invest it by creating the exciting adventure story that you desire, then encourage others to do the same! Each of us is the writer, the architect, and the builder of every one of our days. Remind others…and yourself…of this powerful truth! Live passionately and with self-determination! Plant the inspired seeds of this positive message in others! Take ownership of your life daily and "Create a great day!"

Question:
What would a great day look like in your life?

Jay mulled over the question and opened his notebook to the next blank page. This lesson was a perfect reminder that creating a great day was more often the result of positive intention and desire. He began writing a list of all the things he now knew contributed to the creation of a great day:

To create a great day, I need to remember:
1. *Creating a great day is about having a designated purpose and working the plan associated with that purpose. It's about knowing what I want to accomplish on that day.*
2. *Creating a great day is about responding and not reacting to situations. It's about taking control over my thoughts and feelings, despite what is happening around me.*
3. *Creating a great day is about choosing to have a positive mental attitude even when it's hard. It's about controlling the meaning I give to events and individual moments.*
4. *Creating a great day is about finding ways to encourage and be of service to others. It's about being a Battery Charger, uplifting and building people.*
5. *Creating a great day is about growing in body, mind, and spirit. It's about taking time to exercise, learn, and reflect.*

> *6. Creating a great day is about knowing I gave today my very best, despite whatever may have resulted. It's about maximizing my time and efforts.*

Jay smiled. He felt he was *getting it*. He felt that his thought processes were becoming more and more like those of Amicus. While he chronicled his thoughts, the printer slowly turned out the daily lesson.

1:08 P.M.

A combination of indoor and outdoor jobs occupied Jay and Vicki's attention for the remainder of the day. So many tasks around the house had accumulated that the two of them decided today was the day to jump in and finish them up. Jay listened to a baseball game on the radio while he cleaned the garage, weeded, pruned trees, and focused on an odd assortment of other chores.

Listening to the game reminded Jay of the familiar box seats that he probably would be sitting in today if he still worked at JLJ Advertising. A small, nostalgic part of him longed to be munching on a hotdog and yelling out support to the on-deck hitter. A much deeper part of him realized, however, that there was no way in the world that he would trade those prime seats for where he was in his life now, and more importantly, where he was going. Jay felt a deeper inner peace than he had ever known.

That evening, both Jay and Vicki were absolutely exhausted from the physical exertion of their day. Lying on opposite ends of the couch, they were watching a DVD and sharing a big bowl of microwave popcorn. On her way home, Vicki had picked up a couple of movies that had been recommended by a friend: *Dead Poets Society* and *Grand Canyon*. She'd been told that both had powerful messages, and that she'd probably like them.

In *Dead Poets Society*, a remarkable teacher in a very strict boy's boarding school had just taken his class down to the school's trophy case. The students looked at the impressive trophies that had been won in years past, along with photos of the victorious students of the graduating classes. Pointing to one particularly old photo, the teacher tells his class to look closely at it.

He points out that the young students in the photo were once just like them—they had fire in their eyes and were full of big dreams and ambitions. "That was seventy years ago," he comments. "Now they are all pushing up daisies. How many of them really lived out their dreams? Did they do what they set out to accomplish?"

Then, with all the passion that a whisper can muster, the teacher tells his thoughtful group of students, "*Carpe diem!* Seize the day!"

When the scene panned across the trophy case, Jay was hit by a wave of inspiration. He briefly ignored the movie and reflected on the main character, the teacher. Jay was impressed with the character's deep passion and enthusiasm for life. This colorful instructor was convinced that he must inspire the hearts and actions of his students, and must spark their abilities to dream. It was his personal mission. It gave his life fire. Right then, Jay felt that he, too, wanted a mission. He longed to develop that same passion and heart, no matter what career he chose.

Sunday, June 8th... 7:57 A.M.

Jay slid out of bed, fully refreshed from a terrific night's sleep. Careful not to wake Vicki, he momentarily bypassed his early morning floor exercises, heading downstairs instead. Sitting at the breakfast table, he began disassembling the double rubber banded newsprint monstrosity that was called the Sunday paper. Jay poured a glass of orange juice and selected a banana out of the fruit bowl.

Jay's habits around reading the newspaper hadn't changed much since he was a kid and had first learned to read. He immediately turned to the Sports section where he memorized all of Saturday's box scores and dissected every star player's performance. Once satisfied that he could squeeze no more out of that section, he went to the front page and the headline news.

An article on an environmental/developer conflict in Arizona reminded him of the other movie they had watched last night: *Grand*

Canyon. Although he still was turning newspaper pages, Jay's mind was now elsewhere. He was thinking about something one of the movie's main characters had said. Jay recited the line from the movie, "My life and problems are pretty humorous to the Grand Canyon."

Three weeks ago, Jay thought his problems were insurmountable. He had lost proper perspective. Now, however, he had found a balance. He felt an inner peace knowing that he had arrived at a new, deeper understanding of life. Viewing *Grand Canyon* simply reinforced that feeling. The movie was about keeping life and problems in perspective, about facing whatever happened with courage and composure. It also exemplified exercising the choice to move forward, no matter what. These themes resonated in Jay.

He laid the newspaper down. He had read enough of today's unsettling news concerning the economy, international events, natural disasters, man-made disasters, and what appeared to be world-wide scandal. Throw in twin losses by the Dodgers and the Angeles, and the news of the day wasn't giving Jay's morning much of a lift.

"After reading this, what I need is a shot of Amicus!" He headed for the stairs. Again, Jay was struck by the realization that Amicus had promised him only twenty-one lessons. This was the twentieth. Jay sighed. The weight of this thought did not sit comfortably in his mind or his gut. He silently wished that the lessons could continue.

"Only one more after this. I hope Amicus has a graduate program I can enroll in when this is finished!" Jay halfheartedly chuckled to himself.

The screen flashed on, illuminating Amicus' words.

LESSON 20: *CARPE DIEM!*
(Seize the Day)

Good morning, friend! It's great to have you here this morning! *Lesson #20*, eh? Can you believe how fast the course has gone by? Can you believe, too, how much external change is possible when you commit to internal change? Exciting and energizing events actually can happen, can't they? Possibility and opportunity really are everywhere!

Accompany me for a moment, Jay; let's imagine again. From our previous lessons, you've come to learn that great events happen in life when they are first dreamed in the mind. So, one more time, put on your visionary glasses and follow me while I take you on a futuristic trip. I want you to travel seventy-five years into the future.

Picture in your mind a teacher showing his students an old photo. He's holding up an 8 x 10 color photo of a group of fifty or so unrecognizable people sitting in some bleacher rows. Can you see the teacher holding up the photograph? Now, zoom in closer. Visualize details in the photograph; the people are sitting in four equally numbered and stacked rows. Look at their faces; look closer. Do you recognize them? You should. They are all people in your life now. Today, Jay. There's your wife. There are former neighbors, best friends, former classmates, past coworkers, and your son. There's the checker at the grocery store, the postal carrier, and, in the back row, you recognize Julie from Java Now. You're there, too. Can you find yourself? There! There you are! Right in the middle, front row! Wow! All the people in your life are there in one complete picture! How great!

Now, Jay, I want you to move your attention away from the photo being held by the teacher. Listen to what he is saying to his students: "That was seventy-five years ago, class. All of them are now pushing up daisies. How many of them really lived out their dreams? Did they achieve what they set out to accomplish?"

Hmmm. Thank goodness it's not the year 2085! Thankfully, it's still your time to *carpe diem*. There is time yet for you to seize the day.

Everything that has taken place in your life up to this point...all of your yesterdays...are but memories in a photo album. They have passed. They're gone. What matters is today. What matters are your dreams for tomorrow and whether or not you make the choice to chase them.

Jay, now is your time to seize the day. Now is your time to chase rainbows and make wonderful things happen for yourself and others. Visualize the invisible. Believe the incredible. Now is your time to attempt the impossible. Do it now, because some day, my friend, it will no longer be your time.

Dr. Anthony Campolo conducted a study in which fifty people over the age of ninety-five were asked: "If you could live your life over again, what would you do differently?" The top three answers were: 1. *I would reflect more*; 2. *I would risk more*; 3. *I would do more things that would live on after I am dead.*

Pretty telling, don't you think?

So…seize the day! Seize every day! Forget about days gone by and set your attention on the now! Make a difference in this world! Stretch yourself! Move past your fears, stand up despite your shaky knees, and get out on life's dance floor! Tomorrow is too late! Don't wait! Don't kill time until there are no more photos left to be taken! Today is your day, Jay! Today! *Carpe diem!*

Question:
What risks should you be taking to make your life great?

"Risks?" Jay thought. "Great! Just what I love!" Jay was joking sarcastically with himself. But he now had an inkling in what career direction he should head.

11:00 A.M.

Jay and Vicki attended the late morning church service. Jay listened to the music and was impressed by the ardor and confidence the singers exuded while performing in front of hundreds of people. He imagined that at one time they each must have been terrified to get up in front of others and sing, but today they all seemed so natural. In each of their lives, Jay thought they must have one day boldly stepped out of their comfort zones and taken a risk. For him they were a reminder and a motivator for overcoming fear.

Jay experienced a rush of energy sweeping through his body. An incredible wave of power moved through his core as he felt his thoughts connect with his spirit in perfect harmony. His mind was painting a clear picture of what would give his life purpose. His heart was pumping passion into his thinking beyond anything he had ever felt before. The choir added the virtuoso's touch to a very powerful inner moment. Jay's confidence was alive! At that moment, Jay felt unshakable. With an amazing awareness, he knew he was in control of his own destiny. And he knew he was going to make something positive happen.

After the service, Jay whispered to Vicki, "Let's hang out for a bit at the coffee hour. I feel like mingling and meeting some new people." He winked and added playfully, "Let's see if we can make someone smile." Vicki smiled and nodded back at him. Jay was already one-for-one in attracting smiles.

For the next thirty minutes, Jay and Vicki socialized. Once quite reserved in such settings, Jay now gained a sense of comfort in meeting and talking with people he hadn't previously known. Vicki always had a natural tendency to mix well, so she easily followed Jay's lead. The two of them spoke briefly with half-a-dozen different people and several families before they left for home. It had been a new experience, but it was just an extension of everything Jay was feeling about stepping out of his comfort zone.

Upon returning home, Jay quickly slipped into his running clothes. His mind was racing and energy was pulsating through every fiber of his being. He wanted to run, to race. He wanted a challenge.

"I've got a ton of energy to burn, Vic. I'm going to run to Hillman High School and back. I'm ready for it!"

"Jay! That's seven miles round trip! Don't push too hard! It's hot out!"

Vicki was playing the role of concerned wife, but she knew Jay would be fine. She had watched firsthand Jay's improving fitness level and was impressed by his dedication. She knew he'd been working up to this point for a few weeks. Proudly, she watched Jay tie his running shoes, then head out the door.

After a good stretch, Jay set his stopwatch and took off at a moderate pace. He focused on his breathing and his arm movement. Soon, he fell into a relaxed and comfortable stride. One mile passed, then two. A third mile evaporated; now the school was only half-a-mile away. He felt smooth; he felt great.

Jay was falling into a runner's zone in which his mind could quit focusing on the movements of his body; he started to relax. Now that his fitness level had reached a point where physical pain was minimal, Jay had the mental freedom to delve into topics other than how much his muscles ached.

"This feels good...smooth and easy...good work! Just relax and find your groove, Jay...yeah...just like that! Good job! Be your own pace-setter...you're not racing anybody else."

The revelation struck him: "Hmmm...be my own pace-setter... yeah...that's right! Don't let others' expectations of me cloud my own expectations for myself. I don't have to keep pace with anyone else. I'm not them. I'm me."

He continued, "Don't compare yourself to what others are doing or what they've done...you're you, Jay...you're you. Be your own pace-setter!"

Jay started smiling while he ran. External visuals disappeared as he focused internally. Jay started by visualizing himself at work for Families with Friends. Then he saw himself in the advertising business chasing national customers. Next he had his own business. He knew which way he was leaning, but he needed to be certain. He compared which would be more exciting, which would bring greater rewards, which would contribute more positively to his life and the lives of others...which gave him the greatest sense of value and pride.

Then it hit him...an epiphany. "Wow! It doesn't really matter... does it? My work is not my worth! My work doesn't determine my self-esteem!"

"It doesn't really matter which I choose. The key is that whatever direction I end up going, I can make a difference...a big difference! As long as I bring my best to the party...my best effort...best thinking... best creativity and attitude...I will find connection with my best self and everybody will win! Clients...co-workers...me! Everybody wins if I stretch myself!"

Jay felt an amazing wave of relief. With career decisions looming, Jay gained the peace of understanding that no matter what direction he went, he would still have value to himself...and to others. "It matters most not WHAT I do...but HOW I do what I do!"

Jay had long since made the turn and was now one and a half miles from home. He was running effortlessly and free from any sort of muscle fatigue. He was invigorated by his effort and motivated by his internal dialogue. Possibilities seemed to abound. He felt he could attempt anything and succeed. Jay's mind continued to race with his feet.

Suddenly, he was hit with a second realization…except this one was far less positive: tomorrow marked *Lesson #21*…his last. After tomorrow, his time with Amicus would come to an end. Jay felt the looming void of life without Amicus.

Since the beginning Jay had known there were only twenty-one lessons. The ultimate termination of the lessons had always been a fact, but he had chosen to avoid thinking about it as much as possible. At first, the lessons had been a novelty; they were different and fun. Then they became crucial in moving Jay through his next emotional challenge. Now they were the daily sustenance that fed his spirit and attitude.

"Life without Amicus? Wow! What am I going to do without his presence…and coaching?"

"Oh no! My Final!" Jay had forgotten that at the end of his lessons he was to take a test that Amicus had referred to as a Final. Amicus' words suddenly came back to him in their perfect, original form:

You will have twenty-one lectures to complete in this course. After the last lecture, I will return and you will take a Final. However, this Final will be different from all others that you have ever imagined. In this Final, you will not be quizzed by the professor's questions, but rather you will ask me three questions. Do not worry about what you shall ask; it will be evident to you when the day comes.

"Yikes! I forgot all about my questions!" Jay's voice carried past the walls of his mind as the words slipped past his lips. A surge of panic struck. "What am I going to ask him? Am I supposed to prove what I've learned? Man…I need to make the questions great! But what are they?"

Jay ran a few hundred yards in distress. His physical state changed dramatically as his thoughts became distorted. The mental alarm that had registered inside his head turned to emotional worry and then physical fatigue. No more than a couple of minutes prior, Jay was running on cloud nine. As quickly as his mental energy changed from positive to negative, so did Jay's ability to run.

He slowed down, and the last mile became a painful grind. Jay gutted it out. He didn't want to give up on his seven-mile goal, but he wasn't enjoying the end of the run either—not at all. He had let the meaning that he had given to Amicus' impending Final dictate the state he was feeling. All it had taken was looking at the event as something negative to worry about; instead, he could have seen it as a potentially positive life-changing moment. As Jay crossed the sidewalk crack marking his finish line, this lesson cast down by the universe became quite apparent.

Bent over and puffing, Jay talked to himself, "Positive thinking… positive emotion…positive life motion…c'mon, Jay. You almost let bad thinking hijack your run today! Good job…you finished and met your goal…but darn it! Control your thoughts and quit sweating the small stuff!"

Still bent over, with hands on his knees, Jay smiled. It was a tired smile to be sure, but nonetheless, the smile was there. He chose to give himself credit for two things. First, he'd just finished running farther than he'd run since high school…seven miles! That was fantastic! Second, he was pleased with his newly found self-awareness. He was evolving. Sure, he wasn't perfect, and his thoughts still often raced out of control with worry, but he was learning how to apply the brakes. This felt good. What a difference this newly acquired ability would have made during his trials of adjusting to life beyond JLJ. Maybe complete self-mastery was a dream, but Jay was feeling that every day he was gaining more and more mastery over his thoughts and attitudes. And that was worthy of a smile.

Monday, June 9th...

Jay had already been up for two hours when the phone rang. It was a few minutes before 9:00 A.M. "Good morning, Jay! This is Laura Walston."

The suddenness of Laura's morning call caught Jay off balance. He skipped a breath before he brought his thoughts into line with the moment. Of course Jay knew that Laura's call would be coming soon, but now that it had arrived, he felt alive in the moment.

"Here we go!" Jay thought to himself. And then he answered. "Good morning, Laura! How are you today?"

"Jay, I have some very good news. This morning we made the decision to offer you a position as our man on the national scene." She didn't wait for him to reply. "We're very much hoping that you'll accept the position and the compensation package as we've discussed. We believe you're the person that Brown & Bigelow Creative needs out there! You're the guy, Jay!"

"Wow, Laura, that's great news! Thank you so much for your confidence in me and your offer. I'm very flattered. When do you need an answer?"

Laura laughed. "Well, I guess a part of me was hoping that you would say 'yes' immediately, but I fully understand. Why don't we say that we'd like to hear from you by the end of the week. Fair enough?"

"Thank you, Laura. I'm absolutely thrilled to have received your offer. Thank you again for your confidence in me. I have the highest personal respect for Brown & Bigelow and would be proud to represent such an extraordinary organization. I'll discuss things with my wife and contact you before the end of the day on Thursday. Thank you so much for allowing me some time to make this decision."

As soon as Jay hung up the phone with Laura, he called Vicki. She was ecstatic. Pretending to be a cheering crowd in a vast stadium,

Vicki roared muffled sounds of celebration into the phone. Then she asked, "What now?"

Jay chuckled. "I guess we have a bit of strategizing to do, don't we. I have until the end of the day Thursday with both offers. We'll map them both out on paper, and go from there. Plus, let's not forget this could also be my big chance to go at it under my own umbrella, Garfield Creative. What do you think? Sound impressive?" Jay had a smile to his voice. It felt great to have options. It felt great to be desired. Jay and Vicki talked for five more minutes before Vicki had to hang up and assist a waiting customer.

Jay eased himself into his big, brown leather chair and proceeded to work on calming himself. He tempered the adrenaline that flowed through his body by practicing some deep breathing exercises. As he inhaled a long slow breath, oxygen began to flood his system. He exhaled slowly, consciously. He repeated this calming breath exercise a few times.

With each breath, a silent, short prayer was taking form, "I am so grateful for the exhilarating direction my life is taking." He was in the middle of experiencing a perfect one hundred and eighty degree turn, and it felt amazing.

After calming himself, Jay headed upstairs and took a seat behind his desk. The unbridled energy that he had felt minutes ago was directed now at the computer screen. This was Amicus' final lesson…and Jay wanted to absorb every bit of wisdom from it that he could. His eyes burned into the monitor, and he began to read.

LESSON 21: SEE THE BIGGER PICTURE!
(Walk with Honor, Character, and Integrity)

You've done well, my friend. Your mind, heart, and spirit are multiplying in power on a daily basis. I know that you can feel the difference. Your life illustrates the difference.

Creating success is a science. Opportunity and possibility will always begin to show their faces when effort is exerted. It's cause and effect. You are living proof that good fortune—professional and personal—can be predicted if the compelling messages of the previous twenty lessons are to be applied to

your everyday life. Because of your commitment in applying these success-activating principles, you now enjoy a vibrancy and positive life momentum that is literally unstoppable. You are developing a confidence and a passion that is ultimately powerful, and you are watching your world change for the positive right before your eyes.

Please know, however, that there will come a time again… many times in fact…when the sky of your life inevitably turns dark, and life will challenge you to ignore what you now know. One of the certainties of life is that it's a roller coaster of ups and downs, twists and turns. It will be punctuated by events that are uncontrollable, people who are unchangeable, and problems that are unexplainable. You will again experience days in which it seems more comfortable to disappear inside your shell and hide. But don't.

Instead, recall the life-changing messages that you've been given. As water nourishes and heals the body, the truth and potency of these lessons will nourish and empower your spirit during hard times. They'll help lift you upward despite life's gravitational pull yanking you downward. Stay connected to them and similar messages; thus you'll assure yourself of always having a bright candle of hope to see you through the darkest of days.

And now you are ready for *Lesson #21*.

What is the grand finale of your lessons? What ties together everything that you've learned? Very simply, Jay, don't dedicate your life to always striving. See the bigger picture.

True joy—deep, heart-felt, passionate living joy—will not be found in climbing the world's highest mountains. It will not be found behind the wheel of an expensive car, in a new relationship, or behind the job title of a prestigious position. Those experiences might add to the number of pleasurable moments in your life, but don't equate pleasure with joy, peace, or harmony.

Joy is found in loving your occupation so much that you would do it without compensation. Peace is found in not struggling with your circumstances, but in flowing with them. Harmony is found when you dedicate yourself to a life lived with honesty, character, and integrity.

The bigger picture in life consists not in chasing the tangibles of wealth, money, or fame, but in pursuing the intangibles of joy, peace, and harmony. The bigger picture consists of what you present to the world internally, not what it appears that you have externally. When you bring your best to the world, it will reciprocate. That's when you become an inside-out person.

One of history's legendary immortals who definitely saw the bigger picture was the great Roman Emperor Marcus Aurelias. The most powerful man in the world during his nineteen year reign, Aurelias climbed the ultimate mountain of status. Power, fame, and wealth were all his in extraordinary abundance, but Aurelias had the foresight to know that it all was trivial in comparison to the bigger picture. Aurelias could have written a very credible book on how to have everything in life. Instead he wrote one of history's greatest manuals on how to live life in accord with the bigger picture. In *The Meditations*, this man who had everything shared his ideas on what was truly important:

> *What then is immortal fame? An empty hollow thing. To what then shall we aspire? The just thought, the unselfish act, the tongue that utters no falsehood, the temper that greets each passing event as pre-destined, expected, and emanating from the One source and the origin.*

His writing wasn't about the benefits of having and using power. It wasn't about striving for the definitive, life changing job title. It wasn't about how it felt to have others applaud you. It was about the bigger picture and learning to live in the present, not the future. It was about aspiring to be an inside-out person.

In our very first moments together, we broke the ice and developed common ground by reveling in the qualities of a more recent statesman…Abraham Lincoln. It is fitting to conclude our last lesson together by once again casting an eye on this big picture visionary.

One day long before his time as president, Abraham was writing to an individual who had requested his services as a lawyer. In evaluating the merits of the case, Lincoln knew that the man requesting his assistance had a good chance of winning, but the man's conduct in the situation had been questionable. Although money was tight for Abraham and he certainly could have used the income, he wrote the following words to this potential client:

> *I can win your case and get the six hundred dollars for you. But if I did so, I should bring misfortune upon an honest family, and I can't see my way to it. I would rather get along without your case and your fee. I will give you a piece of advice without charging you for it. Go home and try to think of some honester way of earning six hundred dollars.*

That's valuing the big picture more than your momentary circumstances. Honesty, character, and integrity were a natural part of Lincoln's fiber. His inner voice dictated loudly that he must do what was right. Personal gain mattered little to Lincoln compared to embracing that which was good and decent. Pursue that same path and discover true success in life.

Regardless of the cost, never lose sight of the bigger picture. True joy, peace, and harmony are found when you accept your role as an instrument of the universe for adding value to the lives of people you know and meet. Dedicate yourself to doing the right thing. Dedicate yourself to service. Walk with honor, character, and integrity in all that you do. Do these things and you will find that you can appreciate the adventure of life and live with greater ease. Do these things and you will find your bliss.

Marcus Aurelias and Abraham Lincoln earned their mentions here not because they lived lives with the hope of being remembered forever, but because they lived admirably. They've achieved heroic status because they were men of character and value. They were *inside-out* living men.

Prescribe to the principles for which they are remembered: humility, honor, and truth. Vow to always stand up for the universal good. See life's bigger picture. And in the process, you will most assuredly become a real-life hero.

Question:
What inner qualities would you like the world to see in you?

PS: *Lesson #21* **is completed! I'll see you again tomorrow for your Final!**

After writing down a few thoughts pertaining to Amicus' final question, Jay began a review of his entire Amicus notebook. He had added two special pages at the front: a table of contents listing the lesson headings, and a separate page listing each of the lesson's questions. Then he read through them.

LESSON 1: AWAKEN YOUR GIANT!
  (Dream Again)
LESSON 2: JUST IMAGINE!
  (Dream without Limits)
LESSON 3: BLOCK OUT NAYSAYERS!
  (Believe in Your Dreams)
LESSON 4: 5,110 DAYS!
  (Visualize Long Term)
LESSON 5: THE POWER OF ONE!
  (Focus Short Term)
LESSON 6: MAGNETS, PAINTBRUSHES, AND
  MIRRORS! (Attitude is the Difference)
LESSON 7: BAMBOO FARMING!
  (Be Tenacious)

LESSON 8: DON'T QUIT!
  (Avoid the Easy)
LESSON 9: THREE MORNING QUESTIONS!
  (Start the Day Right)
LESSON 10: SHARPEN YOUR AX!
  (Avoid Dullness)
LESSON 11: THE MULTIPLIER EFFECT!
  (Multiply Success)
LESSON 12: DIRT OR GOLD!
  (Expect the Best)
LESSON 13: PUT WOOD ON THE FIRE!
  (Action Produces Rewards)
LESSON 14: PREPARE TO HIT .367!
  (Prepare to Succeed)
LESSON 15: HEAD INTO THE JUNGLE!
  (Don't Give Up)
LESSON 16: 1,440 MINUTES!
  (Develop Time Mastery)
LESSON 17: WHACK THE WORRY WEED!
  (Eliminate Worry)
LESSON 18: BE A BATTERY CHARGER OF THE
  HUMAN SPIRIT! (Encourage Others)
LESSON 19: CREATE A GREAT DAY!
  (Take Daily Ownership of Your Life)
LESSON 20: CARPE DIEM!
  (Seize the Day)
LESSON 21: SEE THE BIGGER PICTURE!
  (Walk with Honor, Character, and Integrity)

Jay turned the page and read the corresponding questions that went with each chapter:

Lesson 1: What would you like to do in your life?
Lesson 2: With absolutely no limits to your thinking, what crazy things can you imagine accomplishing in life?
Lesson 3: Think of a time that you held back on pursuing

something you wanted because of someone's "expert" advice. What did the expert's advice stop you from getting?

Lesson 4: What will you accomplish 5,110 days from now?

Lesson 5: How would your life change if you started practicing *The Power of One* today?

Lesson 6: Attitude. Are you attracting, painting, and reflecting what you desire?

Lesson 7: If you adopted the tenacious spirit of a bamboo farmer, how would your world change?

Lesson 8: What does doing the easy thing get you in life?

Lesson 9: What can you do to make sure that you start your day by asking the right questions?

Lesson 10: What routines can you build into your life to make sure that you keep your ax sharpened?

Lesson 11: In what specific ways can you change your daily performance from a "3" to a "4"?

Lesson 12: Are your expectations leading you to find the gold or dirt in life?

Lesson 13: In key areas of your life, what can you specifically do to throw more wood on the fire?

Lesson 14: What can you do to build bold confidence in your life?

Lesson 15: What past failures still await another go?

Lesson 16: What changes do you need to make so that you maximize your daily 1,440 minutes?

Lesson 17: What positive steps can you take to whack a current worry weed out of your mind?

Lesson 18: What five people in your life can benefit right now by you becoming a Battery Charger of the Human Spirit?

Lesson 19: What would a great day look like in your life?

Lesson 20: What risks should you be taking to make your life great?

Lesson 21: What inner qualities would you like the world to see in you?

Jay sighed. He had completed the course. On the one hand, Jay had just finished reading Amicus' last lesson and felt sadness that he was through. One the other hand, Jay felt relief knowing that Amicus, through his words, would now be a part of his life forever. Jay quietly vowed to himself that he would memorize every life-changing lesson. He would live Amicus' words. He would emblazon their meaning in his mind; he would brand their message onto his heart. And in one final promise to himself…and to Amicus, too…Jay acknowledged that he must find a way to share with the world everything he had learned.

Tuesday, June 10th…

Jay hadn't slept at all. A life-altering career decision needed to be made over the next few days, but that's not what had prevented Jay from sleeping. Jay's brain spun on without rest pondering everything associated with Amicus and the Final. Like a harried college student pulling an all-nighter and cramming before the big test, Jay had spent the night thinking and writing. Words poured non-stop onto his yellow writing pad like a water faucet with a broken handle. Before the sun had risen, Jay's pen spurted out seventeen pages of questions, notes, ideas, and thoughts. This was it.

As far as Jay knew, this might be the last opportunity he would ever have to communicate with Amicus. He didn't know. The only certainty was that his life had been touched by an almost other-worldly blessing which had helped him to not only get his life together again, but also to catapult him into a higher realm of living. Jay felt that he never could have achieved this level of growth without Amicus. Today's final conversation was important, and Jay wanted to get it right. Sleep was unnecessary for a day. Adrenalin alone would carry him.

When the evening's mental adventure first began, Jay assumed panic mode regarding his Final. He had written out tens and tens of possible questions that he could ask Amicus. He knew he was allowed only three, but how could he decide which were the best?

"What am I supposed to ask? Only three questions? You have to be kidding! How am I ever going to decide? Are they going to be graded? What if I ask the wrong ones and disappoint him? These questions need to be big!"

Were you the man at the park? Will I see you again? Where did you come from? How do you know me? Did you really meet all the people that you mentioned? How could that be? How do I tell people about you? What's my destiny? What's the one lesson that will help me the most? What's my purpose in life? What happens after I die? Should I have more kids? Should I start a business? Is this where I'm supposed to live or is there a better location for me? How can I walk with more humility? How do I overcome my fears? What religion is the right one? What leaders have their heart in the right place? How can I be more of a leader? Is there really a God? Are you Him?

Night matured into early morning; Jay's nerves had settled and he found peace in knowing what he needed to ask. Perhaps big-picture thinking had finally clicked in, or perhaps the truth of what he wanted to know...what he needed to know...had become clear to him. It was 5:32 A.M. when the three questions became obvious to Jay. On a clean sheet of paper, he neatly wrote each question out and set the paper next to his keyboard as a reference.

Bracing himself for what would follow, Jay turned on the computer. Amicus was already there, waiting on the screen.

Ready to create a great day, my friend?

Although he had never heard Amicus' voice, Jay felt as if the words on the screen actually were audible. They seemed to speak to him in a tone that was beautifully melodic and pleasing to his spirit. The voice inside his head was calm yet enthusiastic, respectful yet authoritative.

Jay responded by typing. "I'm smiling at the chance to talk with you again, Amicus! I'm so glad to be here...and that you're here! I have learned so much...and changed so much...from the lessons! A great deal has happened to me since we first met, and I owe so much to you! I am entirely grateful!"

Thank you, Jay. I am proud of your growth and happy that I could be of service to you.

"I feel so lucky to have met you, Amicus! It has changed my life forever! I wish that I could sit in your classroom every day and learn a thousand more lessons! Knowing that your lesson would be there for me each day has kept me grounded and moving forward. They provided me with more security than you might imagine! (Or maybe YOU could imagine! LOL.) I wish that you would be a part of my life forever."

Oh, but Jay…I am a part of your life now…and I always will be. I am a proud potter who does not like to leave any of his potential masterpieces unfinished. And please know that in my eyes, my friend, you are a masterpiece of extraordinary potential. You are a masterpiece in progress.

"Does this mean that you'll be back and that my lessons really haven't ended?"

Jay, never do lessons end. Never. And as far as me returning? I never leave. When the student is ready, the teacher appears.

"What do you mean?" asked Jay.

You now have my words. You have begun to brand their power into your mind and heart. Because of this, you'll always have me with you; I'll always be there for you. Additionally, in a much more complex way, just understand that our spirits are one and the same. I can never leave that which is a part of me.

Jay tried to digest Amicus' words, but he was given no time to inquire further. Amicus spoke again.

But now, Jay, from your query, it seems you're ready to begin the Final. I won't count either of the last questions. Ready? Let's get to question #1. I am anxious to see how far you've come.

Jay eased back on the current line of his thoughts and inquiry. He squirmed in his chair, then turned to the paper at the left side of his keyboard—his three questions. "Here goes everything!" he whispered to himself. Jay typed the first question as he had written it.

"#1. How can I be certain which career direction to take in order to fully maximize my potential and make my life count?"

So, you want to know what to do with your life? Certainly, this is a reasonable question...and one that has been asked millions of times.

Although an occupation can assist a person in feeling valuable, no single job will ever provide long term emotional and spiritual satisfaction. No, Jay, the key to being able to maximize your potential in life is not about what you contribute in a specific job. It's about the character you are trying to develop so that you can contribute more as a human being. Whether you run the boardrooms or sweep them, power in life is reaching out and positively affecting other people wherever you are... and in whatever you are doing. Your ability to know if you are maximizing your potential comes in the form of how you live each day. It comes in how you treat others...what you say to them, your attitudes toward them. It comes in how you make people feel.

Maximizing one's potential is not about how much money you have or how large your home is (despite the bumper sticker proclaiming "He who dies with the most toys wins"). It's about working hard. It's about under-promising and over-delivering. It's about caring enough to give the best of yourself to others and to everything you undertake. If you do these things, you will maximize your God-given potential. You will be making your life count in an extraordinary way.

Jay didn't bother taking notes. He simply read and let Amicus' message sink in as much as possible. "So, let me get this right...you're saying that the job I take in the next few days is not a matter of a right or wrong path?"

Exactly. The job doesn't make the man or woman. Personal growth does. And that, my friend, is the only direction that matters. A life devoted to achievement alone is hollow. A life devoted to serving others has depth.

"Tell me then, Amicus, how is personal growth defined?"

It's defined by exactly the things you are engaged in, sensing, and experiencing now, Jay. You knew that answer. I'm ready for question #2.

Jay's face grew a little warm after Amicus' slight admonishment, but Amicus had been right. Chuckling to himself, Jay fired off question number two.

"#2. What is the most effective way for me to share the lessons that I have learned with the world?"

With the world, my friend? I am smiling at your zealousness, but admiring your vision and desire. First and foremost, Jay, know that the lessons you have learned are not something everybody is willing to hear. Sadly, most people are not ready or willing to hear the message that you have learned, so don't be dismayed if some reject what you have to share. Most people have developed familiar comfort zones and are threatened by anything that causes them to budge or move elsewhere. The hearts and minds of these people are not open to ideas that prompt reflection and self-examination.

You can plant seeds that help people grow and you can water seeds previously planted, but you can never cause the growth of another individual. Everyone has the power of choice. How you share what you've learned is your choice. It is another's choice to heed or ignore what you share.

Realize this, too. The power of these lessons will be received two ears at a time, one set of eyes at a time, one heart and one soul at a time. Always remember that, Jay. Speak to the individual, no matter how large the listening, reading, or viewing audience might be.

Jay broke in, "But Amicus, I was asking: by what means I should communicate this message?"

Preferably with your heart and mind working together, Jay. The mind without the heart tends to complicate things and remove the passion. The heart without the mind soon runs out of fuel. Use both together and the rest will come naturally. The rest will be made clear.

Jay sagged in his chair. He had been hoping Amicus would give him marching orders and an outline of what he should do to carry out his newly found mission...that of sharing a message of personal empowerment. Amicus had not. Jay sighed. He was frustrated that his answer did not bring him the desired or anticipated results. Amicus was not making this Final easy. Jay was going to have to think for himself.

Ready for your last question, Jay?

Straightening up in his chair, Jay took a deep breath, and without consulting his paper, he typed the third question.

"#3. Some days I really struggle. What do I need to do to have complete self-mastery over my thoughts, emotions, and actions?

A lofty and admirable goal, Jay, but at this point in human development, total self-mastery is just not attainable. Life is extremely complex. If you are to be fully engaged in life, you're going to need to understand that you will find disappointment regularly. Certainly you might have what seem to be nearly perfect moments—even days—but expecting perfection out of yourself every day is not realistic. Just as the body needs sleep in order to rejuvenate and heal itself, you need to build into your life a time to recharge your mental, emotional, and physical batteries, too. You just can't put out one hundred percent of your energy one hundred percent of the time.

When your mind or body feels tired...rest. When your nerves are on edge...take a break. Days in which it is a struggle

to find motivation are often a hint to slow down a bit, quit pushing so hard, and enjoy life more. When you have days like that, don't get angry or frustrated with what you perceive as your own inadequacies in disciplining your mind and attitude. Thinking like that is far too rigid. Learn to forgive yourself. Find balance. Listen to the needs of your body, soul, and mind. And then find something fun and relaxing to do until you're ready to give it another go.

Jay felt a sense of relief from Amicus' answer. "That's good to know. I've had bad moments where I had no juice left in me to push myself further—to learn, to exercise, to do anything. I've been down on myself and felt like a loser. I thought I must not be giving it one hundred percent. I thought I was doing something wrong. This negative thinking would start to snowball, and I'd feel even worse about myself."

Ah, Jay! Don't be so hard on yourself. Some days you just need a flat out break! According to the Bible, even God rested on the seventh day!

And that, my dear friend, was question number three. Your questions show me where your heart is and what you deem important…finding purpose, contributing, being your best. You have done well, Jay. Your grade? *A.*

And now it's time….

Sensing that Amicus was about to say good-bye and walk off the computer screen, possibly forever, Jay typed as fast as he could: "Amicus…could you hold a moment, please?"

Jay held his breath as he waited. Seeing no response from Amicus, Jay quickly looked down at his pre-written text and continued typing. He had known that this moment was coming and had prepared for it. Rolling the dice with this next request, he went with his instinct. There was nothing to lose in what he was about to ask, so his fingers pecked out word-for-word what he had written on the paper hours earlier.

"When taking college Finals, it was common to be given a bonus question at the end of the regular exam. Bonus questions were often the hardest and most difficult to answer, but they were meant to possibly enhance a student's grade if answered correctly. Are you with me?"

But, Jay, you already have an *A*!

"I would like a bonus question for a purpose beyond that of enhancing my grade. The reward of the grade matters much less than the education. Right?"

With that sort of logic at your disposal, you will go far, Jay Garfield! I will agree to your request and grant you a fourth question. However, there is a small stipulation. Much work was required of you before you were in a position to ask the first three questions. Therefore, effort will again be required from you in order to ask the fourth question. However, this requirement will be completed after the question has been asked and answered. Agreed?

Jay hadn't considered that there would be a price for his question, but he understood that with great reward some sacrifice is always involved. He believed that he was prepared to meet Amicus' stipulation, but he was wise enough to ask what it was that would be expected of him.

"What is the requirement, Amicus?"

With your question comes the weighty responsibility, over the next six months, of finding one person to mentor and to whom you will pass on what you have learned. It will be your turn to be the teacher. Who that person will be is for you to choose. Just make certain that you recognize there might be a considerable investment of time and energy. It's a big commitment for one additional question. Do you accept the requirement?

"I do."

Then the fourth question is yours to ask, Jay.

Jay proceeded to type that one question that he had pondered ever since the day he had met Amicus. It was the big one.

"#4. Amicus, who are you?"

Curiosity has captured the cat, eh? I could have expected that you might ask this question, but I am very pleased that you hadn't used one of your original three questions to do so.

Jay, you already know the answer to that which you ask. You may think that you don't...but if you were to examine your heart...the deepest part...you would find the truth. You let your brain distract you, Jay. I did acquiesce to answer your question if you agreed to my terms, however, so I will.

Who am I, my friend? Very simply...I am the inspiration you get while running in the morning. I am the longing in your spirit that cries out for completeness. I am the magic that you see in a child's eyes when he watches a circus.

I am the voice inside you saying, "Go for it!" I am the encourager inside you who makes the checker at the store smile. And yes, my friend, I have been known to occasionally wear a royal blue sweat suit in the park and share the beauty of life with a friend. I am the voice that encourages you when you are down...the motivating words you share with someone frustrated by life...the laughter that comes from the deepest part of your gut...the adrenalin rush you feel when you experience sheer joy.

I am the tear that rolls down your cheek because you're feeling pure love...the arms that you feel around you when you are being hugged...the sparkle in the eye of a wise octogenarian. I am the determination that puts a man into space ...the marvel of one peering through a microscope. I am thoughts. I am feelings. I am actions. And I am so much more... so very much more.

And with that, my dear friend, this course now ends. Remember, though, I will never be gone. I am now...and will always be...a part of you. When you start to drown in the seemingly deep ocean of life...when mere existence seems to become a trial without end...when planting your feet on the

**ground in the morning becomes your biggest goal…know that
I am there with you.**

**You have done well, Jay…and your best days…your greatest
days…are in front of you. Welcome back, my friend! Welcome
to the world of the living! It's time to celebrate…and live!**

With that, the computer screen went quiet. Jay furiously typed
words meant to get Amicus back, but it didn't work. He was gone.
Before the typed words of Amicus also disappeared, Jay rushed to turn
on the printer. The printer slowly eased out the page. When it finished,
Jay noticed something on the paper that he hadn't seen when Amicus'
words had originally appeared on the monitor. At the end of the page
in bold letters was written:

**And remember one more thing. I will be cheering for you
every day, my friend…and smiling.**

With Amicus' final words, Jay became overwhelmed with the
deepest emotion he had ever felt in his life. A combination of joy,
sadness, pleasure, pain, hope, and loss all came pummeling down upon
him like a world champion boxer's gloves on a rookie fighter. With
all of his might, Jay clamped his eyes shut, but even their ultra-tight
closure could not stop the tears that escaped. Jay lowered his face into
his hands realizing that his mentor…his teacher…would not be back.
Amicus was gone.

Saturday, June 28th…8:15 A.M.
(Eighteen Days Later)

Vicki got out of bed, walked down the hall and entered the office where Jay had worked all night. He had spent the night diligently composing a letter that he had just finished editing for the fourth time.

"Wow, Jay! You must really love your new work! You've been up all night! What are you working on that's so motivating?"

"Well, last night I started out double checking all our tax paper work that I'm taking to the accountant on Monday. After I finished that, I started working on something that's been on my mind for a couple of weeks. It's a *Letter to the Editor*, and I think I'm pretty much done."

"A Letter to the Editor? Really? To the *Times*?" Vicki's curiosity was aroused.

Somewhat sheepishly, Jay answered, "Actually…it's a *Letter to the Editor* not only to the *Times*. I'm planning to send it to three hundred different papers."

"Three hundred papers! Wow! Why so many? And this has nothing to do with your work?"

Jay continued. "Well, my goal is to multiply the potential number of people who will read my message. That's why I want to send the letter to three hundred papers across the country—so that it has a better chance of being printed a few times. I've already made a list of places to send it. Who knows if it will get printed or not, but I have to try. Want to hear what I wrote?"

"Of course! I want to know what you're up to!" Vicki took a seat on the chair in front of the desk. She was extremely curious to know what Jay had to say.

Jay smiled, took a deep breath, and began to read:

Dear Editor,

It's my opinion that a majority of people could benefit very much by receiving a small injection of hope and encouragement in a world that so frequently drains us of both. I have committed myself to getting the "snowball rolling" by mailing this article to select and influential newspapers in every state across the country. Your paper is certainly one of those I consider most influential. Without your help, this message will go nowhere. With your help, we begin the lofty mission of restoring hope, cultivating passion, and rekindling purpose in the lives of people everywhere.

Could you please consider printing the following message in a guest column or wherever else you think appropriate? I would be grateful if you could let me know, please, if you do. Thank you!

Jay looked up at Vicki. "And now, here's the actual letter."

Let's Get the Snowball Rolling!

Sometimes it's easy to feel defeated by everything that's going on around us. We gaze in disbelief at the gas pump as it continues to tick away dollar after dollar. We go to the grocery store only to utter, "Wow!" when the clerk tells us our total. At home, we turn on the TV hoping to relax, only to be dismayed by what we see on the evening news. We are shocked to hear that a teacher has molested a student. Our hearts break when we see families losing their homes to floods and fires. We're numbed by the horrific human rights violations elsewhere.

Although these situations are the ones that make headlines, it's only because the mundane madness of our own lives is so universal that it isn't newsworthy. An unsympathetic boss, a rude customer, a friend who doesn't pay us back, a call from a concerned teacher, an older model car not running well…we all feel frustration in varying forms every day.

Unkind words, small lies, selfish actions…no one is immune from the craziness.

Most of us manage to squeak through to face another day. In despair, others decide to walk away from their problems, debts, and promises. Still others cry out for the government to remove the insecurities of life and "make things better." Neither squeaking by, walking away from responsibility, nor relying on government to make us happy seem to be a terrific answer to making life better. There must be another answer. But what is it?

The answer is to turn inward and look outward.

True changes in ourselves, our families, jobs, communities, and our country begin when we stop looking for role models and choose to be one. It doesn't matter if we're a successful business owner, a harried stay-at-home parent, or a struggling college student. Our impetus to change is our own willingness to change.

By improving our attitudes, our actions, and our motives, we can make the world around us a better place. When we focus on being a good neighbor, a good friend, and a good citizen, positive momentum starts to build. When we smile at the bagger at the grocery store and tell her we appreciate her hard work…when we write a note of thanks on a napkin to the hardworking waiter…when we reach out a caring hand to those we know and those we don't know, we start to make a difference. And in the process, we become reunited with what matters in life, and life starts to feel good again.

When we focus on the honorable and develop an unwavering commitment to the truth and a bitter distaste for that which isn't, good wins out. When we say we'll do something, we do it. We become encouragers and not complainers. We stop keeping score. We become a breath of fresh air. Sure, we might not be able to stop massive job layoffs, a downward moving real estate market, or the world's energy crisis, but we can get the snowball rolling.

209

By sharing a positive word with coworkers, we build a positive attitude within ourselves. By raising our expectations of ourselves, we raise the expectations of those around us. We can't control what others do, but we can control what we do. Let's hold our tongues instead of lashing out. If our hearts are bitter, let's learn to forgive. By doing so, we can improve our relationships, our health, and our life. The magic of life is very simple. Smile and be smiled at. Heal and be healed.

Let's put cynicism and corrosive thinking on the back burner and turn up the heat on positive values and doing what is right. Abandon selfish thinking for selfless thinking. Let's be individuals of character, honor, and integrity, and let's make a difference.

Let's look at the person in our mirror and ask, "What positive changes can I make?" By changing ourselves, we positively affect the store clerk, who cheerfully affects the next customer, who lovingly affects her family when she goes home. Her husband continues the chain the next day by inspiring his sales team at work, who sincerely seek to serve each of the next fifty people they talk to on the phone. And that's how we get the snowball rolling.

Say and do something positive for others and encourage them to pass on the gesture. Commit to adopting a better attitude. Commit to speaking with a new voice. Commit to empowering others. Let's become better people from the inside out. Let's each decide to be a goodwill ambassador and change the direction of our country. There is no more noble an existence; there is no better way to leave a legacy.

So what do you say? Will you help me get the snowball rolling?

—A. Friend

Jay looked up at Vicki. Her eyes were moist, and she was smiling. "That's really great, Jay…perfect. Tell me though, who's 'A. Friend'?" As Jay began to explain, somewhere in the back of his mind, he felt Amicus' presence smiling.

8:45 A.M.
(roughly the same time 3000 miles away)

The newest member of the foursome walked to the first tee to meet his three new playing partners…three very successful executives of Fortune 500 companies who had flown to New York for a round of meetings that involved the possible layoffs of tens of thousands of people. To break the tenseness of the meetings, the associates had decided to spend the day teeing-up the little white ball and chasing it around Mother Nature with a few iron clubs. Originally, there had been four associates set to tee-off together. Unfortunately, one of their members had unexpectedly received an important business call not more than fifteen minutes prior to their tee time. She was now forced to miss the day's golfing adventure since the seriousness of the call would keep her sidetracked all morning, solving some serious issues that had suddenly arisen within her company.

Clubs slung over his left shoulder, the newly assigned fourth player stepped up to the tee box. Having just been greeted with the names of his three new playing partners, the intriguing, tall man extended his hand.

With deep, sparkling eyes and an impressive voice, this man in blue smiled and said, "Hello, friends. It's a pleasure to join you! I'm Amicus, and I'm looking forward to creating a great day and hitting a few good shots. Now, John, the available bag slot in your cart seems to indicate that you and I will be riding together today! How wonderful!"

Epilogue...

Thank you so much for reading *Amicus 101: A Story About the Pursuit of Purpose and Overcoming Life's Chaos.* I hope that this book has added value to your world and served as a tool for you to take a closer look at your life and the footprints that you will inevitably leave.

Amicus means *friend* and one of the many great things about life is that we all get to play the role of Amicus in the lives of other people. Over the course of your life journey, you will unfailingly encounter hundreds of people in need of being lifted up and empowered. May this book serve as a small reminder to let Amicus live through you during those times when both your words and actions can mean so much to someone else. You never know when a small *battery charging* gesture can literally motivate another to change the world.

We get but one life. Use yours wisely. Be great and empower others to be the same.

Create a great life!

A self-billed "Battery Charger of the Human Spirit," Shawn Anderson is a possibility thinker and an opportunity seeker. Dedicated to assisting others to maximize potential and create opportunity, Shawn's life mission is to empower 1,000,000 people to lead a more positive and purposeful existence.

At his core, Shawn has always been an entrepreneur. From his first business selling night crawlers to fishermen at age ten, Shawn has proven his resourcefulness in building successful organizations, developing national events (such as www.ExtraMileAmerica.com), and creating a multi-million dollar business from the ground floor. A graduate of the University of California at Berkeley, he is a solidifier of ideas and a magnifier of projects. Shawn's books include:

> *Countdown to College: Preparing Your Student for Success in the Collegiate Universe*
> *SOAR to the TOP: Rise Above the Crowd and Fly Away to Your Dream*
> *Amicus 101: A Story About the Pursuit of Purpose and Overcoming Life's Chaos.*

Shawn also mails out a weekly online motivational newsletter to readers called the *M.A.P. to Success Circle!* which is dedicated to assisting readers to build "Momentum in Attitude and Possibility."

For more, go to www.ShawnAnderson.com.